J. T. EDSON'S
FLOATING OUTFIT

The toughest bunch of Rebels that ever lost a war, they fought for the South, and then for Texas, as the legendary Floating Outfit of "Ole Devil" Hardin's O.D. Connected ranch.

MARK COUNTER was the best dressed man in the West: always dressed fit-to-kill. **BELLE BOYD** was as deadly as she was beautiful, with a "Manhattan" model Colt tucked under her long skirts. **THE YSABEL KID** was Comanche fast and Texas tough. And the most famous of them all was **DUSTY FOG**, the ex-cavalryman known as the Rio Hondo Gun Wizard.

J. T. Edson has captured all the excitement and adventure of the raw frontier in this magnificent Western Series. Turn the page for a complete list of Floating Outfit titles.

J.T. Edson

CARDS AND COLTS

CHARTER BOOKS, NEW YORK

When originally published by Corgi in
Great Britain, the title for
this book was *Diamonds, Emeralds, Cards and Colts*.

This Charter book contains the complete
text of the original edition.
It has been completely reset in a typeface
designed for easy reading and was printed
from new film.

CARDS AND COLTS

A Charter Book/published by arrangement with
Transworld Publishers, Ltd.

PRINTING HISTORY
Corgi edition published 1986
Charter edition/May 1988

ISBN: 1-55773-029-6

Charter Books are published by The Berkley Publishing Group,
200 Madison Avenue, New York, N.Y. 10016.
The name "CHARTER" and the "C" logo are trademarks belonging
to Charter Communications, Inc.

PRINTED IN THE UNITED STATES OF AMERICA

10 9 8 7 6 5 4 3 2 1

For Muthoni Mthiga and everybody else at the Tusker Brewery in Nairobi, Kenya, with my thanks for many a "Tembo, baridia sana" *to soothe the hardships of going on* safari.

Heri na baraka, yaku-yote.

Author's Note

While complete in itself, most of the events in this book run concurrently with those recorded in *Decision For Dusty Fog*.

They precede the narrative related in *The Code of Dusty Fog*.

To save our "old hands" repetition, but for the benefit of new readers, we have included details respecting to the careers and special qualifications of Dusty Fog, Mark Counter, the Ysabel Kid and Waco, plus some pieces of information regarding the Old West—about which we have frequently received requests for clarification—in the form of Appendices.

We realize that, in our present "permissive" society, we could use the actual profanities employed by various people in the narrative. However, we do not concede a spurious desire to create "realism" is any excuse to do so.

Lastly, as we refuse to pander to the current "trendy" usage of the metric system, except when referring to the calibre of certain firearms traditionally measured in millimetres—i.e. Walther P-38, 9mm—we will continue to employ miles, yards, feet, inches, stones, pounds and ounces, when quoting distances or weights.

J.T. EDSON,
Active Member, Western Writers of America,
MELTON MOWBRAY,
Leics.,
England.

CHAPTER ONE

We Can Make Diamonds!

"Excuse me, ma'am, but are you Miss Olga Chernyshevsky?"

"I am, sir. Is there anything I can do for you-all?"

"May I ask whether you are the same 'Miss Chernyshevsky of Richmond, Virginia' to whom this advertisement refers?"

"I am. And, despite my *sex*—trusting my use of the word, '*sex,*' does not offend you, *sir*—I assure you that I am *quite* competent to purchase or to offer an expert valuation of jewellery, antiques, or *objets d'art.*"

Looking to be in her early twenties, the woman to whom the questions had been directed was about five foot eight inches tall. Beneath a grey Wavelean hat devoid of the decorative trimming which generally enhanced such headgear, her black hair was drawn into a tight bun. Her olive skinned face did not have even the modest amount of make-up permissible for a "good"—as such things were judged west of the Mississippi River—woman. However, neither the omission, the horn-rimmed spectacles perched on her nose, nor a serious and coldly haughty expression could obliterate the fact that she was beautiful. Furthermore, if the severely masculine light blue silk shirt and dark blue necktie she had on were intended to conceal what lay beneath, they failed badly. Rather they tended to draw attention to the full firm swell of an imposing bosom and the way in which her torso trimmed to a slender waist. Nor was her dark grey skirt any more successful in hiding richly curvaceous hips which gave a hint of joining shapely and sturdy legs. Brown gloves of thin leather covered her hands, concealing her marital status. The right gripped the neck of a bulky black reticule which had the loop of a drawstring passed over her wrist. However, despite the ethnic origins suggested by her name, her accent was that of a

1

native-born Southron rather than a Russian.

Having turned as she was replying to the first question, Miss Olga Chernyshevsky glanced first at the newspaper held by the man who had addressed her!

However, in spite of guessing why she had been accosted and observing the obvious amiability of the speaker, the scrutiny to which the young woman subjected him and his companion was more critical than flattering!

While the two men were alike in the aura of somewhat shabby gentility they displayed, the likeness ended there!

Holding a derby hat of a style no longer fashionable in his right hand, being of medium height and rotund, the speaker exuded joviality. The sleeves of the spotlessly clean yet cheap white flannel shirt, which showed from the cuffs of a well worn black cutaway jacket, were frayed. His yellowish brown nankeen trousers looked close to being threadbare and the polish which had been applied could not hide the aged nature of his boots. Everything about him implied he had seen much better days and was struggling to maintain appearances.

The second man still had an equally hard used derby on his head. Tall, lean, his sallow features were dour and his expression suggested a tendency to be disapproving of everything around him. Although his sombre black suit and boots had cost good money when new, like the attire of his companion, clearly they had been purchased some time ago and, if his somewhat newer—albeit cheaper—shirt was any guide, during a period of greater affluence than he had known recently.

"My dear young lady," the speaker said, his manner placatory and his accent that of a well educated New Englander. "It is *because* of your competence that we have come to speak with you."

"I see," Miss Chernyshevsky replied, seeming mollified by the explanation. "And what can I do for you?"

"I am Professor Oswald Cadwallicker and this is Doctor Angus Donald McTavish," the shorter man introduced, his manner suggesting the names should mean something. Then he glanced in a pointed fashion around the reception hall of the luxuriously appointed Prudential Hotel. Although the time was three o'clock in the afternoon, there were only a few of the employees in sight. Nevertheless, he went on, "Would it be possible for us to talk somewhere less *public?*"

"We could go into the bar," the young woman suggested.

"The *bar?*" Cadwallicker repeated.

"Great heavens to Betsy!" the young woman ejaculated, bristling with indignation. "Don't tell me that a town like Dodge City holds to such out-moded ideas of masculine superiority that it restricts entry to bars to *men?*"

"I'm afraid it does," the portly man admitted. "And, while I do not subscribe to the idea myself, I feel we would attract rather than avoid attention should we go in there."

"We could go to my room," Miss Chernyshevsky offered.

"That's no' the place!" stated the taller man, his Scottish burr giving the impression that he rarely spoke. "And I'm no' so sure what we've got should be shown to a *lassie.*"

"In that case!" the young woman snorted, clearly offended by the somewhat derogatory tone in which the reference to her gender was made. "You're wasting your time and *mine!*"

"I'm sorry, Miss Chernyshevsky," Cadwallicker put in hurriedly. "You must excuse my friend's dour Scottish way of expressing himself. He didn't have any intention of slighting your abilities in your line of business."

"Oh no!" the woman answered, but she reversed instead of completing the turn she had started to make. "I can see he is *bursting* with enthusiasm over whatever it might be you want to discuss with me."

"Well *I'm* in favour of taking you into our confidence," the portly man asserted. "And, Angus, you know my judgement of human nature is *always* good."

"Aye," the Scot replied, in the way of one who begrudged supplying the confirmation despite knowing it was valid. "I can't gainsay *that*, Professor. Perhaps we could talk to the lassie outside."

"The dining-room will be satisfactory," Cadwallicker claimed, nodding towards the open doors opposite the entrance to the bar-room.

"Aye, it's no' so busy's we couldn't talk privately," McTavish conceded, then tapped his left breast pocket with his right forefinger. "But I trust ye'll be mindful of our *circumstances*, Professor."

"We need only have coffee," Miss Chernyshevsky suggested, deducing what was meant by the gesture. "Or I am quite willing to pay for my own meal."

"That *won't* be necessary, my dear young lady," the portly man refused. "I'm afraid the Doctor's Scottish nature some-

times leads him to be excessively cautious where money is concerned. So, if the dining-room is satisfactory to you, we'll go in right now."

Nodding what was obviously a condescending compliance, the young woman accompanied Cadwallicker and McTavish into the dining-room. It was unoccupied by other customers at that moment and only one waitress was present. What was more, after she had fetched the coffee which was all they ordered, she disappeared into the kitchen.

"Would you care to examine these, Miss Chernyshevsky?" the portly man requested. His manner was secretive as, after having darted a glance around as if wishing to ensure nobody was watching, he removed something from his breast pocket and held it out partially concealed in his fist. "With—er— *discretion*, if you don't mind me saying."

"I'm *always* discreet!" the woman declared haughtily. Loosening the draw string of the small chamois leather pouch she received, she tipped its contents into her left palm which she held hidden behind the reticule she had placed on the table. "They *look* like diamonds."

"They *are* diamonds," McTavish stated. "Of course, you can always take them to a jeweller's and have them verified."

"I hardly need a *second* opinion!" Miss Chernyshevsky snapped.

"The Doctor forgot you are quite capable of doing the verification," Cadwallicker claimed, once again acting as peacemaker. "It is just that, back in Massachusetts, the jewellery trade is still solely a masculine province."

"It's the *same* in Rich—!" the woman commenced with obvious bitterness. Then, giving a sniff, she produced a jeweller's lupe from her reticule and started to examine each of the small, brilliant stones from the pouch in turn. Having done so, she laid the lupe aside and, picking up a glass tumbler, ran one along its side. Studying the scratch which was left, she repeated the experiment with the rest and created the same result each time. "They're genuine all right. Do you wish to sell them?"

"Would you be interested in buying them—and *more* like them?" Cadwallicker asked.

"That depends," Miss Chernyshevsky replied, her manner becoming cautious.

"Upon what?" the portly man queried.

"You must realize that I represent a business known

throughout the South for its hon—*integrity*—!" the woman began.

"We've no' stolen 'em," McTavish interrupted, "if that's what you mean!"

"Nor did Miss Chernyshevsky mean to imply we *had*, Doctor," Cadwallicker asserted soothingly. "But, naturally a young lady in her position must bear such a possibility in mind. I assure you that we haven't *stolen* them, my dear young lady. They are our own property. In fact, you might even go so far as to say that *nobody* else has *ever* owned them."

"You *found* them?" Miss Chernyshevsky suggested, but in a manner redolent of disbelief.

"No, my dear young lady," the portly man denied. "We didn't exactly *find* them. Rather you would be more correct in saying we *made* them."

"Made them?" the woman repeated, looking startled.

"Yes, my dear young lady," Cadwallicker confirmed. "We can make *diamonds!*"

"So you have learned how it is do—!" Miss Chernyshevsky gasped. Then, making an obvious effort, she regained her composure and halted the words for a moment before continuing, "But that's *impossible!*"

"They're there," the portly man pointed out, glancing briefly at his companion who was just as clearly puzzled by the first part of the young woman's comment. "And, whether you believe it or not, we *made* them."

"How?" Miss Chernyshevsky demanded, rather than just asked and her interest was all too plain to see.

"Ye canna expect us to tell you *that!*" McTavish snorted. "Even if *you* could understand—!"

"I can see I'm wasting my time here!" Miss Chernyshevsky snorted, pushing back her chair and starting to stand up. "You clearly would not want to do business with a mere *woman!*"

"You must excuse my friend, my dear young lady!" Cadwallicker requested, once more becoming placatory. "He has had few dealings with members of your—gender."

"You could have said, 'sex', sir," the woman asserted, but she appeared sufficiently mollified to sit down again. "I'm no *prude!*"

"Of course you aren't," the portly man agreed. "And, to show you no offense was meant, this is how our secret came about. We were teachers of geology, but decided there could be a more lucrative and satisfying way of earning a living than by trying to drive our knowledge into the unreceptive heads of spoiled and pampered rich young fools in the college where we were on the faculty. So we resigned and went to work in industry. However, I will admit that we stumbled upon our discovery by accident whilst carrying out some experimental work on an entirely different matter for our new employers." Pausing as he saw the way in which the young woman was running a less than flattering gaze over himself and his companion, he continued, "I admit we hardly look like two men who have made such a discovery. Not being experienced in such matters, we failed to realize that it was one thing to make the diamonds, but *selling* them was a horse of an entirely different colour."

"So did Unc—!" Miss Chernyshevsky began, but once again changed her comment. "I don't see why it should be. They're only moderately sized, but I'd stake my reputation they're genuine."

"They're *genuine* all right," McTavish growled. "That's the rub!"

"How do you mean?" the woman queried.

"Like yourself," Cadwallicker replied, as his companion made no attempt to do so. "The jewellers back East we offered to sell them to wanted to know how they had come into our possession. Unfortunately, we told them the truth."

"Why unfortunately?" Miss Chernyshevsky asked. "Weren't you believed?"

"No more than *you* believe us just now," the portly man answered. "So, as funds were running low, we let two of them watch us produce a batch."

"That would have made them believe you."

"It *did*, which made matters worse."

"How?"

"You've heard of the Diamond Trust?"

"Of course I have. It was they who— They control the diamond trade throughout the world."

"They do," Cadwallicker confirmed, wondering why the young woman kept starting a remark and then changing it before it was completed. "And, as you can imagine, it would not be to their advantage to have genuine diamonds produced by our means. That would have a *most* adverse effect upon the price, which has always been based upon their rarity."

"They tried to get our process, damn them!" McTavish

gritted. "We managed to get away with everything we need to keep on making the stones, for all the good it did us."

"That is true," the portly man agreed. "You were looking at the way we're dressed, Miss Chernyshevsky. That is through no fault of our own. Here we are, with something that should be making both our fortunes and we can't use it without bringing the Diamond Trust about our ears. Which is why we've come west. Not only are we hoping to throw the agents of the Trust off our trail, we thought perhaps we might find somebody out here with the vision to realize what we have and the means to help us exploit it."

"*Exploit!*"

"Exploit. We can make the diamonds, but we need an outlet in the jewellery trade to dispose of them."

"An *outlet!*" Miss Chernyshevsky said slowly, nodding in understanding and glancing at the copy of the local newspaper which was open at the advertisement she had had inserted on her arrival. "Yes, a *reputable* jeweller could sell them—in carefully controlled quantities of course—without attracting attention or questions about their source."

"That is *exactly* what we had in mind," Cadwallicker declared. "And why we came to see *you.*"

"Why *me?*" the woman queried. "There are two jewellery shops owned by most experienced *men* in town."

"We *know*," Cadwallicker admitted. "And we've looked them over. Neither struck us as having the *vision* to realize what we have to offer, even if they would have the *courage* to go against the dictates of the Diamond Trust."

"And you think *I* would have?" Miss Chernyshevsky suggested, but the men could see she was pleased by the implication.

"That was my contention," Cadwallicker declared. "As I said to Doctor McTavish, any young lady with the courage and ability to come out West in such a capacity would also have the foresight we require."

"So you want *me* to provide your outlet?"

"You have the means to do so."

"And how *much* would it cost me?"

"Well, there are certain overheads which regrettably our reduced circumstances prevent us from defraying personally before we can commence production in worthwhile quantities," Cadwallicker explained. "For one thing, we will soon be requiring to replenish the hydro—the *ingredients.*"

"But you still have enough of the *ingredients* to let me see how your process works?" Miss Chernyshevsky inquired.

"We have," the portly man confirmed, then raised his right hand in a prohibitive gesture as his companion showed signs of being about to speak. "No, Angus. I *know* what you're going to say, but I cannot agree. If Miss Chernyshevsky is willing to take the not inconsiderable risks involved in going against the Diamond Trust, then I *insist* that she satisfies herself we can produce them as we claim."

Aye," the Scot growled, albeit with less than enthusiasm. "I suppose the lassie has that right. But has she the *means?*"

"*Means?*" the young woman challenged rather than asked. "I assure you, *sir,* that the firm of Chernyshevsky & Sons of Richmond, Virginia, is an old established business."

"That's as it may be," McTavish replied, contriving to look even more dour than before. "But it's always been my policy to see *proof.*"

"Proof, *sir!*" the young woman snapped. "May I ask what manner of *proof?*"

"Financial proof," the Scot answered.

"We are financially sound—!" Miss Chernyshevsky began.

"Aye, that's as maybe," McTavish replied. "But, although I'm no' from Missouri, I'm a Scot and we like to be shown."

"What my friend means, my dear young lady," Cadwallicker put in, seeking to calm the bristling indignation shown by the woman. "Is we'd like to know *you* have the means to become a partner in our scheme without any—delay, shall we say?"

"*Delay?*"

"We need money not only to purchase the supplies we require, all of which are available here in Dodge, but to move on without delay to avoid the agents of the Diamond Trust. If we have to wait until you can contact your *menfolks*—!"

"I've a goodly sum with me," Miss Chernyshevsky claimed, her frown indicating she had noticed the slight exphasis placed upon the last word of the uncompleted explanation. "But—"

"But you want to make sure it is to be well spent," Cadwallicker finished. "A most commendable idea. After all, we might be men of dubious motives trying to fleece you. We *aren't,* I assure you. Nevertheless, as my friend put it, you aren't from Missouri, but you still need to be shown."

"I'd hardly be likely to take your story at face value," Miss

Chernyshevsky declared. "I would have to know you can do as Unc—do as you claim."

"You've seen those diamonds," McTavish pointed out, deciding against asking about the reason for the revision in the last sentence.

"I have and they're genuine," the woman countered. "But that's *all* I have seen."

"We've another thousand dollars worth of diamonds manufactured already," Cadwallicker claimed. "To save you wasting your time and as evidence of our good faith, we'll sell them and those you are holding to you for fifteen hundred."

"Even if I decide not to go any further in the arrangement?"

"No matter what decision you reach. After all, fifteen hundred dollars will give us the necessary wherewithal to purchase all we need and to go and seek for somebody else with the foresight to appreciate what we have to offer."

"That is satisfactory," Miss Chernyshevsky assessed. "I have fifteen hundred dollars—and more—in the hotel's safe, plus a sizeable account at a bank in town. However, I would need to *see* for myself that you can do what you claim."

"And so you shall, my dear young lady," the portly man promised. "When would you like to?"

"There's no time like the *present*," Miss Chernyshevsky declared and, on thrusting her chair back this time, she stood up. "I'll go and put on something more suitable for being outdoors, then collect the money from the safe to show to you. However, I'm not willing to hand it over—or even take it with me—until *after* I have seen you make some diamonds."

"We've *got* her, Angus," Cadwallicker enthused, watching the young woman go out of the dining-room. "But I thought you'd pushed her too far a couple of times."

"There's no chance of that," McTavish replied. "From what I heard her saying around here yesterday, she's one of those 'anything a man can do, a woman can do better' crowd and that kind always jump when you prod them about only being just a 'wee lassie' who can't be expected to know or do anything."

"Well, she's took the bait hook, line and sinker," the portly man asserted. "But I wonder what she meant by those remarks she kept changing?"

CHAPTER TWO

I Must Have Made a Mistake

"Is *this* where you make your diamonds?" Miss Olga Cherny-shevsky asked, wrinkling her nose in obvious disdain as she looked at the small and dilapidated wooden cabin, with a sad-dled horse hitched to the rail of its porch, situated some four miles from Dodge City and towards which she was clearly being taken.

"It's not very impressive, I'll admit," answered the man who had introduced himself as 'Professor Oswald Cadwal-licker,' leaving 'Doctor Angus Donald McTavish' to handle the reins and guide the spirited horse drawing the buckboard in which they were riding. "But it serves our needs and gives us the privacy we require."

"And who might *that* be?" inquired the beautiful young Southron woman with the Russian name, pointing to where a tall, lanky and lugubrious looking man wearing a dirty round-topped black hat, collarless off-white shirt, bib-overalls and blunt toed black boots which gave the impression of never having seen polish, came out of the building.

"The owner of the property," Cadwallicker replied. "A dull-witted bumpkin, but a good fellow at heart and, being in need of money, willing enough to accept our activities without question."

At the Prudential Hotel, Miss Chernyshevsky had wasted no time in doing as she promised. Coming downstairs from her room after an absence of a few minutes, she was carrying a parasol as well as her reticule. Going into the office of the manager, she had returned and shown the two men a wad of banknotes of such size it caused them to exchange quick

10

glances. However, when Cadwallicker hinted she might care to fetch along the fifteen hundred dollars he had quoted as the price for the diamonds, she had declined and stated her intention of returning the whole sum to the safe from which it had come. Furthermore, she had demanded that they left the bag containing the diamonds behind as evidence of their good faith. Guessing that to say "no" would cause her to refuse to go with them and satisfied they could retrieve their property on their return, they had agreed. After having deposited her money and the sack in the safe, she had accompanied them to the livery barn from which they had already hired a buckboard and a very good horse to draw it.

"Howdy," greeted the lugubrious man, as McTavish swung the vehicle in a half circle and halted it facing in the direction from which it had come. His accent was Kansan and indicative of less education than any of the new arrivals. "See you're back, then."

"That we are, Mr. Godwin, that we are," Cadwallicker confirmed heartily. "And, as we won't be needing your services, perhaps you'd care to go and hunt us up a deer, or something of the like, for the pot?"

"Might's well," the Kansan grunted, showing no interest in Miss Chernyshevsky's presence apart from darting a quick glance her way. Ambling in a most leisurely fashion from the porch, he released the sway-backed horse—which looked as lethargic as he did—and hoisted himself laboriously on to the saddle. Setting the animal moving at a leisurely amble, he went on, "I'll do that."

"A good enough man, as I said," Cadwallicker claimed. He was relieved that the young woman had obviously failed to notice the departing man had no weapon of any kind with which to shoot a Kansas whitetail deer, even if the species *Odocoileus Virginianus Macrourus* had not been practically hunted to extinction in the vicinity of Dodge City. Nor, he was even better pleased to realize, had she proved any more observant elsewhere. Or, if she had detected the bulge inside the front flap of the bib-overalls, she had failed to attach any significance to it. Climbing from the vehicle, he turned and extended his right hand. "May I assist you?"

"Certainly *not*, thank you!" Miss Chernyshevsky refused. "Although I'm only a mere *woman*, I assure you that I'm *quite* capable of climbing down unaided."

Once again exchanging a glance with McTavish, as the woman was lowering herself a trifle clumsily from the buckboard, the portly man sensed they were both thinking it would be an added pleasure to prove her much less capable and intelligent than she clearly believed herself to be. However, keeping his face schooled in bland lines, he suggested they go into the cabin.

"Here it is, Miss Chernyshevsky," Cadwallicker announced dramatically, waving his hand to a fair sized and sturdy wooden box which stood in a corner on the dirt floor of the dusty and poorly furnished main room. "Our passport to *riches!*"

If the young woman was impressed by the comment, she contrived to avoid displaying it. Wrinkling her nose in distaste, clearly disapproving of such grubby surroundings, she followed the portly man and the Scot to the object indicated by the former. After each had removed a key from his trousers pocket, they took turns to operate the locks on the door of the box and McTavish pulled it open. Inside, the walls had a blackened look as if having been charred by heat.

However, it was to the apparatus in the container that Miss Chernyshevsky gave her attention. The base was like a wooden box with a drawer at the bottom. On it was mounted a tall dome covered, except where a small metal fixture having a hammer like that of a firearm attached emerged from the top, with thick wrapping of some whitish material held in place by three buckles.

"That's much like my unc—!" the young woman began. Then, as she had several times during the conversation at the Prudential Hotel, she continued with what was clearly a change of subject. "And this is the *thing* with which you *say* you can make diamonds?"

"Not only *say,* my dear young lady," Cadwallicker corrected, as the Scot disappeared into a room at the rear of the building. "But, as you will see, *can.*"

"Go ahead," Miss Chernyshevsky challenged rather than just requested, but her attempt to appear disinterested and even disbelieving was not entirely successful. "First, though, tell me how you produce this miracle."

"I can do that while we watch Doctor McTavish mixing the ingredients," the portly man claimed. "You know, of course, that diamonds are nothing more nor less than pure carbon which has been subjected to certain treatment by the elements. This machine reproduces the treatment upon the mixture of hydrocarbons, bone oil and lithium, in the *correct* balance of quantities of course, turning the compound into the kind of diamonds you've examined."

While Cadwallicker was speaking, his companion returned carrying another, albeit somewhat smaller, locked box. Opening this by raising the lid upwards, the Scot lifted out a set of glass covered scales of the kind used when small quantities had to be weighed with accuracy. Setting it down alongside the box, he removed the protective dome. Next he produced a chamois leather sack about a foot in length, although nowhere nearly filled to capacity, two smaller boxes and a tightly corked bottle containing a viscid, oily fluid. These were followed by a smaller jug with measurements inscribed down its outside and a mortar and pestle.

"Would you no' be crowding me, lassie?" McTavish growled, glancing up as the young woman approached. "'Tis delicate work, mixing just the right amounts of the compound and the *slightest* mistake spoils it."

"If you stand here, you can see what the doctor is doing," the portly man suggested and, as Miss Chernyshevsky took his advice, he continued with the explanation. "The drum on top of the collecting box is made of brass, which has a good resistance to heat, surrounded by a thick coating of asbestos. This is *very* necessary. In fact, even with the protection, the sides of the box are getting charred."

"So I noticed," the young woman admitted, but without taking her attention from the Scot as he carefully weighed powder from the two boxes and decanted some of the liquid with just as much attention to ensure he used the right amount. "It was the sa— And what does this machine of yours do?"

"At the base of the drum is another compound we have developed," Cadwallicker answered, once more wondering about the halted comment. Continuing to talk, he crossed to the rickety sidepiece in the corner opposite the device and returned with a box containing several bulky brass cartridges. "It is based upon the magnesium flash powder, as it is called, used by photographers to produce sufficient light for their pictures, but with added ingredients which cause it to burn in an *extremely* rapid fashion and with a *tremendous* temperature when ignited by a powerful impact. We attain this impact by using the powder from two ten gauge shells, with the shot removed, to propel a steel piston down on to a sheet of steel with tremendous force. The heat generated is funnelled into a metal container holding the compound and, in combination with the pressure caused by the piston, this is thrust through small holes in the base plate and forms diamonds which drop into sand in the bottom drawer."

"The compound's *ready!*" McTavish announced, showing more animation than previously as if being aware that something *very* special was about to take place.

Going to the big box, Miss Chernyshevsky watched the Scot unfasten the asbestos covering. Opening a flap in the brass dome, he allowed her to see a steel tray forming a depression like a shallow funnel around a slightly hollowed block made of the same material, its surface blackened and scarred by heat, in the centre. After he had poured some greyish powder from the chamois leather sack evenly over the depression in the block, he closed the plate. Leaving the covering rolled up, he extracted a tray with a number of small holes in its base from a couple of inches below the flap. Taking the mortar from his companion, he started to place lumps of the compound he had mixed until it attained the consistency of clay so they rested on the holes. Having done so, he replaced the tray and secured the covering.

"It's all *ready*, Professor," McTavish announced. "Put in the charge and we'll make the lassie a few diamonds!"

"They fall into the drawer at the bottom when they've been made?" Miss Chernyshevsky asked, directing a gesture in the appropriate direction.

"They are driven into it through the holes," Cadwallicker confirmed. "We have it partly filled with sand, otherwise they would destroy the bottom of the drawer."

While answering, the portly man was wondering why the young woman did not ask any of the questions about the process which had been raised each time he and the Scot had carried out similar demonstrations in the past. The most frequently raised had been why, if the process was so simple as it appeared, somebody else had not already discovered and exploited it. He always replied than he and "Doctor McTavish" had only stumbled upon the correct quantities for the compound and system to utilize it by accident and, as the former had to be so exact, nobody else had arrived at the correct combination of weights and method of production.[1] However, no queries were put to him. It almost seemed, taken with the unfinished remarks she had made, that she had seen something similar which produced genuine results where—much to his annoyance, as he had always believed something of the sort would manufacture real diamonds—his experiments had failed. Telling himself that he was sure to have heard of such a resounding success if it had taken place, he discounted it as a possibility.

"May I see inside the drawer?" Miss Chernyshevsky requested, as previous witnesses almost invariably did.

"Of *course* you can, my dear young lady," the portly man assented without the slightest hesitation, the contingency having been anticipated and measures taken to enable such an inspection to be carried out. "In fact, I was just going to suggest that you did so."

"Are ye satisfied *now*, lassie?" McTavish asked, after the examination of the drawer had been made and it was returned to its place.

"I am!" Miss Chernyshevsky confirmed, diverted as was intended by the manner in which she was addressed and failing to see Cadwallicker press what appeared to be a knot in the side of the box with his forefinger.

"Then load her up, Professor," the Scot authorized. "And we'll show the lassie how we *can* make diamonds."

Having slipped two of the brass shells into apertures in the device at the top of the dome, the portly man took a long lanyard from his jacket pocket. He connected it to a hole just below the hammer, which was positioned so the two strikers fitted to it could each fall upon a priming cap simultaneously. Signalling for the young woman to accompany him and with McTavish following, he backed away until putting the width of the cabin between them and the box.

---

1. By a remarkable coincidence, in 1880, J.B. Hannay claimed he had made diamonds as result of heating a mixture of hydrocarbons, bone oil and lithium in sealed wrought iron tubes. In the early 1890's, Henri Moissan declared he had achieved a similar result. He did this by dissolving sugar charcoal in molten iron and quenched the solution in cold water so as to crystallize the carbon under the great internal pressure supposedly generated by contraction as the mass cooled. However, subsequent attempts to duplicate their efforts proved unsuccessful.

"Here we *go!*" the portly man ejaculated and tugged on the lanyard.

Liberated by the pull on the cord, the hammer snapped downwards. There was a bellow of detonated black powder and, to the accompaniment of a reverberating clang of steel on steel, the whole device vibrated sharply.

"Not yet, my dear young lady!" Cadwallicker cautioned urgently, catching Miss Chernyshevsky by the arm and halting the step forward she had started to make. "We must give it a minute or more to cool down."

"Aye," McTavish supported. "We wouldn't want ye to go burning your hands, lassie."

"It should be all right now," the portly man assessed, after keeping the young woman waiting with an increasing impatience for about five minutes. "Go ahead."

"Let *me* open the drawer," Miss Chernyshevsky demanded, for her demeanour could hardly have passed as making a polite request.

"As you wish," Cadwallicker assented. However, knowing the sliding mechanism he had operated by pressing the stud disguised as a knot occasionally jammed, he went on, "Of course, the system doesn't always work."

"You can try it again if it doesn't this time," Miss Chernyshevsky offered. However, the need to do so did not arise. Opening the drawer, she saw half a dozen glittering lumps lying on the sand. Reaching out a hand which shook with emotion, she extracted one. Having produced the jeweller's lupe and conducted an examination, she continued in a voice barely higher than a whisper. "You *can* make diamonds!"

"Well then, young lady," Cadwallicker answered briskly, raising no objection to the woman taking the rest of the gems from the tray. "As you have seen us do it, are you willing to invest in our project? Or do you wish to merely take the stones we've already produced at the agreed price?"

"I'm willing to finance the whole project by five thousand dollars for starters, then as much as you need for the future," Miss Chernyshevsky asserted, crossing to put the gems on the box with the paraphernalia for making them. "But—!"

"But?" the portly man inquired.

"But first I want to make a batch of diamonds myself," the young woman explained.

"That's no' possible!" McTavish stated truthfully, sharing his companion's delight at having been promised a much larger sum than they envisaged; but aware that they could not produce the same effect as they had no diamonds available except for those lying in plain view on the box. "No' possible at all!"

"Why do you need to?" Cadwallicker went on.

"Look at it from *my* point of view," Miss Chernyshevsky requested, her tone redolent of determination to have her own way. "I'm going to be investing a *large* sum in this project, which I admit will prove most profitable—But only as long as the supply lasts."

"We can ensure it lasts, as long as we can buy the ingredients," the portly man asserted.

"I'm not gainsaying that," the young woman replied. "But if anything should happen to the two of you, the supply will be finished.

"Nothing is going to happen to us," McTavish claimed.

"It *might,"* Miss Chernyshevsky countered. "So, either I try, or you can try to find another backer—Unless the agents of the Diamond Trust find you *first."*

"The young lady has a point, Angus," Cadwallicker claimed, having detected a hint of a threat in the last sentence. Although he was not worried by its implications, he was wise enough to give the impression that he was. "It's only fair that we let her *try* to make some diamonds."

"Have it your own way," McTavish told the young woman with seeming reluctance, deducing what his companion meant from the emphasis placed upon the word *'try.'* "But there's only enough of the ingredients to make up one more batch."

"I've warned you that we aren't successful *every* time," Cadwallicker put in, confirming the supposition formulated by the Scot.

"You did," Miss Chernyshevsky conceded. "But I'll take my chance."

"All right then," Cadwallicker authorized, his manner that of one who had delivered a warning and now considered he was exculpated should anything go wrong. "Just so long as you *know* the project doesn't work *every* time. Mix up another batch of the compound, please, Angus."

"Not *you,* Doctor!" the young woman corrected, her attitude suggesting she would brook no argument. "Tell me the amounts and *I'll* do the mixing!"

"As ye will!" McTavish grunted. "I'll tell you what to do and how to do it."

"You may as well leave them there, Professor," Miss Chernyshevsky commented, as the portly man was reaching for the diamonds on the box which served as a work bench. "We'll be able to compare them with those I produce."

"Certainly, my dear young lady," Cadwallicker assented, satisfied that he would be able to retrieve the gems later and wanting to keep the intended victim of the scheme contented. "Unless you've any objections, I'll prepare the apparatus while you mix the compound."

"I would *prefer* to know how to do *everything,*" Miss Chernyshevsky amended.

"Very well," the portly man accepted. "Carry on."

Supplying the young woman with the first quantities to come to his mind, McTavish watched with well concealed amusement the way in which she carefully measured each component to ensure all were accurate. However, his companion darted an annoyed glance his way when it became obvious that he had underestimated the amounts in his quotation.

"That's *good!*" Miss Chernyshevsky announced, studying the residue of the bone oil in the bottle and the powders in the boxes. "There's enough left to make another batch if this one should go wrong."

"Aye, that there is," the Scot admitted dourly, deciding another sequence could be avoided by pointing out it would soon be sundown and they had a reasonably long journey back to Dodge City which would be better made before night descended. "Now grind them all together the way I did."

Showing competence at the task, the young woman worked with the pestle until producing a mixture of a texture which McTavish tested and, as gravely as if he believed doing so had any point, pronounced correct. Then she was shown how to remove the asbestos cover of the device, raise the lid and reset the steel piston so it could be driven downwards again by the mass of gas created as a result of detonating the black powder in the black shotgun shells.

With everything prepared, having shown no sign of noticing the exchange of amused glances which passed between the men while she was carrying out the instructions, Miss Chernyshevsky affixed the lanyard and retired to the far side of the room. Giving a tug, she set the firing process in motion and the rest of the "diamond making" process was quickly completed. Dropping the cord, she hurried forward followed by Cadwallicker and McTavish. Reaching the contraption first and blocking their view, she bent over to pull out the drawer at the bottom.

"Oh no!" the young woman gasped. "Either you gave me the *wrong* weights, Doctor, or I must have made a *mistake!*"

"I did warn you the process isn't *always* successful in producing diamonds," Cadwallicker pointed out.

"It hasn't produced *diamonds* this time," Miss Chernyshevsky admitted, but she seemed more happy than disappointed. Stepping aside, she pointed downwards dramatically and went on, *"Look!"*

"Well I'll be damned!" Cadwallicker gasped, staring into the drawer and, by his side, the Scot let out a similarly startled exclamation. "They're *emeralds!*"

"Yes," the young woman agreed, as the portly man reached with a visibly shaking hand to pick up one of the six glistening green stones which lay on the sand. "My Uncle Boris in Riga, back in the Old Country, had that happen to him a few times when he was making diamonds using much the same system."

CHAPTER THREE

We've Been Slickered

"Your uncle has made diamonds and emeralds this way?" 'Professor Oswald Cadwallicker' asked, his tone suggesting he did not believe such a thing possible despite the pretense that he and 'Doctor Angus Donald McTavish' employed of having done so.

"How is it we've no' heard anything about it?" the Scot challenged, without taking his gaze from the green gems which his companion was gathering from the sand of the drawer.

"He did it in Riga," Miss Olga Chernyshevsky explained. "It's a small Russian city on the Baltic which I doubt whether *you* have ever heard about. Anyway, when the Diamond Trust learned of his discovery, they took steps—although nothing was ever *proven*—to prevent his findings being utilized and ensure no word of what he had discovered was made public."

"They *would* do that," Cadwallicker admitted, but—despite being annoyed by the inference that neither he nor his companion were sufficiently well read to know about it—he refrained from mentioning that he recollected having heard of the city of Riga in connection with the Napoleonic War.[1] "But this is incre—!"

"Aye, man, so it is!" McTavish interrupted, realizing the comment he had halted was continuing to give too strong an

1. Riga, capital of Latvia, was put under a state of siege from July to October, 1812, by the forces of Napoleon Bonaparte—although not under his direct command—during his ill-fated campaign in Russia. It held out and became the most northern point of his conquest in Continental Europe. By doing so, it also became a major turning point in the war. For information about the siege, see: THE COMMODORE, by C.S. Forester.

indication that neither of them had expected anything to be produced by their apparatus. "We've never made emeralds, only diamonds."

"Let's see if we can make some more," Cadwallicker suggested eagerly, jiggling the stones in the palm of his right hand. "All we need to do is duplicate the amounts you used for these."

"Aye," the Scot said and his dour tone was not simulated on this occasion. "That's *all* we need to do."

There was good cause for McTavish to sound disconsolate. Although he and Cadwallicker had always believed it was possible to make diamonds and other precious stones in a manner similar to that being employed and had frequently tried, the apparatus never produced the desired result. Now it had done so, by the sheer fluke of his having given the young woman the correct formula to make it work. Unfortunately, due to the excitement of the discovery, he could not remember the proportions he had caused to be mixed.

"We should have enough of the ingredients to make a few more," Miss Chernyshevsky claimed. "And I'm sure I can recollect the exact amounts you told me to use, Doctor."

"I'm no' so sure you can, *lassie*," the Scot answered. Nevertheless, he was certain a woman with the point of view of equality between the sexes held by the intended victim would be only too willing to supply knowledge which she considered made her equal, even superior, in another respect to men. "Tell me and I'll know whether you've got them right or not."

"Well," Miss Chernyshevsky said, after she had quoted the required quantities. "Am I *right* or not?"

"They're right enough," McTavish confirmed, but the words were directed more to his companion than the young woman until he resumed, "So you can mix up some more of the compound using 'em, lassie."

"I'm *sure* you wouldn't want to entrust such a delicate matter to a mere *woman*," Miss Chernyshevsky answered, showing the indignation which had frequently appeared when she thought she was being slighted on account of her feminine gender. "So *you* had better do it!"

"As you wish," the Scot growled.

Watched by the young woman and his companion, who he failed to notice was showing by far the greater interest, McTavish set about the making of the compound. Never had he taken such great care to ensure an accurate measurement of the hydrocarbon and lithium powder. He devoted just as much precision to pouring the addition of as close as he could manage to the amount of the bone oil which he had been given. Furthermore, even when they had been trying to find a combination of the ingredients to really manufacture precious gems, Cadwallicker had never given so much concentration to what was being done.

Although he never offered to do so when they were engaged upon what—despite having arisen out of genuine research—had developed into a very successful confidence trick, the portly man could not resist the impulse to take an active part in the process. Placing the emeralds with the diamonds on the top of the box, he conducted his own tests of the consistency attained by the Scot working upon the contents of the mortar. Until they were satisfied with the mixing, neither remembered the machine had not been made ready since Miss Chernyshevsky had produced the startling result in it. On the realization coming, both went to rectify the omission. While McTavish held the mortar with a care never before employed, Cadwallicker set to work.

Being so engrossed in the task, regarding it as the fulfilment of their long sought ambition, the men gave the person responsible not so much as a thought. In fact, they had to all intents and purposes forgotten her existence. It never occurred to either to look around and ascertain why, in spite of her implied distrust in masculine ability, she was not standing close behind and watching everything that was done to ensure no mistakes were made.

If a glance to the rear had been taken, it would have given warning that things might be far from being as they seemed!

Instead of following Cadwallicker and McTavish, Miss Chernyshevsky remained by the smaller box. Waiting until sure their attention was devoted solely to the work they were doing, she loosened the drawstring of her reticule. Easing open the neck wide enough to facilitate her intentions, watching the men all the time, she slipped the gems inside. Having secured the precious contents by tightening the drawstring again, she grasped the reticule at the neck with her left hand and took up the parasol in her right. Then feeling behind her with each foot to ensure she did not inadvertently kick something which might either trip her, or otherwise make sufficient noise to bring unwanted attention her way, she started to walk backwards.

Reaching the door through which she had entered, still keeping Cadwallicker and McTavish under constant observation, the young woman eased it open slowly so that its hinges did not make too great a squeak. However, even if it had, the pair were unlikely to have paid any attention. Certainly they showed no sign of being disturbed by the unavoidable small amount of sound she made while, having closed the door behind her, she was leaving the building.

Smiling in a way which made her face lose its haughty aspect, Miss Chernyshevsky swung around on the porch. The sight which met her gaze suggested she had made an error in tactics. Although there was no sign of the decrepit horse upon which he had departed, the man Cadwallicker had claimed to be the owner of the property was sitting with his back resting against the rear wheel of the buckboard. However, seeing her, it appeared he drew the correct conclusions from the surreptitious way in which she was taking her departure. What was more, either through loyalty to his visitors or for some other reason, he clearly did not intend to allow her to go further unchallenged.

Electing to act upon his suspicions, Godwin started to respond with a greater speed than had characterized his movements earlier. Beginning to thrust himself erect, his right hand went into the front flap of the bib-overalls and closed around the butt of the Colt Navy Model of 1851 Belt Pistol—a revolver in spite of its name—which formed a noticeable bulge there. Without waiting until he was fully upright, he started to bring it from its place of concealment. Furthermore, while his forefinger was entering the triggerguard and his thumb coiled around to draw back the hammer as required by the single action mechanism, he also opened his mouth to make some comment.

None of the actions were brought to completion!

Advancing so swiftly she practically bounded from the porch, Miss Chernyshevsky showed she possessed a thorough grasp of the situation and was aware of the most immediate priority. On alighting, she brought up and executed a lunge with the parasol which, despite its unsuitability as an *epee de combat*, a fencing master could only have faulted in minor respects. Certainly it served her purpose perfectly. Driven forward with rapidity and precision, the—fortunately for him— blunt metal tip of the ferrule entered the man's open mouth before he could utter a sound.

Having left his horse a short distance away, Godwin had returned on foot to perform the duty of lookout and, if needed, an unsuspected armed guard which—along with employing the appropriate regional accent and conveying the impression of being far slower witted than was the case—was his part in the confidence trick. Taken completely unawares by the speed and effectiveness of the response, he was prevented from carrying out his intention of warning the men in the building of the intended victim's suspicious behaviour.

Instead of giving the yell to his companions he had been on the point of making, a startled and pain filled gurgle was all the recipient of the attack was able to utter. Being assailed so unexpectedly, he was prevented from completing the straightening of his legs which might otherwise have allowed him to take some kind of counteraction. Nor, despite having reasonable competence in its use, was he any better able to bring his revolver into action. However, in one respect, he still managed to carry out at least part of the task which he was intending to perform.

Withdrawing the parasol, Miss Chernyshevsky pivoted at the hips to give impetus to the method she employed to end the second threat to her flight. Around and up swung the bulky reticule. Judging from the result when it passed beneath the brim of the decrepit black hat and crashed against the side of Godwin's face, it held something much more substantial than the gems and usual feminine articles. Making contact with a solid thud which gave testimony to the strength and, if the manner of its delivery was any guide, the skill at defending herself by such means she had acquired, the improvised weapon sent the lanky man sideways in a helpless reeling stagger.

At which point, the comparative silence in which the attack was taking place was brought to an end!

Just clear of the bib-overall's flap, with the hammer at the fully cocked position, the Colt was ready to fire when turned into alignment. Although prevented from doing the second part, an involuntary reaction caused Godwin to carry out the first. Knocked off balance, his already disrupted wits rendered even less able to cope, he could not prevent his right forefinger snatching at the trigger and discharging a bullet which went nowhere near its intended target. Restricted by the smaller quantity of powder the chambers of the cylinder could accept, the "Navy" revolver did not give such a resounding bark as those of "Army" calibre. Nevertheless, in the young woman's opinion, the sound it emitted was far greater than was desirable under the circumstances.

"Hot damn!" Miss Chernyshevsky hissed, watching her victim sprawling on the ground and the Colt flying from his grasp. *"That* will do it!"

What took place in the cabin immediately after the shot rang out proved the summation was correct!

"What the hell?" Cadwallicker ejaculated, justifying the supposition although he had not heard it uttered, as he looked around from where he was re-setting the piston of the device.

"The lass!" McTavish spat out at the same instant, so surprised by what he saw on glancing to his rear that he dropped the mortar. "She's *gone!*"

"So're the glitters!" the portly man yelled, turning his gaze to the box which served as a workbench and, as he often did in moments of stress, reverting to the jargon of the underworld in his reference to the missing gems. While spinning on his heel, passing under his open jacket, his right hand brought a Remington Double Derringer from the specially made pocket in his vest which allowed it to be produced with some speed. "Come *on!*"

"Dinna fuss yoursel'!" the Scot advised, but he duplicated his companion's actions by arming himself with the same kind of weapon, carried in a similar fashion, while swinging around and starting towards the front door. "Godwin's got her!"

However, regardless of his statement, the Scot accompanied his companion hurriedly across the room!

Aware that the shot would be heard and cause an investigation by the men in the cabin, the young woman was moving while uttering her assessment of the circumstances. Throwing the reticule and parasol on to the buckboard's floor in front of the driver's seat, she darted to the head of the spirited horse. Despite the animal having been made restless by the shot, listening to the startled conversation from inside the building —although the exact words eluded her—she made a quick snatch and set free the weighted tethering rope from where it was connected to the headstall. Then, showing a far greater agility than when descending, she swung herself aboard the vehicle and liberated the reins which had been looped around the whip standing erect in its holder.

Hearing the door of the cabin thrown open, the shriek of its poorly maintained hinges ringing out with a much greater volume than she had produced on taking her departure, Miss Chernyshevsky did not bother to look around. She knew what sight would meet her gaze, so acted to reduce the threat to her future well being that she realized it would pose. Having already noticed the horse was an excellent specimen and in the peak of condition, the latter proved by it having made the journey from Dodge City at a reasonably fast pace without showing any sign of distress, she felt confident of evading the fate which she knew would befall her should she be captured.

Proving once again that to think was to act, letting out a yell reminiscent of the battle cry employed by Confederate cavalrymen during the War Between The States and frequently emitted when cowhands from Texas were celebrating, Miss Chernyshevsky supplied an added inducement by a deft flick from the whip to the signal given via the reins. Already restless, the horse responded by lunging forward with a vigour which did more than just pull the buckboard in its wake.

Feeling the wheels of the vehicle leave the ground and descend with a thump, Miss Chernyshevsky contrived to remain on the seat. However, she was unable to prevent the Wavelean hat being dislodged. What was more, although the violence of the starting did not seem sufficiently powerful to create such a potentially painful result, the black hair with the tight and unflattering bun accompanied the headdress into the back of the vehicle. Obviously being an excellently constructed wig, its loss brought into view brunette hair cut short around her skull. Paying not the slightest attention to the inadvertent removal of part of what was obviously a disguise, she gave thought only to guiding the horse along the barely discernible track down which she had approached the cabin and ensuring it did not slacken its speed.

Bursting from the cabin first Cadwallicker gave vent to a bellow of rage. Like the Scot, he had believed Godwin had fired the shot to either compel the young woman to halt or ensure she had no other choice. The sight of the lanky man lying face down and unmoving warned him how wrong the supposition had been. Nor, hearing the sound of the rapidly departing vehicle, was he in any doubt this indicated there was a danger of her making good her escape. Consumed with a fury increased by the realization that he and his companions had been tricked, the sight of her changed appearance supplying a final unnecessary confirmation, he leapt from the porch.

Coming down, the portly man quickly brought the Remington to shoulder height at arm's length and his left hand joined the right on the butt. Sighting over the round two inch long superposed barrels as best he could with his grasp caused to quiver by the stress of his raging emotions, despite being mindful of the limited range offered by the easily concealed weapon, he squeezed the unguarded trigger. Flame and smoke belched from the upper muzzle, but—not unexpectedly—the fleeing woman gave no sign of having been hit. Snarling incoherently what was intended as a profanity, he drew back the hammer and, in addition to recocking the action, caused the mechanism to lower the changeable position of the striker to where it could reach the priming cap of the second cartridge.

"Hold your fire, man!" McTavish commanded, possessing a full measure of the parsimonious nature traditionally attributed to members of his race. "Don't waste your ammunition. Going as fast as she is, ye'll no' be hitting her with that stingy gun."

Although he dropped his own weapon into his jacket's right side pocket and darted to pick up Godwin's Colt, possibly being motivated by a similar restriction to that he had expressed, the Scot refrained from firing it after having attempted to line the just as rudimentary sights on the rapidly departing figure in the buckboard.

"God damn it, Angus!" Cadwallicker raged, all the blandness having left his face and it was now suffused by rage. *"We've* been slickered. Let's get after her!"

"How?" McTavish asked, being just as angry as his companion, albeit better able to keep the emotion under control and think rationally.

"How?" Cadwallicker bellowed, glaring about him. Then a full appreciation of the situation struck home. "God damn it, *yes.* How can we go after her?"

Under normal circumstances, the culmination of the confidence trick would not have taken place at the cabin.[2] There-

2. Usually after having convinced the victim that the device could "man-ufacture" diamonds, the conspirators returned with him—"Miss Olga Chernyshevsky" having been their first female "mark"—to the place where they had first met. On receiving the money, while McTavish went supposedly to purchase more of the ingredients, Cadwallicker delayed the arrival of the victim at their appointed rendezvous. When they came on the scene, the Scot would emerge from the building selected with what looked like blood streaming down his face and claim he had been com-

fore, the conspirators had failed to anticipate the need to have mounts available there which would have allowed them to take up the chase. Even the horse which Godwin had used had been selected to add to the illusion that he was the owner of the property. It was spavined and wind-broken to such a degree that it would not be able to overtake the spirited animal drawing the buckboard.

"It'll have to be a shanks' mare," McTavish declared bitterly, without offering to go and examine Godwin. "And, unless I'm sore wrong about yon lassie, it's no' the first time she's pulled games like this. So, long before we've walked into Dodge City, she'll be gone from the Prudential Hotel."

"God damn her to all hell's fires!" Cadwallicker spluttered, also paying no attention to the lanky man who was groaning and starting to stir. However, although he was about to point out it had been McTavish's decision to select 'Miss Chernyshevsky'—a name he now guessed was as much an alias as were those employed by himself and his companions—prudence caused him to refrain. Being aware that the Scot had a temper even more violent than his own, if better controlled most times, he went on, "We're *not* going to let her get away with it!"

"That we're *no'!*" the Scot confirmed, his manner redolent of grim determination and giving the suggestion it would go badly with the young woman when next their paths crossed. "The trouble is, I'm willing to bet—and you know I'm no' the man to wager lightly—we'll no' be finding her in Dodge."

"I'd be surprised if we did," the portly man admitted, having regained something of his more usual temperament. "But she's local, I'd say from the way she's handling that buckboard and, as this isn't the East where we know our way

---

pelled to kill an agent for the Diamond Trust who was waiting there. Then, having been given a pre-arranged signal, three men hired locally came into view in the distance. Two wore what appeared to be badges of office and the third was described as being yet another agent by Cadwallicker. Acting upon the advice he was given to take flight, the victim rarely objected when it was suggested they split up. Generally, he was only too willing to get away from the conspirators; particularly as he was warned that he might be considered an accessory to what would be regarded as murder by the authorities. If the ploy failed, either the Scot or Cadwallicker would render the victim unconscious by a blow before there could be an outcry.

around, how're we going to find her?"

"Aye, she's local all right," McTavish agreed. "And, the way she took us in, she's been around long enough to be known. Do you mind that place we were told to go to if we needed any good help?"

"I do indeed!" Cadwallicker replied, guessing what his companion was contemplating. "And I'd be surprised if we couldn't at least learn who she is and perhaps even where we can find her when we get there."

CHAPTER FOUR

In The Good Lord I Trust

"Yes, Horace?" Jonathan Ambrose Turtle inquired, his voice that of a well educated and bred Texan.

"I thought you'd like to know, sir," replied Horace Tumbril. Tall, gaunt, with a perpetual expression of being harassed, he looked like an over-worked clerk grown old in a junior position and disillusioned by life as a result. Nevertheless, he was most competent in his duties as the manager of the hotel side of the business; despite the very special nature of the establishment rendering them somewhat different— even potentially more dangerous—from conventional establishments of that nature. "Everything is ready for the game in Number Seven, sir."

"You've got your '*but*' tone, Horace," the owner of the Honesty John's Tavern estimated, knowing his employee very well as a result of their long acquaintance in the same capacity. "So what's wrong with the game in Room Seven? You don't think any of the players might be figuring on *cheating*, do you?"

"That's hardly *likely*, sir," the manager stated rather than assessed. His manner indicated complete confidence that there was no possibility of such a thing happening, despite continuing, "Is it?"

"I wouldn't *think* so," Turtle admitted with absolute conviction. "So is there somebody sitting in who may want to be told he'd be *advised* to step across our line?"

"Not that I *know* of, sir," the manager admitted, sounding as he would not be surprised if one or more of the players in the impending poker game should need to take advantage of the specialized fitting to which his employer referred.

As was almost invariably the case throughout the evening,

Turtle was lounging at his ease in his massive and comfortable
specially built armchair on a dais alongside the end of the
counter in the bar-room of Honesty John's Tavern at Brownton, Kansas. Tall and almost globular in dimensions, with a
sallow yet amiably pleasant cast of features—despite being
dressed after the fashion of a Deep South plantation owner
from the days when "cotton was king"—he conveyed the impression of being an Oriental potentate surveying his domain.
However, as was always the case, instead of a group of scantily attired and nubile harem girls around him, there were two
cold-eyed and well armed men always in attendance.

Apart from the employment of what were clearly capable
bodyguards, which in itself could have been no more than a
sensible precaution on the part of one whose great bulk and air
of lassitude apparently rendered him incapable of self-protec-
tion, there was nothing about the enormous man to indicate he
belonged to a family which had been prominent in the illegal
activities of Texas even before independence was wrested
from the tyrannical domination of Mexico's *Presidente* Antonio Lopez *de* Santa Ana.[1] Nevertheless, as he never troubled
to deny it, his background was well known. In fact, although
he had never made it public knowledge for obvious reasons,
he had recently been sent to act on their behalf to—as its
current head, Rameses "Ram" Turtle had said—"Get some of
that money our good ole boys with the trail herds are being
fleeced of by those Yankees up there in Kansas."[2]

However, regardless of his instructions and despite such
criminal connections, it was the proud boast of Jonathan Ambrose Turtle that he had *never* knowingly committed a dishonest act in his life!

Nevertheless, in spite of this laudable and truthful claim, it
was a well known fact that even Turtle's most charitable or
sycophantic associates could not with any vestige of truth as-

1. Information about the struggle by the Texicans, as they were called at
that period, to obtain independence from Mexican rule is given in the Ole
Devil Hardin series.
2. Information about a previous, current and later head of the Turtle fam-
ily, Coleman, Rameses "Ram" and Hogan respectively, can be found in:
OLE DEVIL AND THE CAPLOCKS; Part Four, "Mr. Colt's Revolving
Cylinder Pistol," J.T.'s HUNDREDTH; SET TEXAS BACK ON HER
FEET; BEGUINAGE; BEGUINAGE IS DEAD!" And various volumes of
the Alvin Dustine "Cap" Fog series, particularly THE RETURN OF RA-
PIDO CLINT AND MR. J.G. REEDER.

sert the same applied to the greater majority of his customers.
In fact, as had been the case with a similar establishment
having the same name which he had run in Texas, there were
those who might claim the most frequent and numerous of the
clientele of Honesty John's Tavern—which offered the ameni-
ties of a clean, comfortably appointed and costly hotel as well
as a well stocked and equipped saloon—left much to be desired.

On any given night, forming the majority of the customers,
there were invariably men present who could admit—if they
were so inclined—that between them they had committed
practically every crime on the legal statute books of the United
States. In fact, like its predecessors, his place had already
become notorious as a gathering place for outlaws during the
comparatively short time it had been open. However, when
this aspect was pointed out by insensitive people, Turtle had
always declared it was his belief that criminals needed somewhere they could relax and enjoy the company of their own
kind just the same as law abiding folks.

There were aspects of Turtle's latest Honesty John's Tavern, which its predecessor lacked, ideally suited to its most
numerous clientele!

Having been erected so that it bisected the joining of two
counties *exactly* upon their boundary line, a fact attested to
and notarized on a large notice placed prominently behind the
main bar-room's counter, the premises offered certain local
advantages. By stepping over a brass rail nailed to the floor in
the appropriate position, one could escape the attentions of
whichever sheriff arrived with the intention of making an arrest. Furthermore, situated in the centre of Brownton though
the building was, the town marshal and his deputies were so
lax in the performance of their duties that they posed no threat
to the visitors.

Regrettably, however, Honesty John's Tavern did not
present such complete immunity as was rumoured to be offered by the town of Hell in the Palo Duro country of Texas.[3]
Being far better known, albeit somewhat newer in operation,
it was subject to less restrictive visits by the United States'
marshal and his deputies; due to them having greater jurisdic-

3. Details of this town, which offered sanctuary to outlaws for a share of
their loot, can be found in HELL IN THE PALO DURO and GO BACK
TO HELL.

tional authority than was granted to county or municipal peace officers.[4] Aware of this distressing fact, Turtle employed men to continually lurk all around the building and pass warning if such unwelcome callers should approach.

There had been no such warning that evening!

In fact, the only event of note all day had been the arrival of news shortly after noon on a west-bound train that the already close to legendary young Texan, Captain Dustine Edward Marsden "Dusty" Fog, in his capacity of town marshal of Mulrooney, had led a posse to wipe out a band of *Metis* from Canada who had had sufficient lack of judgement to commit an attempted assassination and three murders in his bailiwick.

The information had not been received with the satisfaction law abiding citizens would have given it elsewhere, due to the rivalry between the two towns. Turtle was of a more tolerant nature and, anyway, far less affected by the manner in which —as a result of the rapacious greed shown by some members of the community—Brownton had failed to attract more than a fraction of the business brought north by trail herds for shipment to the meat hungry East.[5] Furthermore, he had a Texan's close to chauvinistic pride in his home State. Therefore, he had remarked that—judging by the story of how the incident had taken place, there having been no casualties suffered by the posse despite the wanted men being inside a cabin and warned of their presence—it had been a mighty fine piece of work.[6] Such was not an attitude to be well received by those who heard it, but his position in the community made him oblivious to the opinion of others.

Taking in everything with a gaze which rarely missed even the smallest detail or unimportant happening, Turtle felt content with his lot that evening!

With a good number of customers present, most of whom were spending lavishly in spite of the prices at Honesty John's Tavern being higher than elsewhere in the town, business was excellent!

A further source of satisfaction for Turtle was that a poker game was shortly to be commenced in one of the second floor

4. An explanation of the jurisdictional authority of various law enforcement agencies in the United States of America can be found in Item 15, APPENDIX FIVE.

5. How this came about is recorded in: THE TROUBLE BUSTERS.

6. Told in: DECISION FOR DUSTY FOG.

rooms. Despite the conversation he was having with Tumbril
implying something could be wrong, it promised to be most
lucrative. All the players were sufficiently wealthy to ensure
the stakes were very high and the "cut" he invariably extracted
from each pot when such an event took place promised to be
substantial!

"Then what is it?" the globular owner asked, having the
greatest respect for the competence of the lanky man and
aware that he would be almost impossible to replace, but
wishing—not for the first time—he would change his irritat-
ing habit of waiting for information to be sought rather than
giving it immediately.

"It's *M'sieur* Chavallier, sir."

"And what about *M'sieur* Arnaud Chavallier?"

"He wants to *join* the game, sir," Tumbril said, his nasal
New England voice implying such a suggestion was ill advised in his opinion.

"And?"

"And I saw him play the last time he was here, sir. He'd be
out of his class *completely* in that company."

"Has he paid his bill?"

"*Naturally,* sir," Tumbril confirmed, showing annoyance at
it even having been thought he would be so remiss as to have
overlooked this most important aspect of his duties. "He queried why it should be necessary, as he did last time. So I reminded him of your policy of, 'In the Good Lord I trust, but
mortals pay cash' and he yielded with no better grace than
before."

"Bad grace or not, there's no reason in the world why we
should stop him playing," Turtle asserted judiciously. "Just
point out the game is *completely* honest, but for high stakes
and between men of considerable ability. After that, if he still
wants to play, on his own head be it."

"Very well, sir," the manager assented. "I was going to do
that; but, knowing *him,* I thought it would be received *better*
coming from *you.*"

Watching Tumbril walking away, looking—as always—
like a dejected whooping crane which had been painted black
and suspected something even worse was about to happen,
Turtle resumed his scrutiny of the bar-room. When Arnaud *le
Loup Garou* Chavallier did not enter, he assumed his stricture
had been accepted on receipt without it being brought to him
for confirmation. Satisfied he had done all he considered it

was his duty to do as host by giving the warning, he resumed his interrupted scrutiny of the bar-room.

About five minutes later, a woman entered and caught the eye of the globular man. As she came in he thought that her appearance did not look as though she would be likely to enhance his profits to any great extent!

Rather the newcomer might have arrived seeking some menial kind of employment such as a laundress, a roommaid, or even as a swamper; regardless of the latter generally being considered a masculine occupation and reserved for those of their gender who were capable of nothing better. Certainly, being just over medium in height, dumpy and seemingly round-shouldered in build, there was little about her to suggest her ambitions extended to acceptance as an addition to the less than decorously dressed, shapely and attractive young women mingling with the customers.

Judging by the shapeless black hat with a dangling veil concealing the features behind it, secured to a stringy and straggly mass of brown hair with a jade-headed pin, through the less than fashionable black dress beneath an equally cheap and close to threadbare coat of the same colour, to the much newer sharp toed and high heeled black boots showing beneath its hem, the woman—who gave the impression of being well past the first flower of youth—might be a newly-made widow. However, covered by black gloves made from thin leather and, like her footwear, of better quality than the rest of her attire, no clue as to her status could be obtained from her hands. The right grasped a bulky parasol and the left was clamped about the neck of a largy and lumpy looking reticule.

However, as frequently happened all through nature, appearances could be deceptive!

Glancing at a waiter who was approaching and guessing his intention was to ask the reason for her visit, the woman leant her parasol on the wall by the door. Then, making a stretching motion and flexing her shoulders, she straightened them in a way which added an inch or two to her height. Reaching up with her liberated hand, she removed not only the hat but the untidy "hair" to which it was attached. Doing so brought into view very short cropped genuine brown hair and a beautiful face with the golden tan suggestive of excellent health which indicated she was considerably younger than was suggested by the less than flattering attire.

"Give one of these to the man outside and the other's

yours," the newcomer requested, in the accent of a well bred Southron, taking two silver dollars from her reticule and holding them out. "Have him bring my gear in and see it's taken up to whichever room I get."

"Yes, Mi——*ma'am*," the waiter responded, making the amendment as he recollected his employer insisted no names should ever be mentioned until authorization to do so was granted by the customer being addressed. Even if he had not recognized the newcomer, the way she had said 'whichever' and not 'if' with reference to being given accommodation would have indicated she believed she would be welcomed as a guest. "I'll be honoured to see to it for you!"

Smiling and retrieving her parasol, the beautiful young woman strolled across the room toward the bar. Although no names were mentioned, it was obvious that the waiter was not alone in identifying her. However, accepting what was known to be a stringently enforced house rule, none of the customers who greeted or—if beyond hearing distance—exchanged waves of salutation, referred to her by name. Those of the clientele who were less well informed, but equally aware of the insistence upon anonymity required by the owner of Honesty John's Tavern, refrained from trying to satisfy their curiousity—or seeking confirmation of their suppositions—from the better informed.

Those who either did not know the newcomer, or merely harboured suspicions as to her identity, watched Turtle in the expectation of gaining an indication of her status!

In both the establishments he had operated, the globular man had established a certain procedure for greeting customers!

Such honest citizens who arrived were ignored, unless of sufficient social prominence to make this impolitic!

How an outlaw stood in the ranks of the criminal element could be determined by the response accorded. If amongst the lower echelon, or poorly thought of for any reason, he too would receive no attention. Should he be of a slightly higher level, he would be given a nod or even a few words. Beyond that stratum, the response also varied.

In fact, one's position as a successful law breaker was clearly shown by the number of steps Turtle took on rising and approaching to meet the new arrival!

Rumour had it that, one night in Texas—despite the amount of publicity he was receiving as the most successful

robber of banks and trains ever to have followed that illicit
trade, as well as being considered in some circles to be a noble
defender of the 'poor and downtrodden' against the evil
"railroaders" and a reincarnation of the legendary Robin
Hood[7]—Jesse Woodson "Dingus" James received only three
paces, although just prior to his arrival the man generally reported as being his second in command, Coleman "Cole"
Younger, was granted the infrequently bestowed distinction of
five.

Aware of this, several of the clientele started to make hurried wagers. The least informed were betting the new arrival
would have to go all the way to the dais. Others selected the
number of steps they estimated she would receive as a greeting and indication from Turtle. One man found plenty of
takers when he estimated she would be accorded more than
five. Such a figure was only rarely granted and only two
Texan gun fighters, John Wesley "Wes" Hardin and William
B. "Bad Bill" Longley, both of whom had been driven beyond
the law by the evils of the Reconstruction period after the War
Between The States,[8] had even been given more.

Thrusting himself out of the armchair and descending from
the dais with an ease which seemed surprising compared with
the air of lethargy he presented while seated, supplying an
indication that he could move with surprising speed despite his
bulk,[9] the globular man caused one set of wagers to be settled!

However, other bettors watched eagerly to ascertain the
result of their respective and varied selections!

It was soon obvious the newcomer was considered worthy
of an approach, rather than a mere standing up!

7. According to legend, learning a widow was about to have a mortgage
foreclosed and lose her home to an unscrupulous landlord, Jesse Woodson
"Dingus" James gave her sufficient money to pay him off, with the instructions to ensure she received a receipt for the full amount and the
requisite documents, then robbed him after he had left her property.
8. How John Wesley "Wes" Hardin fell foul of the repressive laws of the
Reconstruction period is described in: THE HOODED RIDERS
8a. Wes Hardin makes "guest" appearances in: PART TWO, "THE
QUARTET," THE HALF BREED; its 'expansion', HOLD FOR RAN-
SOM and Part Two, "Cousin Red's Big Chance," THE HARD RIDERS.
9. Although weighing over two hundred pounds, Roscoe "Fatty" Arbuckle, a famous comedian of the silent movie era, not only performed all
of his own stunts such as taking falls, but is reported to have frequently
won bets by beating much more slender men in one hundred yards sprint
races.

"One! Two! Three! Four!" more than one watcher was counting. Nor did they stop there. "Five! *Six!*"

The sum was only one less than accorded to Hardin and Longley!

"Miss *Chernyshevsky,* isn't it?" Turtle inquired, halting and extending an enormous right hand.

"It is, Jonathan," the beautiful young woman confirmed, experiencing no surprise at the firmness and strength of the grip—which was not tightened to impress her, or she knew it would have been most painful—she received while shaking hands. "But you may call me, 'Olga'."

The manner of the response had been caused by the newcomer being aware that the globular man disliked having anybody sufficiently well acquainted, prominent, or—if not considered worthy of the privilege—ill-advised, to use his first name and shorten it any way!

Although perhaps apocryphal, a story was told of how, having been greeted as 'Johnny', Turtle had replied with offended dignity, "I was a *fourteen* pound baby"—a typical Texas-style exaggeration as the actual weight had only been *twelve* pounds—"and am hardly diminutive now, so do *not* shrink my given name."

"I'm delighted to see you, my dear," Turtle boomed. "By the way, if you should be interested and unless you are too tired after your journey, there is rather a good *friendly* poker game in Room Seven."

"I'm not in the least tired and seven has always been my *lucky* number," claimed the young woman who was still calling herself 'Miss Olga Chernyshevsky', glancing to where the waiter and the man who had brought her from the railroad depot were carrying her baggage inside. "So, as soon as I've taken a bath and changed, I'll drop by and take a few hands."

CHAPTER FIVE

I'm Getting Ready!

"All this talk about co-operating with *England* is fine," Steven King claimed, in a voice raised sufficiently to ensure it was heard by the man a short distance away from his party; but for whom the words were really intended. As an aid to hold the attention of his main audience, in addition to supplying free drinks, he was giving his nasal 'Down East Yankee' voice the Irish brogue he normally strove to eliminate. "But it's little enough liking those god-damned Lime-Juicers have for *us* when they aren't wanting to put their hands in our pockets."

Tall, lean, with thinning dark hair and in his early fifties, everything about the speaker indicated he was not the typical habitue of the Buffalo Saloon in Mulrooney, Kansas. Despite his hospitable behaviour, there was an expression of harsh piety about his sallow face which was frequently borne by those whose religion was the kind which—according to legend—took a gun to church to ensure they received what they were praying for. His black suit, white shirt, sombre necktie and Hersome gaiter boots were expensive, yet excessively plain as if to denote a disinclination to squander hard-earned money on luxuries or fripperies.

"How do you mean, sir?" inquired one of the burly gandy dancers, most of whom were just as obviously Irish as he was and who were gathered around the New Englander's table enjoying what under normal conditions would have been unthinkable largesse towards members of their class.

"I was over there last year," King explained, contriving to sound as if he was confessing to some unsavoury crime. "In spite of them being so *willing* to let us build a railroad into Canada's will make them a whole heap of money, with pre-

39

cious little of their own being spent on it, I saw a play and there were illustrations in *all* their newspapers showing how *they* think all us Americans look and behave. You *wouldn't* have liked it. I know I *didn't*. According to them we're *all* loud-mouthed, arrogant, uncouth, loudly dressed and forever chewing tobacco and spitting out the juice."

It was eight o'clock in the evening!

The day before, King had been attending an important meeting at the Railroad House Hotel. It was to discuss the proposed extension of a spur-line, going north from Mulrooney, which would link with an inter-continental railroad under construction in Canada. While he was in favour of the project and was willing to back his conviction with a large proportion of his fortune, he had more culturally imbued than financial objections to the intended British involvement in the project. Before he could seek support for his point of view, the manager had come in and said there was a matter which it was imperative should be brought to the immediate attention of the assemblage.

The reason for the visit to the Conference Room—as the management of the hotel called the venue for the meeting—by the town marshal, Captain Dustine Edward Marsden 'Dusty' Fog, and his first deputy, Mark Counter, had been as urgent as was implied by the manager. They had come to warn the delegates of a dangerous situation which had arisen. Evidence suggested that a summation expressed earlier that the threat posed by Arnaud *'le Loup Garou'* Chavallier's *Metis* had ended was incorrect. Some of them had murdered Sir Michael Dinglepied and his personal secretary, Shaun Ushermale. One of their number was being held prisoner at the jailhouse.

The measures arranged by the marshal for the protection of the delegates had been effective, but the New Englander had resented being compelled to take them. He had felt his permission for such precautions should have been asked for with the humbleness and respect which he considered his position in society demanded. That the man who showed such scant regard for one of his prominence was not only a Texan, but had served with Confederate States with great distinction during what King invariably termed the 'War Of The Southern Rebellion,' did nothing to lessen his ire. Nor, having a dislike for Great Britain almost equal to the close to paranoiac hostility middle class-middle management elements—not all of them of 'liberal' persuasion, although these were the most rabid—in that country had already developed towards the United States, was he any better enamoured of the aftermath.

Filled with the culturally induced antipathy towards everything to do with Great—as it was *then*—Britain, although he usually tried to avoid letting his Irish origins be apparent, King had utilized the time during which he and the rest of the assemblage were compelled to remain under guard at the hotel by trying to arouse hostility against the two remaining aristocratic members of the British Railroad Commission!

Unfortunately for the New Englander, subsequent events had caused his efforts to lose whatever advantage he might have accrued![1]

Sir John Uglow Ramage, Lord James Roxton and the English-born member of the Canadian delegation, Colonel George A. French[2] had been allowed to accompany the marshal's posse; an option none of the Americans were offered. While King had hoped this omission could be used for his purposes, he found none of his fellow delegates were in any way put out by having been excluded. To make matters worse, when the posse had returned after concluding their mission with complete success, the participants claimed Ramage had been chiefly responsible for the affair being brought to a most satisfactory conclusion without casualties amongst them.

Much to his annoyance, instead of resenting the British trio being allowed to participate in what should have been a matter of law enforcement by Americans from the local population, King had discovered his countrymen attending the meeting had developed a growing respect for them. Nor had his at-

1. A report of the meeting is given in: THE CODE OF DUSTY FOG.
la. The events connected with the way in which the menace of the *Metis* was dealt are recorded in: DECISION FOR DUSTY FOG.
2. In May, 1873, Colonel George A. French organized what a later generation would term a "para-military" law enforcement force which was to be called the "Canadian Northwest Mounted Rifles." However, due to the Government of the United States having registered protests over the presence of a military body operating close to its border with Canada—wishing to maintain the spirit of co-operation he had established with various peace officers while visiting America—he substituted the word, "Police" for "Rifles" and this was accepted as a satisfactory compromise by both countries.

tempts to belittle their activities met with any success. Harland
Todhunter, whose company was building the spur-line, had
been loud in their praise. Even the delegates from Montana
and Dakota Territory, having attended the meeting to compete
for having it routed through their respective Territories, had
shelved their differences temporarily to give an equally vocif-
erous acclaim. The only person from whom King had felt
certain he could count upon support, was Bruce Millan for
whom he had no particular liking as a man or on account of
his radical politics, and he had been called away from
Mulrooney by what was claimed to be urgent business and had
given no indication of when he would return.

Being disinclined to go to the Fair Lady Saloon, where he
had felt sure his sensibilities would be further offended by
watching the other Americans "fawning around those blasted
Lime-Juicers" in the celebration of the posse's successful activities, King had found himself at a loose end. Rather than
remaining alone at the Railroad House Hotel, he had set out to
ascertain what other kinds of relaxation Mulrooney had to
offer.

Nothing the New Englander had seen had come up to his
requirements until he was passing the Buffalo Saloon!

King recollected that he had heard there was a connection
between this establishment and the one owned by the beautiful
and—he was willing to admit to himself grudgingly and re-
luctantly—very competent Miss Freddie Woods. By all accounts, there had been a feud culminating in a fist and hair
pulling fight between the female employees of both and, surprising as it might strike some people, the development of
close bonds of friendship when it ended in what could only be
termed a mass draw.[3]

Having had his curiosity aroused by the recollection, the
New Englander had looked over the batwing doors into the
main bar-room. It was well lit, clean, comfortably furnished
and well filled with representatives of several kinds of businesses which brought revenue to the local population while
passing through the town. However, at first, he had considered it did not offer anything better than the rest of the places
he had passed.

Just as the New Englander was about to walk on, his atten-

3. The feud is described in: THE TROUBLE BUSTERS.

tion was attracted by hearing an Irish 'come-all-yeez' type of song being chorussed vigorously at one end of the bar![4]

The singers were a bunch of half a dozen men King recognized as being railroad construction workers and four saloon-girls!

Despite his "roots" having been in the "Emerald Isle," they were at a somewhat higher social level than the men in the group and the New Englander would have ignored them if he had not seen another party further along the counter. Nor did he consider the soldiers, buffalo hunters and, especially, the Texas cowhands who were present in scattered groups as being sufficiently near his social status to warrant the pleasure of his company.

While the three almost equally well built and ruggedly good looking young men drinking beer seated at a table by the left side wall possessed the requisite social standing, King had no desire to join them as doing so was likely to cost him money without any gainful return for its expenditure. He knew the two wearing the everyday attire of members of the clergy were Father Brian O'Riordan, whose "cloth" would have made him acceptable company otherwise, and Reverend Dennis Thatcher, belonging to a church which he had been taught from childhood to be abhorrent. The other was the chief desk clerk—also the son of the owner—from the Railroad House Hotel, Walter Braithwaite.

That the first two should be in such a location and on what was obviously such amicable terms despite their different theological backgrounds surprised the businessman. However, anybody who lived in the town could have explained that they both followed a more liberal line than was generally adopted by the older members of their respective denominations. He did not know they had joined Braithwaite in the bar-room as offering an informal—and neutral—location to discuss organizing a series of "Boston game" football matches of the kind they had all played in Eastern colleges and they were seeking to popularize in Mulrooney.[5]

4. "Come all yeez"; an Americanized corruption of the Gaelic word, 'comailes,' meaning a rousing Irish ballad.
5. Being based upon a variant of soccer first played in the British Isles at Rugby public school during 1823, the "Boston game" and other regional varieties in the United States would evolve into the highly organized professional and amateur game of "American," or "gridiron" football. Be-

What caused King to enter, instead of passing on, was another group obviously enjoying themselves further along the counter. It consisted of one of the British aristocrats who had aroused his ire, the youngest member of the town marshal's office—who nevertheless had played a *very* important part in preventing the attempted assassination bid at the railroad passenger depot and was, he assumed, there to supply protection for Roxton—and two girls whose attire was hardly that of "good" women and were so alike, except for the colour of their hair and having different accents, that they might have been related.

On going inside, the New Englander had crossed directly to the bar!

Knowing King's feelings towards them neither Roxton nor the deputy had suggested he join their party. Nor, on the surface, had they apparently noticed how he appeared to have suddenly developed a pronounced Irish brogue when he had invited the singers to join him in a drink. Although the gandy dancers had shown surprise, as his clothing and general appearance indicated he belonged to a stratum of society which was generally disinclined to mingle with their kind on a social level, they had accepted. After a couple more songs and rounds of drinks, which he paid for although he was not noted for being free-handed in his home town, he had started to pave the way for his reason for entering.

"Can you hear that bleeder?" demanded Barbara 'Babsy' Smith, her voice giving a strong suggestion that she could have been born within the sound of the bells in St. Mary-le-Bow at Cheapside, in London. Bristling with indignation and glaring along the bar at the New Englander, she went on just as heatedly, "He ain't half running poor old Blighty down!"

Barely over five foot in height, not long out of her 'teens, the speaker had tightly curled blonde hair taken in a pile on top of her head under a large brimmed and flower decorated hat tilted at a jaunty angle. Her face was pretty and, except when annoyed as at that moment, had an expression indicative of a vivacious nature and a love of life. Being out for an

coming popular at various Eastern Colleges and universities, with the main emphasis being on kicking although carrying the ball was becoming increasingly an accepted tactic, it was played on occasion with up to twenty-five men in each team.

evening's entertainment in the company of what she referred
to as "two gentlemen friends," she wore neither the sober
attire of her duties as personal maid to Freddie Woods nor the
much more revealing costume donned when working downstairs in the bar-room; being an accomplished and well liked
entertainer in her own right. Instead, following the precept she
often declared that a girl with as good a figure as she knew she
possessed should be willing to show it off, she had achieved a
compromise by having on an outfit just bordering upon the
indecorous without going beyond the standards her well liked
and respected employer expected. The clothes she had selected were a trifle more garish than some might have considered socially acceptable and fitted so snugly, they did nothing
to hide the rich curves of her firmly fleshed close to buxom
figure.

"Chap had a point, though, dear girl," Lord John Roxton
asserted, his tone giving its usual suggestion of ennui. "He's
exaggerating more than a little about the newspapers. The
Times wouldn't even *think* of including illustrations of *anything*. But I must admit I was *dragged* to see that blasted play
by Vera Gore-Kauphin, which was another *good* reason for
avoiding her in future. It was written by one of her *crowd* and
I thought at the time how uncharacteristic it was of the Americans I'd met."[6]

Not quite six foot in height and in his mid-twenties, Roxton was lean in a wiry fashion. Flower-pot red from much
exposure to sun and wind, rather than having taken a tan, his
face was good looking with a crisp rusty-red moustache and a
small—somehow aggressive seeming—sharp pointed tuft of
whiskers on his projecting chin to emphasise its hawk-like
lines. His poise and demeanour were those of one who enjoyed an active existence and had lived hard in his time. The
suggestion was correct. He had spent much time on expeditions in various far from civilized parts of the world with his
father and had recently carried out an exploration on his own
account along the River Amazon in South America.[7] He was

6. Information regarding Vera Gore-Kauphin is recorded in: THE RE-
MITTANCE KID and THE WHIP AND THE WAR LANCE.
7. The tradition of hunting and exploration in South America was continued by Lord James Roxton's son, John; see: THE LOST WORLD, by Sir
Arthur Conan Doyle.

wearing a jaunty grey Homburg hat, a brown three-piece suit which bore the unmistakable cut of a top grade tailor in London's Saville Row, a soft white shirt with an attached collar, a necktie of one who had received part of his education at Eton public school and brown boots having an almost mirror-like polish.

"We're not *anything* like that," asserted Phyllis 'Ginger' Winchell, who had just about forgotten her christian name. Her accent was indicative of having been raised in Chicago, but not as part of that city's higher social circles. She too was small and close to buxom and, apart from having fiery red hair in a similar style, dressed in much the same fashion as the little blond. "Fact being, we're ever such nice folks, aren't we, Your Duke-ship?"

"*You* certainly are, my dear," Roxton admitted, accepting the entirely wrong honorific with cheery good grace. "And so are the *vast* majority of your fellow colonials.[8] I just wish, though, that so many of you hadn't asked me why I don't wear a *monocle*."

"I thought all you English dukes and such wore them," Ginger claimed.[9]

---

8. Like many of his generation and class, albeit perhaps a trifle tongue in cheek in most cases—as it was in his own—Lord John Roxton held to the belief that the world was divided into two parts, Great Britain and its colonies. Therefore anybody who was not British was considered a "Colonial."

8a. For our views on the subject, see the dedication for: KILL DUSTY FOG!

9. A popular misconception in the United States all through the Nineteenth Century was that all members of the British upper class wore monocles. This could have been helped to gain strength as a result of a few like the Earl of Hawkesdon, known as "Brit," who did so: see: RIO GUNS.

9a. Having learned of the supposition, the very competent British lady criminal, Amelia Penelope Diana "Benkers" Benkinsop wore a monocle as an aid to creating the character she was playing at one period during her visit to the United States in the mid 1870"s; see: Part Three, "Birds of a Feather," WANTED BELLE STARR.

9b. Further information about the visit is given in: BEGUINAGE IS DEAD! and Part Five, "The Butcher's Fiery End," J.T.'S LADIES.

9c. Information regarding a descendant of "Benkers," Miss Amelia Penelope Diana Benkinsop, G.C., M.A., B.Sc (Oxon), owner of Benkinsop's Academy For The Daughters Of Gentlefolk in England—who also followed the family tradition of retaining the full name regardless of whom

"Some do, old thing," the lean aristocrat replied, as gravely as if the conversation was on the highest level of diplomacy. "But most don't and, what's more, I *never* take crumpet——!"

"That's *not* what I heard," Babsy commented, darting an arch glance at the little red head.

"I get the feeling I'm missing something there," Ginger said, being unfamiliar with the term in the context employed by the no bigger blonde.

"That's *not* what I heard, neither," Babsy declared, flickering her gaze to Roxton.

"The Lime-Juicers didn't even support the Union in the War Of The Southern Rebellion," King said, before the comment of the little blonde could be taken further. If he had been less interested in trying to provoke Roxton, he would have noticed his reference to the civil conflict which had torn apart America so few years ago and still evoked unpleasant memories had brought frowns of disapproval from more Texans than just the young deputy town marshal. In fact, several cowhands who were present began to exchange angry looks and mutter amongst themselves. These were increased rather than diminished as, feeling strongly on the next subject due to having had a considerable loss of revenue incurred, he continued just as loudly, "They let those damned Reb pirates use their ports as bases to go out pillaging our unarmed merchant ships on the high seas."

"And, if that international tribunal which is sitting gives the verdict many of us are expecting, it will cost Britain a tidy sum in compensation," Roxton remarked, proving himself to be a good prophet.[10] "What are you doing, old chap?"

---

the father might have been—is given in: BLONDE GENIUS and Part One, "Fifteen, the Hard Way," J.T.'S LADIES.

10. In 1872, an international committee sitting in judgement on what became known as the "Alabama Arbitration Tribunal," over protests levelled by the United States of America against Great Britain's role in the War of Secession, ruled in favour of the complainants. For allowing vessels of the Confederate States' Navy such as the commerce raiders, *Alabama*, *Florida* and *Shenandoah* to not only be built in, but to operate from its ports—and being actively involved in running essential military supplies to the South through the blockade of the U.S. Navy, with officers of the Royal Navy serving on "half pay" given encouragement to participate, and other activities considered detrimental to the Union's cause—

"I'm getting *ready*!" the deputy answered in a Texan's drawl, albeit far from succinctly, removing his badge of office.

Perhaps an inch taller than the aristocrat, Waco—the only name acknowledged by the peace officer—was a few years younger.[11] Blond haired and with a figure filling out to powerful manhood, his good looking face had lines suggestive of a maturity beyond his years. He had on a low crowned, wide brimmed black J.B. Stetson hat of the style favoured by cowhands from Texas, a tight rolled scarlet silk bandana knotted around his throat and trailing its ends over the front of his open necked blue shirt almost to the level of his newish Levi's pants' waistband. Their legs turned back in cuffs about three inches deep, which were intended to serve as a repository for such small items as nails when working on foot. An unfastened brown and white calfskin vest and high heeled brown boots with sharp toes and decorated by a carved five-pointed star motif, albeit the spurs which usually adorned them having been removed, completed his ensemble. Despite being at the most in his late 'teens, he wore his gunbelt and the twin staghorn handled Army Colts in its low-tied fast draw holsters with the easy assurance of one well versed in their use.

Dropping the badge into the crown of his hat, the youngster placed it on the bar. Then, untying the pigging thongs securing the tips of the holsters to his thighs, he unbuckled and removed his gunbelt. Signalling for a bartender to come, he pushed them all across the counter.

"What's up, Waco?" the man asked.

"You'd best get ready to send somebody down to the firehouse and the jail, Wally," Waco replied.

"Are you expecting *trouble?*" the bartender inquired, aware of why the first destination had been stipulated and glancing around.

"You could say that," the youngster replied, his tone and manner grim. "Seeing's how I'm fixing to *start* the son-of-a-bitch *myself* right now."

---

the Government of Great Britain had been ordered to pay compensation to the sum of $15,500,000.00.

11. Why Waco acknowledged only one name, as well as his background and special qualifications, can be found in: APPENDIX FOUR.

CHAPTER SIX

Maybe It Wasn't Luck!

"Good evening, Miss *Chernyshevsky*," Horace Tumbril greeted, with as near as his doleful New England tones ever came to showing pleasure. "Are you gracing us with your presence?"

"I'm hoping to," replied the beautiful young woman who had been accorded a considerable honour by Jonathan Ambrose Turtle on her arrival at Honesty John's Tavern. Smiling at the men seated around the table, after a quick glance at the only other member of her sex in Room Seven, she went on, "Unless my 'presence' will be unwelcome to these gentlemen, of course."

Although generally not susceptible to female charms, having reached the age where flirtation—or more—with members of the opposite sex, even when as beautiful and well endowed as the one he was addressing, had lost much of its former attraction, Tumbril concluded there was little chance of objections if the way in which the players already present were looking at the new arrival was any guide!

Since leaving the bar-room and going to the accommodation she had been allocated, the beautiful young woman had made quite striking changes to her appearance!

Bare-headed, Miss Chernyshevsky now had on an equally realistic—albeit *far* more attractive—blonde wig. Being an extremely experienced poker player, she had dressed in a fashion calculated to distract her male opponents. The neckline of her white blouse was cut close to indecorously low and left her shoulders uncovered. It had short puff-sleeves which bared her arms from the top of her strongly muscled—but not to the point of losing femininity—biceps, such as peasant girls often wore in Mexico. The material was so thin, it presented an all too obvious proof that it alone covered a bosom which was so firm and full that, having no other support than the flimsy material through which her nipples showed in bold relief, the mounds jutted forward with little sagging despite their imposing bulk. Extending to foot level, her glossy blue skirt gave only slight hints that she was wearing flat bottomed canvas pumps. Being aware that such things were likely to arouse suspicion, her fingernails had been trimmed right down and she was not wearing jewellery of any kind.

"Gentlemen, allow me to present Miss *Chernyshevsky,*" Tumbril requested, acting in his capacity as dealer for the game. He would not be playing, other than riffling the deck and serving the cards to the contestants. In addition to collecting the percentage of each pot which was levied by Turtle, he was responsible for the other "house" rules being enforced and, being known to possess the knowledge to detect any kind of crooked gambling tricks, ensuring no cheating occurred. "Ma'am, these are from your right, Mr. *Smith,* Mr. *Brown,* Mr. *Jones,* Mr. *Arbuthnot*——*!*"

"I like to be *different,*" drawled the big and well built middle-aged man wearing clothing of Texas' style who was identified fourth.

"I *always* wanted to meet a gentleman called '*Arbuthnot,*'" the "blonde" claimed, as soberly as if she believed the names she had been given were genuine. Every one was a wanted man with a high price on his head, as well as being leader of a successful gang, who various peace officers would be delighted to capture. Although all the quartet were just as aware of her true identity, there were those present who did not. Wishing to retain anonymity where they were concerned and being sure the desire would be respected by those better informed, she continued in a formal tone, "But please do call me, 'Olga'."

"Mr. Goldberg, I believe you know," Tumbril went on, apparently disapproving of such frivolous utterances, and nodding to a short and stout well dressed man of Hebraic appearance who occupied a chair a little distance away from the big central table around which the players were seated.

"I do indeed," Miss Chernyshevsky agreed, nodding a friendly greeting. She did not think that anti-Semitism had compelled the man in question to remain apart from the

others. Knowing him to be present as a loan broker to those in
need of funds, she went on, "Hello, Abe. I hope I don't need
to come to *you* tonight."

"Win and spend it in good health, B——*Olga,*" Abraham
Goldberg replied amiably, making the amendment as he received a glance redolent of warning from the lanky manager-
cum-dealer.

"This is a *guest* from Canada," Tumbril continued, indicating the last player at the table. "Mr. Arnaud Chavallier."

"*Enchante, mademoiselle,*" said the final man requiring in-
troduction and the only one for whom it was really necessary.
He continued speaking in English with a noticeable French
accent, drawing a frown from the other woman present. "I did
not expect such *pleasant* company when I came to join the
game."

"Delighted, M'*sieur* Chavallier," Miss Chernyshevsky acknowledged, although—while she knew nothing of the misgivings expressed in the bar-room—drawing the conclusion
that Tumbril did not care for the latest player to be introduced.

On sitting down to start the game, Arnaud *'le Loup Garou'*
Chavallier had hung a round topped, broad brimmed brown
"plainsman's" hat, of a kind well suited to wear on the wind-
swept open prairies of Canada, on the back of his chair by its
barbiquejo chinstrap. Doing so displayed that, although he
was a prominent leader in the most hostilely dissident section
of the *Metis* nation, he kept his light brownish hair cut much
shorter than was fashionable amongst the men of his race.
Deeply tanned though they were and surly of expression at
that moment, his handsome and sharply defined features were
only marginally suggestive of his quarter Assiniboine Indian
blood. Looking somewhat younger than his actual thirty-odd
years, he had a good—albeit not exceptional—width to his
shoulders and a slender waist. Even at the table, running a
lascivious gaze over Miss Chernyshevsky's openly exhibited
physical attractions, he conveyed a genuine impression of
being able to move with rapidity when necessary. He had on
an open necked dark blue shirt, an unfastened fringed buckskin jacket and a pair of yellowish-brown Nankeen trousers
tucked into brown Wellington-leg boots.[1] Around his waist

1. "Wellington leg": in this context, not the modern waterproof variety of
footwear. It referred to boots having the legs as high as the knee in front,

was a black gunbelt with an ivory handled Colt 1860 Army Model revolver in its low tied cavalry-twist holster on the right, balanced by a long bladed J. Russell & Co. "Green River" hunting knife similarly equipped at the hilt in a sheath of Indian manufacture at the left.

Having heard the news from Mulrooney, although he had brought the *Metis* to Kansas and was responsible for the schemes which ultimately led to their death, *le Loup Garou* had felt no remorse over their fate. The only sorrow he had experienced—and still did—was caused by having spent a considerable sum of money, extorted from members of his race in Canada who were otherwise unsympathetic to his aims, purchasing arms and other equipment for the mission upon which he was engaged. Being too clever to run any undue risks, he had remained in the comparative safety of Honesty John's Tavern while his men were seeking to carry out his orders. He had already sent off a telegraph message to ask for replacements to continue his attempt to ruin the spur-line before it could come even close to Canada, but had insufficient money to keep him in the style he desired until they arrived with more funds.

On being told of the poker game by one of the hotel section of the Tavern's bellhops—a luxury Turtle provided as part of the services for which he charged a high price—considering himself a far more skillful player than was the case, Chavallier had decided to recoup some of his lost finances by joining in.

"And this is *Miss* Irene Beauville," Tumbril said, clearly as an after-thought and, to anybody who knew him as well as did the beautiful "blonde," with even less enthusiasm than when presenting Chavallier.

"Good evening, Miss Beauville," Miss Chernyshevsky greeted, looking to where the latest person to be presented to her was lounging with a sprawl of an almost feline grace upon a settee which—along with a coffee-table close by and an armchair on the opposite side of the room—were supplied for the benefit of players who wished to relax away from the table. Concluding correctly that the manager's disapproval probably stemmed from the pair occupying a room together without making the pretense of being man and wife, a propri-

---

but cut away at the rear, after the style made popular in the Napoleonic War by General Arthur Wellesley, the Duke of Wellington (1769-1852).

ety he expected under such conditions, she inquired, "Aren't you in the game?"

"She *isn't!*" Chavallier stated, before the woman could reply and his manner indicated clearly he considered the matter was not open for discussion.

Also a *Metis,* by the standards of either race from which she had had her origins, Irene Beauville was an exceptionally fine specimen of the female gender. Close to five foot eight inches in height, she was in her early twenties and had her tawny—almost blonde—hair cut much shorter than was fashionable with both of her peoples. Not so deeply tanned as Chavallier, her face had a savage beauty; while also giving an indication of an arrogant nature, even when it was not marred by the scowl of disapproval which came on hearing the denial. She was wearing a multi-coloured short sleeved blouse with an extreme decollete, which clung like a second skin to her magnificent bosom and was knotted, instead of being buttoned, to leave her midriff bare. The material was so thin and tight, as was the case with the garment worn by the equally well endowed "blonde," that the nipples of her large firm breasts thrust forward so prominently they seemed in danger of bursting through it. Below them her waist trimmed until filling out to well rounded buttocks set upon curvaceous hips and shapely, clearly well muscled thighs and calves. These were but inadequately concealed beneath a flaring black skirt which ended high enough to display bare ankles and low heeled sandals with cross-straps extending upwards. She had a Plains Cree Indian bear-teeth necklace. A wide Navajo silver and turquoise bracelet encircled each wrist and several obviously costly rings decorated her fingers. As she was not playing, she was free from the restrictions which were responsible for Miss Chernyshevsky refraining from exhibiting jewellery of any kind.

"That is a *pity,*" Miss Chernyshevsky claimed, trying to be friendly and receiving a bitter scowl of resentment in return. Giving up the attempt at sociability, as she concluded her good intentions were unwelcome, she looked around the table and went on, "I trust you will all be tolerant and bear with me if I should make any *mistakes,* gentlemen. I so *very* seldom play cards."

"The game, *lady* and gentlemen, is straight five card draw poker," Tumbril announced, noticing that only Chavallier of the men at the table seemed to take the "blonde's" patently untrue assertion at its face value. "No limit. No wild cards. No skip straights, blazes, or other local variants of hands.[2] Jacks or better to open. Any player may split openers, but must announce it is being done and lay aside the discard so it can verify at a showdown that they were held. Anybody has the right to cut the deck, but the final cut must be made by the player to the left of the one having the deal. Is that all *understood?*" Receiving indications of concurrence from the players, he went on while breaking the seal and opening a deck of cards, "Shall we say, 'lady first,' or would you prefer to cut for the deal?"

"Give me your rings, bracelets and that damned necklace!" Arnaud Chavallier snarled, using his cupped hand to protectively shield and look at the full house of three kings and two aces he had acquired, despite increasing the odds against making any improvement by holding the ace of clubs as a "kicker" to his original pair of kings, on drawing two cards.[3]

From the outset, it had been as apparent to all the other players as it was earlier to Horace Tumbril that the *Metis* was far from being in their class!

As a result of the combination of the cards running badly for him and his lack of skill compared with his opponents, Chavallier was now needing assistance to cover and call the bet in the latest pot!

Apart from the *Metis* having refrained from asking Irene Beauville to come and look at, or kiss, his cards to bring him

2. "Skip straight": a sequence of five cards with numbers running alternately instead of concurrently—i.e., ace, three, five, seven and nine—considered when allowed as beating an ordinary straight and sometimes, dependent upon the "local" rules in force, even a flush.

2a. "Blaze": five picture cards. When allowed, even the lowest possible combinations of two pairs—i.e., two kings, two queens and a jack—or three of a kind—three kings, a queen and a jack—are considered to beat a flush.

3. "Holding a kicker": retaining a pair, generally accompanied by an ace or a king. The chances of making any improvements by this means are 1 in 3.86, as opposed to 1 in 3.48 when drawing three cards. While the odds against receiving a card matching the "kicker" are 1 in 5.9 and 1 in 6.25 if only a pair is held, they become progressively higher and, therefore, less favourable, as the value of the hand obtained increases.

luck—which was considered a gaffe of the highest order by competent poker playing "wolves"—there was hardly an error of an inexperienced "rabbit" he failed to employ.[4]

The recipient of the demand, for it had been that rather than a polite request, looked far from delighted by it!

"If you're going to use my jewellery," Irene answered just as sharply, disliking having been spoken to in such a fashion in English and responding with the French dialect peculiar to the *Metis*. "I hope you know what you're *doing*. Are you *sure* you've got the winning hand?"

"I *am!*" Chavallier snarled in the same tongue. Barely concealing his anger and impatience, he went on just as wrathfully, "So get your fat butt off that settee and hand them over!"

Anger darkened the face of the beautiful and sensual *Metis* girl, making her look as savage as a stick-teased bobcat and about as dangerous to touch!

However, knowing her companion had a temper which suggested how he had acquired his sobriquet, *le Loup Garou*, the *Metis* girl had better sense than continue to refuse!

Being too wise to take further liberties—even in a room with masculine strangers present who might intervene in her behalf if Chavallier lost his temper—and in spite of her obvious reluctance, Irene thrust herself up from her comfortable perch with a cat-like grace and speed. Scowling and showing disapproval, she removed the Plains Cree Indian bear-claw necklace from around her throat and tossed it on the table with an angry gesture. Then she stripped the Navajo silver and turquoise bracelet from each wrist and followed them with the rings off her fingers, slamming rather than just placing them in front of her companion.

"How much for them?" Chavallier inquired of Abraham Goldberg, ignoring the reaction he had provoked from the yellowish-blonde haired girl. Then, accepting the sum quoted with less than good grace, it having been lower than he expected—although it was fair and he felt sure he would not have been offered even that price by any of the players—he looked at the remaining opponent in the pot and said defiantly, "I'll see you!"

---

4. A description of several of the errors committed by inexperienced "rabbit" poker players is given in: SET A-FOOT.

"Four deuces," replied Miss Olga Chernyshevsky, turning over the cards upon which she had been betting.

"Four deuces?" Chavallier repeated. "But you stood pat!"

The comment, which sounded closer to a protest, was made as a result of the *Metis* remembering how he had based his strategy upon the "blonde" refraining from drawing in an attempt to improve the cards she was holding. On two previous occasions, he had been up against her under similar circumstances. Each time he had thrown in his hand instead of calling and was led to assume—as only the rankest "rabbit" ever let anybody see the cards held unless having had money paid into the pot for the privilege of "calling"—he had been bluffed out by an inferior holding.

Promising himself he would not fall for such a ploy again, *le Loup Garou* had awaited his opportunity and at last felt it was being presented. Despite her standing pat, he had seen an ace amongst the cards thrown on to the centre of the table by the other players as being inferior to his and Miss Chernyshevsky's respective hands. The opportunity to acquire such potentially useful information had advised him that in addition to having a hand superior to a straight or a flush, he could beat any full house she might be holding. Therefore, he had bet heavily in the expectation of winning the pot.

Unfortunately for Chavallier's strategy, a full house—no matter how high—did not beat even such a small four of a kind.[5]

"I didn't think I *needed* another card," Miss Chernyshevsky replied, having planned her play so as to lay the trap into which her opponent had fallen. "My wasn't I *lucky?*"

The words were uttered in the "blonde's" Southron drawl, with a well simulated innocence which brought grins to the faces of all but one of the male players!

Although more circumspect, as neither was an active participant, even Tumbril and Goldberg showed they too found the comment amusing!

The couple from Canada were the exceptions to the friendly reaction!

However, although Chavallier did no more than slam down his cards and glower across the table, his companion showed even less restraint!

5. An explanation of the relative hands in the game of poker is given in: TWO MILES TO THE BORDER.

"Maybe it *wasn't* luck!" Irene hissed, wanting to take her temper out on somebody and using English—albeit with an even stronger French accent than that of Chavallier—for the first time, as she watched her jewellery being put away by the Hebraic looking man.

The amusement left the faces of the men!

Every masculine gaze, even that of Chavallier, was turned to the beautiful "blonde"!

Knowing Miss Chernyshevsky, the outlaws, Tumbril and Goldberg waited with baited breath to see how she reacted to what came close to being an accusation of cheating!

"Excuse me, *gentlemen!*" Olga requested, the words coming through barely parted lips, as she pushed back her chair and came to her feet without so much as a glance at the other girl. Although she had no reason to do as was suggested by the excuse she intended to make, she continued, "I must go *somewhere*. Perhaps the atmosphere will be *cooler* when I come back."

Watching the "blonde" walk by with what she sensed was a deliberately sensual gait to be studied appreciatively by every pair of masculine eyes—even those of Chavallier—the *Metis* girl let out a furious hiss. Already bored and far from pleased by the way in which Chavallier had refused to let her leave when she suggested going to their room, her always quick and uncertain temper went beyond its boiling point. Wanting to vent her growing anger upon somebody, she caught the other girl by the bare shoulder.

Jerked around, Miss Chernyshevsky was taken by a punch to the jaw which sent her reeling backwards against the wall!

Before anybody could make a move to interfere, or the "blonde" was able to even get ready to protect herself, Irene had darted over to deliver a hard slap with each hand to her cheeks.

CHAPTER SEVEN

That Just Can't Be Dusty Fog

"What's wrong, ma'am?" Captain Dustine Edward Marsden 'Dusty' Fog asked solicitously, walking forward through the moonlight with all his attention devoted to the person he was addressing and to whom he was extending his right hand. "Let me help you up!"

Even as he was speaking, the town marshal of Mulrooney discovered appearances could be deceptive!

Being most competent in the performance of his duties, even though the present period of office was only the second time he had "worn the tin star,"[1] Dusty Fog was aware of the value of remaining alert even on what had so far been a quiet and—knowing nothing of the trouble which was in the process of beginning in the Buffalo Saloon at that moment—uneventful evening. Nor, as he was walking through the area given over to shipping pens for the cattle which he and other Texans brought from their home State in order to be sold at a much more lucrative market than existed elsewhere,[2] did he need to keep constantly reminding himself there could be even a greater reason for caution than usual.

Earlier that day, the town marshal's office had received a

1. The first occasion Captain Edward Dustine Marsden 'Dusty' Fog served as a peace officer is recorded in: QUIET TOWN.
2. The nature of the only large scale market for cattle in Texas after the War Between The States, which was still the case at the period of this narrative, is described in: THE HIDE AND TALLOW MEN.
2a. How a large herd of half wild Texas longhorn cattle was brought to the railroad shipping pens in Kansas is explained in: TRAIL BOSS.

warning from a generally reliable source that there could be a plot about to liberate a prisoner who was being held at the jailhouse awaiting trial for an extremely vicious murder!

Vague as the rumour had been, Dusty was too experienced to discount it. Kenneth Little hailed from the "hill country" of the Ozark Mountains in Missouri. While being brought back from Hays City, where he had been arrested after making his escape from Mulrooney, he had boasted that he had a large family who would come to his assistance as soon as they learned of his situation. He had also claimed he was a member of the "Bald-Knobbers." They were a group which had originally been formed for self protection during the years of turmoil preceding the War Between The States, but—like many such associations—had attracted the worst elements of the region and developed into a force more criminally inclined than beneficial.[3]

Even discounting the latter assertion, knowing the strong family bonds of "hill folk," the marshal had felt sure the kin of his prisoner would not be swayed from coming to the rescue by thoughts of the especially brutal crime which had caused the incarceration!

However, until coming across the figure in the vestments of a nun crouching on hands and knees against the corner of a building, groaning as if in considerable pain, Dusty had seen nobody. Nor, although he did not consider his watchfulness a waste of time, had anything occurred so far to justify it. He would have been more wary if the subject of his interest was a man. However, not only did the person he was addressing look to be a female, but there was a convent in the town. Being an order devoted to nursing and giving comfort to the sick, its incumbents were not infrequently to be found in what would otherwise have seemed unlikely parts of the town.

To make matters worse, Dusty told himself in the moment that the realization struck him, an incident which had occurred shortly after he took office ought to have warned him that the sight of such attire did not necessarily mean it was worn by a woman who had taken the vows in some religious order![4]

Unfortunately, before the realization struck home, it was

3. Information about the "Bald-Knobbers" in later years can be found in: THE SHEPHERD OF THE HILLS, by Harold Bell Wright.
4. The incident is recorded in: THE MAKING OF A LAWMAN.

too late to avoid the consequences of the error in judgment!

The situation into which Dusty had walked so unsuspectingly was, in fact, an obviously well planned attempt to lull him into a belief that he would have nothing to fear from coming to offer his assistance!

Causing the awareness of the true state of affairs to come, albeit just an instant too late, the shape stopped groaning and twisted around to grab Dusty's outstretched wrist in both hands!

At the same moment, even as the marshal was starting to try and pull himself free and his left hand was moving towards its holstered weapon, he discovered there had been another— even more important—purpose to the sound being emitted than merely helping to dispel any suspicions he might have harboured!

Two men, whose presence some slight sound might have betrayed if it was not masked over by the moans, came swiftly from around the corner of the building!

Both being just over medium height and stocky in build, the pair were wearing a style of clothing common in certain "hill country" areas of Missouri. There was a noticeable family resemblance about them to suggest who they might be. What was more, it was obvious from their actions that they had been waiting in concealment and were not merely passing by chance. One was holding a Colt 1860 Army Model revolver ready for use. However, although the other had not drawn a similar weapon from its low cavalry twist holster on his gunbelt, it was he who dealt with the attempted resistance. Whipping around his right hand, he grasped a small leather wrapped billy of the kind frequently used by bouncers in saloons and dance halls to quell recalcitrant customers.

The weapon thudded against the top of Dusty's head!

Despite the protection offered by his low crowned and wide brimmed Texas-style J.B. Stetson hat, which partly deflected the blow and was knocked off, the marshal went down stunned!

"Damn it!" growled the figure in the nun's habit, albeit in a masculine voice which established he was from the region of the Ozark Mountains around Mutton Hollow where the so-called 'Bald-Knobbers' held their strongest sway. "I hope you didn't sap him down *too* hard!"

"I've dropped too many for *that*," answered the wielder of

the billy, having a similar inflection in his voice. "He'll be waking up in a minute or so at most."

"I know he's got a badge on and all," said the third member of the ambush, gesturing with his revolver towards the victim sprawled unmoving on the ground. Looking to be in his early twenties and slightly younger, he clearly had a close blood relationship with the previous speaker. "Are you *certain* sure this be *him*, Cousin Sam?"

"Hell, *yes!*" ejaculated the man who struck the blow. "Brother Amos's got something there. He surely don't look *nothing* like I've allus heard him to be."

"It's *him* all right!" the 'nun' claimed definitely as he stood up. Removing the habit revealed he was a few years senior to the other two. Being dressed in a similar fashion and armed with a low hanging Remington New Model Army revolver, although his clothes looked a little more expensive, he was clearly from the same area and related to them. "I was surprised, like you, when I first saw him. Fact being, I said to myself, 'That just *can't* be Dusty Fog'. But I'll be 'ternally damned if it warn't and it still be!"

There was some justification for the comments!

Despite the competence he had acquired in other fields and regardless of the efficient way in which he had run the office of the town marshal since arriving in Mulrooney, Dusty Fog looked nothing like the general conception of how one with his already close to legendary reputation should be.[5] For one thing, even aided by his high heeled tan coloured boots, he was no more than five foot six in height. Having lost his hat as he collapsed, his neatly trimmed dusty blond hair was rumpled untidily. In his early twenties, while moderately good looking, there was nothing particularly eye-catching about his tanned face when in repose. The tightly rolled scarlet silk bandana, dark green shirt and Levi's pants he was wearing had been purchased recently.

However as he lacked Mark Counter's way of showing off clothes, he contrived to give them the appearance of being somebody else's cast-offs and they tended to emphasise rather than detract from his small stature. Nor did the badge of office attached to his left breast pocket and the well designed gunbelt

---

5. Details of the background and special qualifications of Captain Dustine Edward Marsden "Dusty" Fog can be found in: APPENDIX ONE.

with twin bone handled Army Colts in its cross-draw holsters make him any more noticeable or dangerous in appearance under the prevailing conditions.

"Well anyway," John McDonnell remarked, not without a shade of relief in his tone. "We've got him!"

"Yeah," growled Samuel Little, also having had no delusions about the risks involved in what he and other members of his family had come to Mulrooney to do. He had no intention of letting himself, or his cousins, become complacent because they had succeeded in their purpose even better than he had anticipated when making arrangements with his twin brother. "Now get them guns of his'n unloaded and we'll do what we've come for."

"I'll go through his pockets while you're doing it, Brother John," Amos McDonnell offered. "Badge toters 'most allus carry stingy guns hid on 'em to be used sneaklike."

Giving a non-committal grunt, as he suspected the real reason for the proposal made by his sibling and considered it ill-advised in the present company, the elder brother extracted the Army Colt from their victim's right side holster. He did not need to take the time to empty the loose powder, .44 calibre bullets and retaining wadding from the six chambers. Because of the manner in which the charge was detonated by the "cap and ball" firing system, removing the percussion caps from their nipples at the rear of the cylinder served to render the revolver innocuous. Having done so, he returned the weapon and took out its mate for similar treatment.

"He got a stingy gun?" Little inquired dryly, as the younger brother was straightening up at the conclusion of the search.

"Naw!" Amos answered, sounding aggrieved at the victim for being so remiss. Holding out the thing he had found in the right hip pocket of the Levi's pants, he went on in an equally disgruntled fashion, "Only *this!*"

"You *wouldn't've* kept no cash money, even had he any on him," Little stated, also having guessed the real reason behind the search for a small concealed weapon and keeping a careful watch on his younger cousin while it was taking place. "We're not god-damned *thieves,* so you can put that back where it come from. It's nothing's can do us any harm."

As far as appearances went, there seemed to be justification for the last words!

The item taken from Dusty's pocket and about to be thrown

away in disgust by Amos gave no indication of its purpose and looked completely innocuous. It appeared to be a six inch length from a broom's handle made of Osage orange—the *bois d'arc* tree regarded by Indian bow makers as being the hardest, finest and most durable of woods—with the ends rounded and having had half a dozen grooves carved around the centre.

Knowing the peculiar kind of code of ethics practised by his cousin, who—along with his twin brother, Saul—exerted undisputed leadership over their branch of the Bald-Knobbers —Amos replaced the device in the pocket from which it had come!

The would-be thief was just as aware that, no matter whether or not his older sibling approved of retaining any worthwhile loot, he would not have been permitted to do so!

Unlike the leaders of some Bald-Knobber and similar groups, Sam Little refused to use the membership for the purposes of terrorizing the local population into paying what a later generation would refer to as "protection" money, or to commit robberies against any except the most wealthy individuals. Instead, he insisted they devoted their illicit attentions to such targets as banks and railroads; who were regarded with suspicion and as oppressors by the poorer people throughout much of the South and the Mid-West.

Having made things temporarily too hot to hold them in the region over which they foraged, by agreement with the other groups of Bald Knobbers, the twin brothers and six members of their family had come to Kansas. It was their intention to pass the time, until the situation back home became more amenable, in sampling the possibilities offered by the busy trail end railroad towns. They were aware that peace officers tended to keep a watchful eye upon parties of men who arrived without any obvious reason, particularly in such potentially lucrative locales. Lacking a motive they could offer, such as having brought a herd of cattle, they had travelled in three separate parties without arousing suspicion. As had proved the case elsewhere, they had arrived in Mulrooney without finding anything they considered worthwhile.

However, before the Bald-Knobbers could locate a prospect and commence their activities, trouble had struck!

Always wild and vicious, especially when in liquor, Kenneth Little had gone to the brothel owned by Mrs. Lily Gouch after drinking heavily elsewhere. Being able to conceal his true state, he had succeeded in gaining admittance and selecting a girl. When she had refused to comply with his demands for more than just normal sexual relations, he had flown into a rage. To compound his iniquity, he had mutilated rather than just torn open his victim with a knife. Seen doing so, and being a state of intoxication which added to a fund of almost animal cunning and courage, he had leapt through a second floor window. Despite having cut his left arm badly in the process, he had made good his escape and fled to Hays City.

Although furious at their sibling, in accordance with the code by which they had been raised in the Ozark Mountains, the twins had also been determined to prevent him from suffering the consequences of his vicious crime. Saul had followed him, with the intention of sending him to the comparative safety of their home area until he could be put beyond the reach of the United States' law. Remaining in Mulrooney to look for prospects to rob, a need which had grown more urgent as he and Saul realized just how much money would be needed to get Kenneth out of the country; it having become obvious that the local authorities were employing every available assistance in their efforts to apprehend the younger sibling, making it imperative his safety should be quickly ensured—Sam had studied the various members of the town marshal's office and learned all he could about their daily routine.

The knowledge was to prove useful in a different context to that envisaged when the surveillance was commenced!

Instead of remaining sober until a safe location was attained, Kenneth had become drunk and, fortunately before he had committed another serious offense, was arrested in Hays City. Recognizing him from the description circulated, the marshal had telegraphed the news to his contemporary in Mulrooney. Although Saul had hoped to effect an escape while his sibling was being brought back by train to stand trial, no opportunity had arisen. Refusing to be deterred from their purpose, the twins had concocted separate, yet complementary—albeit, as each sought to be considered the sole and undisputed leader of their section of the Bald-Knobbers, not entirely amicable nor mutually agreed upon—schemes.

In fact, the twins had not parted on the best of terms!

Refusing to be swayed from his purpose, Saul had gone to

attend to one of his ideas with the assistance of two members
of their group. A third kinsman had set off upon an assignment which he had concocted and, despite his twin's objections, had won from the rest agreement for it to be carried out.
For his part, Sam, though disgruntled by the latter arrangement in particular had come with the McDonnell brothers to
the area in which he had declared they would be best able to
acquire a vital element for the plan he was putting into effect.
He would have settled for any of the deputies who might be
making a patrol in the area, but was especially delighted when
he saw he would be able to have the added potency offered by
being able to employ the marshal. As he had anticipated, the
disguise he had adopted—one he often used for a similar purpose of lulling suspicions when engaged on robberies—had
proved successful.

All that remained was to continue with the plan!

And hope everything was going as well elsewhere!

"I wonder how Cousin Saul's getting on?" Amos McDonnell remarked, returning the harmless looking piece of wood
to where he had found it and seeking to avoid any further
lecturing upon—although he had never heard the term—the
kind of double standards by which Sam Little looked at life.

"It don't matter shit, spit, nor piss in the bucket how he's
getting on," the oldest of the trio claimed, hoping his twin
brother would not be able to play any major part in the rescue
of their sibling; as doing so would weaken his own ambitions
to gain control of their band. "Nor whether Cousin Ezra does
what he's supposed to neither, 'cepting all hell'll pop happen
he gets caught at it."

"Cousin Ezra's slicker'n a greased weasel at sneaking
around without getting catched," John McDonnell claimed,
tending to favour Saul as the future leader despite having been
assigned to help the other candidate. "He'll do what he's been
set on to do."

"Which'll be fine, so long's Brother Kenneth don't start
getting notions and does's he's told for once," Little countered, regarding the participation to which he and the elder of
his assistants had referred as being more of a possible threat
than a helpful adjunct to his scheme, even though he had not
been able to prevent it being put into effect. "'Cause, *providing's* Fog comes out of it, we'll have him cut free and without

needing *nothing* Brother Saul, nor Cousin Ezra for that matter, might do."

"Look," John growled, in the fashion of one whose doubted judgement was being justified, pointing to where Dusty Fog was stirring. "I telled you's I *didn't* hit him too hard!"

"And not afore time," Little stated, suspecting the feelings of the speaker where the leadership of the band was concerned. Glancing all around and seeing no sign of human life, he continued, "Sooner we get moving, the better. Somebody might come along any minute and see us. Which should they 'n' they get nosy, that'll be just too *bad* for them. We're going to get Brother Kenneth loose and may the Good Lord help *anybody's* stands in our way!"

CHAPTER EIGHT

Better Than the Battle at Bearcat Annie's

Although Arnaud *"le Loup Garou"* Chavallier and the other men had come to their feet when the attack was launched by Irene Beauville, not one of them offered to intervene!

However, while the rest watched with signs of enthusiasm, Abraham Goldberg hurried across the room and went out leaving the door open!

Having delivered the slaps, which jolted their recipient's head from side to side, Irene sank her hands into what she believed was a mass of blonde hair ready to be pulled in a most painful manner as a prelude to other punishment being inflicted!

On commencing the jerk with all her far from inconsiderable strength, the beautiful *Metis* girl discovered her error in no uncertain fashion!

While Irene would quite willingly have torn out a double fistful of the blonde locks she was clutching, the last thing she expected was what happened. Instead of meeting resistance from them being embedded in the head of her intended victim, which experience gained in fights with other women had led her to anticipate, it appeared the whole scalp was torn off. All the "hair" came away with such inconceivable ease in her grasp, she was close to being numbed by amazement. However, as she took a step back involuntarily and under the impulsion of the thwarted pull, she was not given an opportunity to recover from the surprise.

Caught unawares by the punch which propelled her against the wall, the young woman who called herself "Miss Olga Chernyshevsky" had not regathered her wits when the savage flat hand blows caused additional pain and threatened to reduce their ability to function still further. However, granted the brief respite, she quickly proved she was far from incapacitated and made the most of it. Presenting a somewhat ludicrous sight with her brunette hair cut so short about her skull and the make-up she had applied—which was more than when seeking to present a "prim and proper" appearance to the confidence tricksters in Dodge City—she launched a retaliatory attack.

Bringing her left leg up, Olga placed her foot against the yellowish blonde's mid-section and gave a thrust. Letting out a startled squeal, Irene was sent backwards. Following, the brunette tackled her around the shoulders and they reeled onwards together to land on the armchair at the side of the room. Held down for a few seconds, her assailant giving her yellowish-blonde locks a tugging with one hand while the other clutched at and twisted her face in an equally painful fashion, finding she was being hurt caused Irene to respond effectively.

Receiving a kick in the ribs from the side of a shapely bare leg, Olga was dislodged and driven away. Thrusting herself upwards, the *Metis* charged and was met with another tackle. Reeling across the room, to the accompaniment of encouraging yells from the watching men, their arms encircled one another's torsoes and hands scrabbled wildly in search of a hold on opposing flesh. By the time they arrived and fell on to the small coffee-table in front of the settee at the opposite side, Irene's blouse was flapping open, the knot having been wrenched apart, giving irrefutable proof she was not wearing anything underneath it. What was more, having had its neckline ripped downwards for some inches, the upper part of Olga's attire displayed a similar omission and the blue skirt had been subjected to a tear at the waist which indicated, by displaying black material instead of bare flesh, that she had considered some form of undergarment was required in that area.

Neither girl was allowed to try and make adjustments to her clothing. The table tipped over to deposit them on to the floor, from where they struggled upwards and the blonde once again employed a more productive tactic by delivering a most competent punch which flung the brunette on to the settee. Diving forward, Irene grabbed Olga by the throat with both hands. Gasping as she found her breath was being cut off, the brunette

exerted all her considerable strength upon pushing with her
hands against her assailant's shoulders. Although contriving to
force Irene's torso until almost at arms' length, she was unable to
extend the distance far enough to cause the throttling grip to be
released. Accepting this was the case, she changed her methods
to a more efficacious way of gaining liberation.

Removing her hands, the brunette knotted the right into a
fist and, as Irene involuntarily tilted forward, swung it.
Caught by a punch which packed more power than she would
have expected when deciding to work off her anger at Chavallier having lost all her jewellery to the other girl, the blonde
could not retain her choking hold. What was more, lifted erect
by the impact, she was given further evidence that the brunette
was far from the easy victim she had envisaged. Coming from the settee with a rapid motion, Olga swung a second
punch with her right to Irene's chin. Before the *Metis* could
recover any semblance of control, it was followed by an
equally hard left.

Although Goldberg informed Jonathan Ambrose Turtle of
what was taking place in Room Seven, nobody else on the
first floor of Honesty John's Tavern was aware of it. Hearing
the commotion as the *Metis* girl erupted through the door,
although the earlier indications of conflict had been drowned
by the hum of conversation and music from a small band at
the end of the room, all the male and female occupants of the
bar-room forgot whatever they were doing and looked up with
interest. The sight which came to their gaze was particularly
pleasing to the men.

Propelled backwards through the door, which fortunately
for her was still open, Irene crossed the narrow passage outside the room. Striking the bannister before she could regain
control of her movements, she broke through. Rolling help-
lessly down the stairs, although her skill as a rider allowed her
to reduce the punishment slightly, brought into view her
wildly flailing shapely bare legs and, at one stage, an undergarment comprised of a very small triangular strip of red cloth
passed between her thighs and knotted about her hips.

Charging out of the door, Olga clearly had no intention of
bringing the incident to an end by retiring to her own room!

Instead, the brunette went after the blonde in a manner
indicative of being willing—in fact most eager—to continue
the fight!

However, the speed with which Olga was moving proved her undoing!

Starting to slip over the smooth material it was covering, provoking appreciative whoops from the male spectators on the first floor and who had come from Room Seven, the brunette's badly torn blue skirt slid downwards. This brought into view and entangled equally well formed legs encased in black silk stockings which were supported by scarlet suspender straps attached to not quite so diminutive, yet *far* from decorous, lace trimmed black satin drawers. Tripped by the ruined garment, the brunette toppled and followed the blonde in a fashion suggestive of possessing an equal skill in matters equestrian.

Despite arriving on the floor of the bar-room first, the after effects of the punches which had caused her to reach there were such that Irene had only just got to her feet when the brunette descended and rose. Grabbed by the hair with one hand, she received another punch to the side of the jaw from its mate. However, although she reeled, she was not incapacitated and contrived to retaliate in kind, just as vigorously, when her assailant came towards her. Then, being followed just as she was compelled to make an equally involuntary withdrawal, Olga was dumped backwards on to a table from which the occupants scattered hurriedly—taking their glasses with them—as they realized what was going to happen.

"Shall I go stop them, boss?" inquired the taller of the Turtle's bodyguards, his manner indicating he was hoping the answer would not be in the affirmative.

"*No!*" the owner of Honesty John's Tavern refused emphatically. Knowing "Miss Chernyshevsky," he felt sure she had not provoked the hostilities. He was equally aware that, especially as the *Metis* girl showed signs of providing a worthy opponent, his customers would deeply resent any interference in what was already regarded as being exceptionally good entertainment. "Let them fight it out. 'Less I miss my guess, it'll be better than the battle at Bearcat Annie's is said to have been."[1]

Tipped over by the weight of the furiously struggling pair, the table dumped them on to the floor. They churned over and over, letting out a cacophony of squeals, yelps, gasps and

1. The battle at Bearcat Annie's is recorded in: QUIET TOWN.

furious exclamations, with more skillful tactics replaced by instinctive feminine brawling. While it was going on, Irene's skirt was torn and slipped away gradually to show her shapely and practically unclad rump. Then it descended further and was kicked free to leave her wearing only the flapping blouse, which revealed more than it concealed, and the minute loincloth. Indiscriminately clutching hands added to the damage already inflicted upon Olga's blouse so it too hung open to display her otherwise uncovered torso and holes appeared in her stockings as they started to come free from suspender straps. Both lost their less than adequate footwear, but neither gained more than a momentary advantage until it appeared to go to the brunette.

Finding she was lying back down upon her supine assailant, Olga contrived to sit up with the blonde head caught under her crooked right arm. Interlacing her fingers and spreading apart her shapely well muscled legs as an aid to leverage, she started to put on the pressure. Croaking as the constriction made itself felt, Irene scrabbled and hit at her captress's back. Her way of life was not conducive to growing long nails, which reduced her ability to scratch, and she was restricted in the power she could put behind the blows. Nevertheless, in addition to wrenching the blouse apart down its back, she managed to inflict some pain to the other girl. It was not sufficient to acquire liberation, but caused her to be presented with another means of escaping.

Although determined to make the most of what she knew must prove a weakening hold, the assault on her back caused the brunette to loosen it before it achieved its full potential. Before the encircling arm could be tightened again, the blonde rotated her head until her face was pressed against the perspiring mound of flesh exposed by the damage to the peasant-style blouse. Feeling the constriction being reapplied, she opened her mouth and bit. As soon as the teeth started to close on the vulnerable area, Olga squealed and parted her hands. Snatching herself free and bouncing away on her rump, her reaching fingers ascertained the skin of the breast had not been broken.

However, the relief which came from the discovery was ended rapidly!

Thrusting herself into a sitting posture the moment she was free, the blonde shuffled after Olga. She curled her hands under the brunette's armpits and, failing to grasp the bare breasts as was her intention—more by chance than deliberate design—acquired what wrestlers call a "full nelson." In their divergent efforts, one to apply pressure and the other seeking escape, they came to their feet. Drawing her torso forward, the brunette jerked it to the rear so her curvaceously and thinly covered buttocks rammed into Irene's stomach. The attack elicited a pain-filled croak and caused the encircling arms to be unwound hurriedly so their hands could clasp at the point of impact.

Twisting around as soon as she was free, before the succour could be attained, Olga grabbed the flapping sides of the blonde's still otherwise intact blouse with her hands. Falling over backwards and hauling Irene after her, the brunette brought up her right foot as her shoulders reached the floor. Subjected to a thrust against her midsection, the blonde was pitched in a half somersault through the air over her attacker. Once again, the skill she had acquired from countering unexpected falls from the back of a horse allowed her to alight less heavily than would otherwise have proved the case. However, on rolling over so as to rise, she discovered her assailant was already up.

The top of the brunette's left ankle lashed around to catch Irene under the chin. Jerked into a kneeling posture, she received a second kick to the body which sent her rolling across the floor. Then her hair was seized and she was hauled erect by it. Subjected to a left hook into the *solar plexus,* she was folded on to the right fist which rose to meet her descending jaw. The blow not only straightened her out, she was driven backwards through the side window in an eruption of splintered wood and shattered panes. Nevertheless, as she alighted on the ground outside, she was still sufficiently in control of her faculties to roll clear when the brunette hurtled after her in a plunging dive.

Coming to her feet, Irene might have been thankful for having made the departure from the Tavern without sustaining cuts from the glass she had broken. Instead, being hurt and suffering to an extent which caused her to be oblivious both of her lucky escape and her unclad state, she decided she had had enough. Without offering to inform her opponent of her desire, clasping her hands to her bare back, her dazed state caused her to stagger away from the building in the direction of a large wooden trough filled with water which Turtle maintained for the benefit of his customers.

Partially winded by descending upon something less yielding than the body of her intended victim, Olga once more showed no inclination to call off hostilities. Thrusting herself on to hands and knees, being able to see all she needed by the light of the moon, she located her quarry and stood up. Trampling on and causing the trailing ruined stockings to be dragged from her feet as she went, she set after the blonde. Although the tackle she launched almost missed, the brief contact she made knocked Irene over and, with the flapping blouse dragged from its wearer being discarded, they went down together.

Rolling apart as the first of the people from the building appeared around the front corner, the girls scrambled to their feet. Sent staggering by a punch, the blonde proved still capable of fighting back regardless of her wish to quit. Ducking, so the reaching hands of the brunette missed their objective, she wrapped her arms around the now bare approaching legs and, snapping their knees together, lifted. Raised and pitched over before she could resist, Olga broke her fall with a similar ability. She felt fingers scrabbling at her head, but her short cropped hair offered little purchase. Realizing this, Irene grabbed the brunette by the neck with both hands. Hauled upwards from behind in this fashion, much to her surprise, Olga was released while contemplating protective measures against whatever might be coming next.

Seeking to escape the attack she did not doubt would be delivered, Olga started to move forward. A foot came against her thinly covered buttocks and shoved hard. Caught with her left leg raised for a step, she was sent across ground which became slippery in a way she was too engrossed elsewhere to understand and was only able to prevent herself from falling by catching hold of the end of the trough. This proved less than a blessing. Turning, she found Irene had come after her faster than she anticipated. The punch she received toppled her backwards. However, having given the blow considerable impetus and finding the surface underfoot just as insecure as had its recipient, the blonde followed the brunette into the water.

Although neither girl was in any condition to appreciate the fact, the muddy nature of the ground around the trough was produced by the kind of coincidence no writer of fiction would dare include in his books. Shortly before sundown, the specially made vehicle which brought water from a nearby stream to replenish the trough had lost a wheel just before the contents were decanted and they were spilled. More had been fetched to complete the filling, but the first had soaked and softened the immediate area. Nor, as the sun went down soon after, had it been dried out to any great extent.

Inflicted by the weight of the two well endowed and far from tiny girls descending into it, the right side legs of the trough sank through the softened soil. Tipping over, it deposited them along with such water as they had not already splashed out when arriving, on to a surface which was already close to ankle deep in gooey sludge. Startled yelps burst out when they felt cold and clammy mud splurge around them as they rolled over locked in a far from gentle embrace. The sensation came as such a shock that they involuntarily broke away from one another.

However, the separation was not protracted!

Quickly forcing herself into a sitting position, Olga saw Irene was doing the same!

Still paying no attention to her less than adequately clad condition nor the clamour from the excited spectators who were approaching, the brunette scooped and hurled a double handful of mud at the blonde. Blinded and having more of the goo enter her partially open lips as she was gasping in air, Irene could not prevent herself being pushed on to her back and straddled across the torso by two curvaceously bulky thighs. Her throat was grasped and her head raised to be banged against the ground. Spluttering sludge from her mouth on responding vocally to the pain, which was less than it would have been before the accident produced the greatly softened state of the ground, some primeval instinct for self preservation warned she must clear her vision quickly if she wanted to escape the latest rough treatment.

Acting upon the impulse, the blonde clawed the mud from her eyes. Looking up, she took in the sight of her assailant's body which was already carrying a liberal coating of the mud. Ignoring the picture Olga presented, although it was greatly appreciated by the male spectators as was her own almost naked and equally sludge covered appearance, she sought to gain freedom by means similar to those responsible for her predicament. Collecting as much of the thick black goo as she could gather in her hands, she flung it into the brunette's face. Then, feeling the pressure on her stomach relax and the hands leave her throat, she surged once more into a sitting position.

Without waiting to do more than reach a semi-kneeling posture, the girls flung themselves together. Colliding with a "thwack!" which resembled two pieces of wet beef being thrown against one another, the contact brought them briefly to their feet. Starting a primitive wrestling tussle, they staggered in a circle without leaving the muddy area. Scrabbling ineffectually at the sludge-covered bare back of the brunette, having found the mud it had gathered rendered the very short brown hair even less receptive to pulling, Irene's fingers hooked under the waistband of the lace trimmed black satin drawers. The snatch she made without even thinking of what might happen snapped the supporting elastic and, already sagging under the weight of the mud which had encrusted them they started to slide over the wearer's hips. Continuing the descent, despite her instinctive attempt to catch them with one hand, they entangled her legs. However, feeling her equilibrium destroyed, she contrived to take her assailant down with her.

Watched by a very appreciative and vocally supportive audience, the two beautiful and shapely combatants churned over and over through the mud. There was no longer any scientific fighting. Instead, oblivious of everything other than a mutual desire to gain victory, they employed the purely instinctive tactics of women in physical conflict. To the male spectators, there was something erotically stimulating about the sight of the constantly changing and increasingly more mud covered mound of wildly rotating femininity.

In the course of their vigorously thrashing efforts, giving not the slightest sign of being aware of the sticky blackish sludge through which they were moving, each combatant was constantly seeking ways to dish out punishment in recompense for the suffering being inflicted upon her person. When not engaged in trying to tear at hair, the effectiveness of the efforts being reduced by the shortness of both sets of locks and the coating of mud which rendered it impossible for either to be identified by colour, four hands were unceasingly roaming at random over two magnificently endowed bodies. While each set of voluptuous contours was being punched, slapped, grabbed, clutched at and jerked indiscriminately, they were continually being assailed by jabbing knees and encircling legs.

The conflict did not all take place upon the ground!

Twice the embattled pair struggled until they were standing still locked in mindless tussling on their feet and encircled by one another's arms. On the first occasion, their bosom-grinding, hand-flailing embrace ended with legs becoming entangled inadvertently and returning them to the muddy battle ground. Next time, they stumbled against the edge of the trough they had overturned and, tripping, went down with only the briefest separations on landing. However, no matter what was being done, the sounds they made involuntarily to punctuate their efforts were reduced to gurgling splutters resulting from mud entering mouths and requiring to be spat out as well as spreading ever further over their bodies.

If she had been in any condition to think of it, Miss Chernyshevsky might have found comfort in one aspect of the latest stage of the conflict. She had lost her drawers, kicked off to remove the impediment they were placing upon her freedom of movement as they had slid downwards. However, in a very short while the state of total nudity to which she had been reduced was at least partially obscured by the all-pervading sludge. What was more, having had her tiny breechclout just as inadvertently wrenched away while her assailant was crawling through her forced apart thighs to momentary freedom after being held supine beneath her, Irene could have counted herself blessed in a similar way. Although the most private portions of her anatomy were displayed by the loss, the garment having been just large enough to prevent this earlier, they too quickly acquired a coating of mud which gave each of the combatants the appearance of being clad in an all-over body stocking extending from the top of the head to the soles of their bare feet.

After brawling mindlessly for over a minute, the girls somehow found themselves kneeling face to face. Each was showing the exertions they were enduring, made even more severe by their surroundings, starting to take toll. Movements had been slowing perceptibly. Slaps and blows had continued to be delivered, but arrived closer to tired shoves than the earlier crisp blows. Breathing had been rendered increasingly difficult by the necessity to frequently eject mud which had entered the mouth, or snort it out of plugged nostrils. However, while the sludge also impaired vision from time to time, they were at such a close proximity this was less of a detriment to their respective activities. In fact, whether able to see or not, they were moving by primeval instinct rather than conscious guidance.

Somehow forcing themselves erect from their knees, leaning breast to breast and with chins on opposing shoulders, the embattled pair interlaced their fingers and began an involuntary trial of strength. For a few seconds, they strained against one another in a way which made them an impressive sight for the masculine onlookers in particular. The coating of mud which covered each from head to foot limned their whole bodies, defining every muscle, curve and protruberance to its best advantage. Even after their exertions, they were still so evenly matched that, in spite of the less than firm ground underfoot, it seemed they had reached a condition of stalemate.

Striving to attain a great leverage, Irene's right foot slipped a little. Before this could cause an adverse effect, it was stopped by coming into contact with the base of the overturned trough. Close to exhaustion though she was, she realized the advantage this contact might offer. They had moved apart until almost at arms' length and the strain to which Olga was subjected had caused her legs to spread apart. Swinging up her right foot, bracing herself against the trough with the left, the blonde directed it between the obligingly separated thighs until the front of her ankle struck at their junction.

Although the kick failed to attain the full power it would have done earlier in the fight, it arrived hard enough to hurt the vulnerable point it had reached. Croaking out breathlessly in pain, Olga wrenched her hands free. Starting to stumble away from her attacker, with fingers clasping at the stricken region, she bowed forward at the waist. Much to her horror, she felt herself grabbed by the sides of her neck and dragged forward until her head was stuffed so it protruded from between Irene's thighs. As they closed upon her neck, feeling the blonde's hands scrabbling on her rump, the full gravity of her situation struck the brunette. Clearly the intention was to lift her and, toppling backwards, drive the top of her skull against the ground.

Fortunately for the brunette, there was no convenient hand hold available!

In fact, Olga might have counted having been reduced to total nudity a blessing of magnitude!

Before Irene could realize that the mud-slickened buttocks did not offer anything which could be gripped, then decide to encircle her waist as an aid to lifting, the brunette forced her weary and suffering body to react to the threat. Wrapping her arms around the blonde's thighs, for a moment she felt she could do nothing more. However, desperation gave her the stimulus she needed. Calling upon her last reserves of strength, she straightened and raised the *Metis* girl on her shoulders. A wail of alarm burst from Irene as she felt herself being elevated until, having gone beyond the point of balance, her legs were released. Feeling herself passed over her assailant's back, exhaustion prevented her rider's instincts from offering the protection they had earlier, and she descended flat on her back in a spray of disturbed mud which nevertheless served to cushion her arrival somewhat.

Not sufficient, however, to save Irene!

Tottering as the weight she had raised departed, Olga could not retain her balance. Falling backwards, she landed rump first alongside the supine and weakly moving blonde. Seeing Irene slowly forcing first head, then shoulders and finally torso upwards, she compelled herself to make another effort. Twisting until kneeling on her right leg, she linked both hands and swung them with all the force she could muster so they slammed upwards beneath the blonde's jaw. As Irene was slammed down, determined to end the fight, the brunette sank both hands into her hair. Obtaining a purchase on the slippery locks for long enough to serve her purpose, she hauled upwards until her opponent was sitting in a limp and unresisting slump. Although the *coup de grace* she delivered with a fist to the chin was unnecessary, she was in no condition to appreciate the fact.

Forcing her protesting body to continue moving, Olga straddled the torso of the unmoving blonde with her knees. Before she could do any more, the complete absence of resistance finally registered. Weakly shoving Irene's head from side to side a couple of times with her hands, to satisfy herself it would be safe to do so, she rose slowly to her feet. She was too mentally and physically drained of energy to hear and see, much less respond to the enthusiastic approbation her success was eliciting from the onlookers. In fact, although she had risen victorious, her legs would not support her. Crumpling on to her knees, she was unaware that Turtle had removed his coat and given it to one of his saloongirls with instructions to drape it around her and, helped by as many others as might be required, carry her back to Honesty John's Tavern.

CHAPTER NINE

Blokes Have all the Bleeding Fun!

"Excuse me, *hombre*," Waco said, having walked forward and confronted Steven King. "Didn't I hear you say something *wrong?*"

"What do you mean, deputy?" the New Englander asked and, although he did not care to be addressed as, *'hombre'* instead of 'mister,' or preferably, 'sir,' his manner was condescending as he considered befitting one of his superior station in life when speaking to a mere public servant.

"Not *deputy,* 'cause I'm off watch tonight and you'll see's how I'm not wearing my badge," the blond youngster corrected, gesturing at his unadorned vest, as he was desirous of absolving the town marshal's office of blame for what he was hoping to bring about. "I've come to tell you's how I'm right proud to be a Johnny Reb born 'n' raised and don't take *kind'* to what you just said."

"*Nothing* I've said was any of *your* concern!" King asserted, having lost the Irish brogue he had assumed as a means of winning over the group he had joined at the bar.

"When I hear somebody saying, 'the War of the Southern Rebellion,' it right quick gets to be *my* concern," Waco explained, with truth, although he might have let the designation pass unchallenged under the pleasantly relaxed circumstances which had at first prevailed when he and his party entered the Buffalo Saloon. It was part of their 'seeing the sights' evening together which they had been promising to spend since first becoming acquainted. He went on, "I just natural' have to come and tell him the rights of it."

"Which are?" the New Englander growled, sensing danger.

"The only thing we rebelled about was having to let lousey

Down East Yankees like *you* try to tell us how we'd got to live," the youngster replied. "Which I'd reckon *anybody* would do."

"Did you hear that, gentlemen?" King asked, bringing back the brogue and looking at the railroad construction workers. "He doesn't *like* us!"

No fool, despite his less likeable qualities, the New Englander had a suspicion that there was more than just the objections of a 'right proud to be a Johnny Reb born 'n' raised' behind the intervention. In fact, he considered such behaviour went against the normal habits of the young Texan; whose behaviour while explaining certain matters pertaining to the killings by the *Metis* shortly after the interrupted meeting at the Railroad House Hotel had impressed him. Concluding he was the target for reprisals on account of what he meant to do, he was hoping to obtain recompense for the money spent buying drinks by seeking protection from the recipients.

"Then that's soon enough settled!" stated the youngest gandy dancer, acting as the shrewdly perceptive businessman from the East had hoped and before any of his companions could speak.

Without realizing it, King was falling into a trap!

Being a shrewd judge of character, Waco had felt sure he could not provoke the New Englander into personally striking the first blow, and he had anticipated what the response to his behaviour would be. What was more, having studied the group while approaching, he had guessed correctly when selecting who was most likely to be first to respond to a request for protection no matter how it might be presented. Therefore, despite having halted with his back to the candidate, he was not surprised to feel his shoulder grasped and a pull exerted to swing him around.

The surprise proved to be on the part of the young Irishman!

Turning what he expected to be an unsuspecting victim around, the gandy dancer hurled a looping round-house punch with his left fist. While packed with some power, it was slow and inadequate when dealing with one who had received the instruction in matters fistic which had been given to Waco since he had become a member of Ole Devil Hardin's floating outfit. Ducking so the fist passed above his blond head, he rammed a punch of his own with considerable force into his would-be assailant's *solar plexus*. Giving vent to a startled and agonized croak, the gandy dancer was driven backwards folding at the waist.

"Don't you try to *jump* me!" Waco yelled, the moment he had removed the threat posed by the young Irishman.

Having made what he would be able to claim was an excuse for his next action, the blond Texan pivoted to deliver a powerful backhand punch with speed and a good aim. Caught on the side of the jaw, King was sent sprawling against two of the most brawny members of the railroad party. Having extracted partial revenge for what he felt sure was the reason why the businessman had sought out the company of the gandy dancers and spoken in such a derogatory manner about England, Waco was not allowed to devote more of his attention to the task of retribution at that moment. Letting out a bellow, his intended attacker came rushing into the fray.

"Pray do *excuse* me, ladies," Lord James Roxton requested, as politely as if addressing *very* important guests at a garden party in the grounds of Windsor Castle, as he realized what Waco was meaning to do. Tossing his rakish Homburg hat over the bar, he removed his jacket and threw that in the same direction. He was speaking and acting with greater rapidity than was his habit in less urgent circumstances. *"Business, you know!"*

As with his predecessor, the tactics of the youngest gandy dancer were reliant upon muscle power rather than skill. Stepping clear, with the grace of a *matador* in contention against a willing but inexperienced bull, the Texan avoided the outstretched hands which intended to grab him. As the Irishman blundered by, Waco turned to deliver a kick to the seat of his pants which changed his reckless charge into a headlong and uncontrolled rush. Before he was able to regain direction over his movements, he crashed against a table at which half a dozen United States' Cavalry soldiers were entertaining a couple of attractive saloon-girls. Although they all attempted to rise before he reached them, none succeeded completely and, as the table was overturned, all were deposited on the floor.

Despite the success he had had so far, Waco was not allowed to continue without retribution. Swung around by one of the men against whom he had sent King reeling, he took a punch which flung him into the arms of two to his rear. Incensed by the interruption to what had been an enjoyable sup-

ply of free drinks, even though they had not formed any liking
for the donor, they hung on to his arms so he could receive
further chastisement. The man who had hit him moved forward to administer it.

Scrambling to their feet, the blue uniformed soldiers were
clearly in no mood to forgive what had happened. Bending,
the burly corporal who was senior member of the group
swiftly dragged up and knocked the young Irishman back in
the direction from which he had come. However, that did not
end the participation of the Army. Seeing one of their kind
treated in such a fashion, the gandy dancers at the nearest
table rose with the intention of taking revenge. Rushing at the
soldiers, they started to launch a furious attack in retaliation.

Seeing Waco's predicament and identifying him as one of
their own, albeit not from their respective outfits, two groups
of Texans rose to come to his rescue. Guessing what was
intended, all the unengaged gandy dancers at the bar rushed
eagerly to counter the intervention. Never willing to miss the
opportunity for a fight, others of their kind rose to join in.
However, in the heat of the moment, some of them assailed a
party of buffalo hunters who—to give them credit—had no
thoughts of participation when rising to their feet.

After that, the conflict extended its sphere of influence like
ripples spreading across the surface of a pond when a stone
was thrown in!

Soon it was involving practically all the people on the
"drinking" side of the bar!

Neither the distaff side of the saloon's employees, nor the
two members of the clergy amongst the customers were excluded!

"Blokes have *all* the bleeding *fun!*" Barbara 'Babsy' Smith
complained, watching Roxton tackle the man who was about
to hit Waco.

"Don't they *just!*" Phyllis 'Ginger' Winchell supported,
possessing an equally volatile nature and quota of high spirits.
Then, looking at the saloon-girls of the party along the bar
who were approaching in what was obviously an irate fashion,
she went on amiably, "Hey, Bridg——!"

"Them two jaspers you and that *foreigner* brought in've
spoiled our party!" accused the tallest girl, whose hair was
almost as fiery red as that of Ginger, speaking with a pronounced Irish accent.

"What did you *call* me?" the close to buxom little blonde demanded, her Cockney voice at its most strident, before her friend could reply.

"A god-damned *foreigner!*" Bridget Murphy supplied.

Being newly arrived in Mulrooney, the shapely and junoesque Irish red head had only heard of the way in which the feud ended. It was her contention that, had she been present, the Buffalo Saloon would have emerged victorious. However, although she had had Babsy pointed out as a prominent and most competent participant on behalf of the Fair Lady Saloon, the knowledge she had acquired omitted one important detail. Lacking this information, she could hardly have said anything more liable to arouse the ire of the little blonde.

"*Foreigner,* is it?" Babsy screeched.

To the little blonde's somewhat insular way of thinking, much as she liked the United States and Americans in general, she was *British*. Therefore, no matter where in the world she might be, it was the local population who were the foreigners as far as she was concerned. Enraged by what she considered an insult of magnitude, but far from being disappointed by the opportunity it presented, she snatched off her broad brimmed hat and sent it after her male companions' discarded property over the counter. Then, bending at the waist, she charged to ram her head into the larger girl's midsection. Despite being cushioned slightly by the upswept pile of curly blonde hair, the attack evoked a squawk of pain from Bridget. Driven backwards, she tripped with her assailant following her down. On landing, they each grabbed hair and commenced as lively a fight as was going on elsewhere.

Regardless of being an employee of the Buffalo Saloon, Ginger's nature and liking for Babsy would not allow her to remain a passive observer, particularly as Bridget was accompanied by a brunette with whom she shared a mutual dislike. Hurriedly discarding her headdress in the same way as the rest of her party, she announced her intentions by actions not words. Slapped hard across the face, the brunette retaliated immediately and just as vigorously in kind. A moment later, the four girls still standing were mixed in a hair yanking tangle—although Ginger was not subjected to the full attentions of the other three—which caused them to trip over and join the little blonde and larger red head on the floor. Arriving they continued their efforts without caring who was being assailed.

What was more, seeing what was happening, the rest of the saloon-girls came over to participate instead of taking the more prudent course adopted by their male fellow workers.

Although Reverend Thatcher and Father O'Riordan were impelled by the best of motives when they came to their feet, they discovered—as had other potential peace-makers in the past and those who would make similar attempts in the future —that "the way to hell was paved with good intentions!"

Because he was on the nearer side of the table and, there-fore, closer to the action, the representative of the Protestant Church was first to discover the truth of the stricture. Sent his way by a kick from a buffalo hunter, a burly gandy dancer collided with him. Swinging around with a fist drawn back to supply offensive rather than precautionary protections, the man restrained his inclination to hit out on seeing the black attire and "reversed" white collar worn by his intended target.

"Forgive me, Father!" the railroad construction worker supplicated, in the instinctive manner of an Irish Catholic who found himself on the point of committing an act of what he considered to be *lese*-clergy rather than -*majeste*.

"Sorry," Thatcher responded without thinking of the possi-ble consequences, as he had frequently done when a similar error of classification was made. *"Wrong* denomination!"

"Oh?" the gandy dancer ejaculated. "That's all right then!"

Saying the words, the man lashed out with the fist he had been on the point of lowering. Taken at the side of the jaw, Thatcher was sent across the room. Crashing his way between a knot of fighters, taking two of them down with him, he sprawled in a sitting position against the wall. Being of the same persuasion as his assailant, losing the wrath with which they turned their attention his way, they were aghast at what they realized must have happened. Seeing the man they sus-pected was responsible approaching, they rose quickly and started to try to make amends for what they considered to have been an unforgiveable act.

"Forgive him, Father!" one of the men requested, as he and his companion started to help the victim up. "He must be dru——!"

"Like I said!" Thatcher snapped, before the explanation could be completed. Wrenching himself free from the hands which had raised him to his feet, he lunged to meet his assail-ant repeating, *"Wrong* denomination!"

Uttering the final word, the Reverend proved he had acquired more than just theological training at the Eastern college from which he had graduated to take the "cloth." Putting to use the skill at boxing he had developed, he slipped the latest punch sent his way. Having done so, he ploughed his right fist into his assailant's midsection and it proved as efficacious as the one delivered by Waco to start the mass brawl. It was followed in very rapid succession by a hook to the descending chin and a right cross to the jaw. Taken by a "one, two, three" combination, which would not have disgraced a professional pugilist trained in the fighting with gloves which was now threatening to supplant the old fashioned bare-knuckle style, the gandy dancer returned to the centre of the room faster than he had come.

However, having dealt with the attacker, Thatcher was not allowed to resume his attempt to act as a peacemaker!

Showing less respect for his "cloth" than the three Irishmen, a buffalo hunter tackled the Reverend and he became as involved in the general fracas as everybody else!

Following Thatcher, Father O'Riordan meant to stop the gandy dancer repeating the attack. On his way, he came into contact with a cowhand who inadvertently knocked against him. Swinging around to counter whatever danger the meeting posed, having had a sturdy Baptist upbringing, the Texan was not influenced by the vestments which met his gaze. Driven back a couple of paces by a hard if less than skilful punch, the priest demonstrated he too had acquired fistic skills in addition to formal studies at the University of Notre Dame. Dealing with his intended assailant in much the same way that his opposite number from the Protestant Church had used against the gandy dancer, he removed the threat. However, he too was immediately the recipient of other attentions which caused him to forget pacificism in favour of active and competent militancy.

Having no distinctive attire to afford him at least partial protection, Walter Braithwaite was just as quickly absorbed into the battle. What was more, proving equally as capable as his theological companions, he was able to obtain satisfaction for a number of frustrations caused by the nature of his work. While he was employing a pair of skilful fists with vigour and precision, regardless of at whom and why he was striking, he was really directing the blows at various of the hotel's clientele to whom he was compelled to give politeness—no matter how unjustified such civility was on account of the treatment accorded in return—in his capacity as senior desk clerk. Therefore, although he did not come through the exchanges unscathed, he was soon enjoying the fight as much as he had when in contention against members of other collegiate fraternities back East.

After feeling at his jaw when his wits returned, using the support offered by the bar rail and top of the counter, King dragged himself erect from where he had been pushed down by the men with whom he collided. He realized the blow had not been delivered by accident and suspected the blond youngster intended to repeat it if granted an opportunity. Seeing Waco and Roxton were fully engaged elsewhere, the lean aristocrat proving a most effective brawler with fistic skills backed by what was obviously a sound working knowledge of the French kicking techniques known as *savate,* he decided he was being granted an opportunity to make good his escape.

The ambition of the New Englander was thwarted from a source he would never have envisaged!

Having contrived to straddle Bridget's torso with her knees, Babsy was subjecting the mop of red hair she grasped with both hands to a pounding on the floor. However, while wild with excitement, she was still conscious of what was going on about her. Seeing King starting to push himself away from the counter, she guessed his intentions. Already aware of what had provoked Waco to behave in such an untypical fashion, a glance informed her that he was unable to interfere. Nor would there be any aid from "Jimmy" Roxton—as the aristocrat had insisted he was called—as he was just as fully occupied. It was, the little Cockney decided, a moment to apply the woman's touch. What was more, fortune was favouring her, as a quick glance established that Ginger was equally well positioned to render assistance.

"Grab that skinny bleeder, Ginge'!" Babsy yelled, leaving her perch—much to Bridget's relief—to dive and grab the New Englander around the legs.

Hearing and understanding, the little red head also quit her straddling position on the chest of the brunette. Thrusting up from the floor, she clutched King by the tail of his coat and hauled at it. Caught completely unawares, he was toppled backwards. On alighting, he was assailed by what gave him the impression of being a couple of thoroughly aroused and furious bobcats. What was more, his troubles were only just beginning.

Rather by accident than deliberate intent, Bridget, the brunette and several other girls followed the pair to contribute to a mauling which was far worse than anything Waco would have been allowed to inflict under the prevailing conditions. After about thirty seconds, which seemed *vastly* longer to him, his assailants disintegrated into fighting segments of their own. They left him looking *very* much the worse for wear. In addition to having the makings of an excellent black eye, his cheeks bore scratches and he had lost several hanks of hair. His jacket was minus a sleeve and torn up the back. Looking as if assailed by several cats, his shirt was in tatters and his collar and tie were gone. Ripped along its inner seam, the right leg of his trousers showed somebody had left a set of deeply indented teethmarks in his calf.

All in all, Steven King was cursing the impulse which had led him to try and take out his petty spite against Lord James Roxton in the saloon!

What was more, much as he wished to resume his painfully interrupted departure, the New Englander could see no sign of the fighting all around him ending of its own accord.

CHAPTER TEN

Cool 'Em Down a Mite

At the first sign of the trouble spreading in the bar-room of the Buffalo Saloon, the male employees followed the instructions they had received for coping with such a contingency. All the bartenders on the "sober" side of the counter, except the man to whom Waco had confessed his intentions, started to remove to a place of safety the contents of the shelves. Then they released the securing pegs and caused a shield of wooden planks to drop into position in front of the big mirror which was one of Buffalo Kate Gilgore's favourite fittings.

Moving just as quickly, the waiters grabbed up and took into the street as many glasses and bottles as they could carry. As soon as the rescued glassware was on the sidewalk, two of them returned to perform a similar protective function to that behind the bar for the two large front windows which bore the name of the establishment and a painting of buffalo on the move. Then they rejoined their companions and awaited the developments they felt sure would shortly be forthcoming.

It was not dereliction of duty that made the one bartender abstain from helping with the precautions. Being the senior of them, he had a different purpose in mind. Going through the door behind the counter, he left the saloon and hurried to carry out the instructions received from the blond youngster. Arriving at the firehouse, he called out the reason for his visit. Leaving the cheerfully enthusiastic occupants to make their preparations with all speed, he ran to his next destination.

"Howdy, Wally," greeted the only deputy in the office of the town marshal as the bartender entered. "I'd think you'd come sparking Big Sarah, only she's not on watch tonight."

"I know," the man replied, being on very close terms with the woman in question; who alternated between doing duty in the capacity of matron to attend to female miscreants and being one of the 'barmaids'—as Freddie Woods called her

89

female employees who worked behind the counter—at the Fair Lady Saloon. "Is Cap'n. Fog here?"

"Nope," the deputy denied. "He's off making the rounds, but don't you go getting funny notions about what Sarah and him might be up to. She's *way* too smart to settle for *second* best when I'm around, all ready 'n' willing: and Dusty's too scared of what Freddie would do to him should he go chasing other gals."

"You on your lonesome, Mark?" Wally inquired, having deduced why Waco had started the fight and wanting to grant time for retribution to be meted out to the lanky New Englander who had been its cause.

"Derry and Pickles are in the back with that son-of-a-bitch who killed the gal down to Lily Gouch's fancy house," the peace officer replied. "And, with Lon hanging around there 'cause we've got word's his brothers could be in town trying to save his hide by scaring witnesses out of talking, it's me or *nobody* for whatever's ailing you."

"Then Buffalo Kate's in *real* trouble," the bartender asserted with a grin which robbed the words of any sting.

Although the town marshal was not in his office at the jailhouse, Wally considered the self-proclaimed "only deputy available" would be more than capable of dealing with the situation!

A good six foot three in height, with a tremendous spread to his shoulders and his torso trimming to a slender waist set upon long and powerful legs, Mark Counter would have stood out in any company.[1] In fact, men of his great size were the exception rather than the rule.[2] Having been on the point of

1. Details of the background and special qualifications of Mark Counter are given in: APPENDIX TWO.
2. Two men who came close to matching Mark Counter in height and bulk were his cousin, Trudeau Front de Boeuf, and Tiny Crumble.
2a. Some details of the less than honest career of Trudeau Front de Boeuf and his even more disreputable mother, Jessica, are given by inference—albeit under his family sobriquet, "Cousin Cyrus" and with no reference to her—in: Part Two, "We Hang Horse Thieves High," J. T.'S HUNDREDTH. They make personal appearances in: CUT ONE, THEY ALL BLEED; Part Four, "A Different Kind of Badger Game," MARK COUNTER'S KIN and Part Three, "Responsibility To Kinsfolk," OLE DEVIL'S HANDS AND FEET.
2b. Tiny Crumble appears in: THE GENTLE GIANT.

setting out for a patrol around the streets, he was putting his white J.B. Stetson hat—its crown embellished by a black leather band sporting half a dozen silver conchas—on curly golden blond hair kept cut short in the accepted cowboy style. His tanned features were almost classically handsome, but exuded a rugged force. Being the attire of a Texas cattle country fashion plate, all his clothing was made of the finest materials and specially tailored for him. Such an excellent fit could never have come from the shelves of any store. His brown *buscadero* gunbelt, carved with a decorative "basket-weave" pattern, carried two ivory handled Colt 1860 Army Model revolvers in fast draw holsters and, showing signs of being well maintained, clearly had seen much use. Despite weighing over two hundred pounds, he gave no suggestion of being slow, clumsy, or awkward on his feet. Rather he carried himself with a springiness that indicated a potential for very rapid motion when required.

"Trouble at the *Buffalo?*" the blond giant inquired, sounding mildly incredulous, on being told what had caused the visit by the bartender. "Waco reckoned as how he was taking Lord Roxton there with Babsy and Ginger."

"They're there, all right," Wally affirmed, wondering how the next item of news he meant to impart would be received and ready to give his opinion in exculpation if necessary. "Fact being, it was *Waco's* started off the fussing."

"He *must* have had a *real* good cause," Mark claimed, knowing the change for the better which had been wrought to the youngster's character on being accepted as a member of the OD Connected ranch's floating outfit. However, he did not wait for confirmation. Instead, he strode towards the rear entrance of office calling, "Hey, Derry, Pickles, I'm going out."

"You should've gone ten minutes back!" replied the mock irascible voice of the aged jailer, Albert 'Pickles' Barrel, from the section at the back of the building given over to cells. "Shut the front door when you go out and don't make too much noise when you come back."

"I'll mind it, pappy!" the blond giant promised. "And don't you go taking no more of Derry's hard earned money off him at cribbage while I'm gone."

"There's no chance of *that!*" Deputy Town Marshal Frank "Derry" Derringer declared. Without coming to the open door, he continued, "Would you play with somebody who peeks

when he's dealing, counts his score higher'n it is *every* time
and knocks your pegs out of the crib board, then puts 'em in
again back half a dozen holes?"

"I don't reckon I would," Mark admitted, as soberly as if
he believed all the unfair tricks had happened.

"No," Barrel cackled cheerfully. "And neither will I. Now
stop all that bellering out there and get going."

"I can take a hint," the blond giant informed the bartender.
"Come on!"

Making his way towards the Buffalo Saloon at a rapid
walk, accompanied by Wally, Mark saw that the arrangements
made by Freddie Woods and Captain Dustine Edward Marsden "Dusty" Fog to cope with such a contingency were already being put into effect!

Having moved with the speed which spoke of considerable
training and organization, the three main units of the
Mulrooney Fire Brigade—a title the men concerned had accepted with some pride when it was suggested by their beautiful English lady mayor—were already approaching the scene
of the brawl. By the time Mark came up, the horse-drawn fire
engines were halted. Leaving the teams in place instead of
removing them as would have been done if attending a fire,
the crews swiftly started to unroll hoses connected to the large
brass tanks. While the nozzle captains hauled the operative
ends towards the batwing doors, the others took up positions
at the pump handles and were joined by some of the men who
had been attracted by the commotion.

"Looks like a wild one in there, Mark," Fire Chief Moses
Rubens greeted, glancing up from checking the brass nozzle
of his hose pipe.

"Looks that way, Moe," the deputy admitted, gazing over
the batwing doors.

"Everybody seems to be having such a *good* time," the
burly and cheery featured head of the Fire Brigade claimed.
"It almost seems a shame to spoil their fun."

"Buffalo Kate might not see it that way when she gets
back, 'specially if one of those big old front windows she's so
all-fired proud of gets busted," Mark pointed out, the owner
of the establishment having been called away from Mulrooney
on a private matter shortly after the culmination of her feud
with Freddie Woods had seen them forget their differences and
become partners. "Which being, we're just natural' going to
have to be spoil-sports for shame."

"I'm afraid I don't see *anything* else we can do," Rubens admitted, ascertaining that the man on either side of him was ready. "Let's cool 'em down a mite, gents!"

On receipt of the order, eager hands vigorously started to operate the pumps of the fire engines. Swelling as they became filled, the hoses writhed like living entities. Then, being guided into the bar-room, the brass nozzles erupted jets of water. These were directed in horizontal arcs with precision and effect.

Caught in the chilling and powerful flow, fighters were either swept from their feet or sent staggering!

Watching what was happening, Moses Rubens and the other two nozzle captains changed their point of aim as was required!

Being soaked to the skin, the various recipients of the attentions had different feelings about what befell!

Having a badly ripped shirt and bleeding lip, Waco was being held against the bar by a buffalo hunter and a railroad gandy dancer. The latter had not been amongst the group who Steven King was trying to use against Lord James Roxton and, in fact, was not even Irish. However, with a burly soldier preparing to deliver a second punch to his body, the blond youngster was one who thought the water beneficial. Seeing his predicament, Rubens engulfed him and his assailants in a flow which caused the attack to be abandoned.

Dealing with an assailant, after having used his skill at boxing and *savate* to good advantage against various predecessors, the lean young aristocrat was less enamoured of them all being swept off their feet by Nozzle Captain Siegfried Kretschmer.

Contriving to get back to settling her personal difference of opinion with the larger woman who had called her a foreigner and who the fortunes of battle had separated her from, Barbara "Babsy" Smith, now less than substantially attired and in her stocking feet, realized a crisis point had been reached. In fact, although Bridget Murphy might not have agreed at moments during their far from gentle brawling, the close to buxom little Cockney blonde was starting to believe she had bitten off rather more than she could chew. Held at arms' length by the neckline of the black lace bodice—which was made available for this purpose by the loss of her dress—with one hand, the Irish red head was beyond her reach. Also reduced to her undergarments, having her stockings in tatters and lost her shoes, Bridget was drawing back her other fist to deliver what she hoped would prove a *coup de grace*. Just as she commenced her swing, they were caught by the jet from the hose of Nozzle Captain Phineas Riley. Sent sprawling, what little breath they had left being driven from them, they lost interest in aggression.

Not far away, Phyllis "Ginger" Winchell and the brunette who had incurred her animosity were in no better shape as far as being adequately clad was concerned. They too had sought to keep their affair private by seeking one another out whenever they lost contact. Their fight was also approaching a settlement. However, the little red head was better off than her blonde friend. Straddling her supine and obviously much weakened opponent, Ginger was in an ideal position to end all opposition by banging the head she was grasping by its hair on the floor. Before she could deliver a second bump, they too became a target and the matter was driven from their thoughts along with all notions of continuing.

After having saved Babsy from imminent defeat, Riley noticed Reverend Dennis Thatcher going hurriedly towards where Father Brian O'Riordan was under attack by two cowhands. Drawing an erroneous conclusion over the reason, which was actually to render assistance, the nozzle captain acted upon it as he considered befitting a good Catholic. Seeing his colleague wash the Reverend over, being an equally stout adherent to the Protestant faith, Kretschmer felt it incumbent upon him to take reprisals. However, in doing so, he inadvertently alleviated the predicament of the priest with a greater ease than Reverend Thatcher could have achieved.

Before the contents of the three fire engines' tanks were exhausted, the efforts of the Fire Brigade had brought an end to all hostility!

Waiting until Chief Moses Rubens and the nozzle captains withdrew through the batwing doors, Mark entered the barroom!

Halting just across the threshold, hands thumb-hooked into his *buscadero* gunbelt, the blond giant gazed about him!

Something of a connoisseur of such things, having participated in more than one similar brawl, Mark concluded he had rarely seen evidence of one being better!

In fact, the handsome giant found himself regretting that

duty had prevented him from being present to join in!

Gasping for breath, soaking men and equally bedraggled women stood or sat on the floor showing signs of the fray and exhaustion. Others of both sexes had been swept from their feet by the jets of water and were starting to rise. There were some who lay still, having been rendered unconscious as a result of the fighting. However, as far as Mark could see, there had not been any use made of firearms. Nor had any ready-made, or extemporized, cutting weapons been employed. In fact, everything implied the battling had been restricted to fists, feet, the occasional set of teeth and pieces of furniture used as clubs.

While considerable damage had been done to the fittings of the bar-room, it was mainly confined to the furnishings on the customers' side of the counter and nothing irreplacable was ruined. A couple of side windows were shattered, but the protective shields over the pair at the front of the building— much larger and far more costly to replace—had saved them. Afforded a similar defense against being inadvertently smashed, the big mirror behind the bar had also come through the fracas unscathed.

Having concluded his examination, the blond giant walked forward!

Making an effort to control his desire to grin, Mark gave his attention once again to the participants!

"I suppose the question now is," the big blond drawled. "Who-all started it?"

"You might say's how I did," Waco confessed, looking more cheerful than contrite.

"I hope you've got a *real* good excuse," Mark declared, studying the signs of conflict left on the blond youngster's face and trying to sound stern despite the twinkle in his eye. "Because Dusty's surely going to need one when he hears what's come off here."

"Sure and wasn't it all a little bit of a misunderstanding?" suggested the biggest of the gandy dancers who had formed the singing group. Thinking of what had led up to it while fighting, he had reached an accurate conclusion over the reason for Waco's actions and wanted to make amends. "And a darling of a fight it was, to boot."

"I'm right pleased you think so," the blond giant answered. "Because you're *all* going to pay for *everything* that's got busted."

"I'll attend to the damages, old boy," Lord James Roxton offered immediately, having strolled over in his usual languid-seeming fashion. His face was showing fight damage similar to that of the young Texan and his clothes were even more dishevelled. *"Noblesse oblige* and all that sort of twaddle."

"That you won't, your honour," the Irishman asserted, but in an amiable and even respectful manner. "There's more than just *you* had the fun of it, sir, so it's only right as we *all* of us should help pay the piper. So, happen Cap'n. Fogg'll give me leave, I'll be finding me hat and making a start on it and bad cess to any's don't want to help out."

"I'll have the bartenders work out what it's going to cost you," the blond giant promised, without troubling to correct a not unusual misapprehension about his identity. Then he gave his attention to the female combatants who were still on their feet and stood, trying to hold together whatever torn, soaking garments remained, in not over successful attempts to retain some semblance of modesty. "You *ladies* had best go get into some dry clothes, you seem to be all *wet*. And, while you're at it, take along your friends who must've *swooned* in the excitement."

"I'll give you a hand with them, luv," Babsy Smith offered, removing the fingers with which she had been ruefully working her throbbing jaw from side to side. Glancing down and realizing just how scantily she was attired, she was grateful for the knowledge that she would be able to borrow clothing from her little red haired friend to make improvements to her appearance. Then, running a gaze over her opponent, she continued with a grin, "Cor, I bet *we* don't half look a *sight*."

"I've felt *better*, I'll be admitting," replied Bridget Murphy, to whom the offer had been made. Feeling at her swollen and discoloured right cheek, she winced and went on, "You're all right for a *foreigner*."

"So are *you*," the little blonde grinned, noticing the last word was not uttered with its earlier disdain. "Come on, luv. Let's get started."

Satisfied he could leave the distaff side of the affair to look after one another, Mark swung his gaze to where the two members of the clergy were approaching. Each sported a blackened eye, a thickened lip and, in addition to their suits being damaged, had lost his white collar.

"What have we here?" the blond giant queried dryly. "The church militant?"

"There's a perfectly simple explanation for all this," Reverend Dennis Thatcher claimed. "We've been engaged in a theological discussion."

"These little things are sent to try us," Father Brian O'Riordan supported. "Only it's thinking I am we may have tried a *little* too hard."

"I suppose *you've* been seeing if you can find fellers *loco* enough to play that blasted 'Boston game' of yours?" Mark suggested to Walter Braithwaite, who showed just as much sign of having been very actively engaged in the brawling.

"Strange as it might seem, that's *exactly* what I've been doing," declared the desk clerk of the Railroad House hotel. With his voice taking on a note of blatantly conscious virtue, he continued, "But, throughout *all* the trouble here, I was just an innocent bystander."

"I know what *that* means," the blond giant affirmed. "You could hit *everybody* who came near enough without bothering to find who-all they were siding." Then his attention was attracted to the cause of the trouble, who had been rendered unconscious while trying to leave the room by a blow from one of the gandy dancers which was intended for Lord Roxton. Being unaware of the facts, he concluded somebody must have devoted a considerable amount of effort to reducing the New Englander to such a dilapidated condition. Wondering why this should be, he went on, "You'd best help Mr. King back to his room, Mr. Innocent Bystander."

"Certainly," Braithwaite assented cheerfully. He had seen Babsy lead the attack, but could not guess why she and the other girls had singled out the New Englander for such attention. *"Whoever* left him like he is didn't do things by *halves*. He looks like something half a dozen or so cats dragged in, then tried to throw him out again."

CHAPTER ELEVEN

We'd've Stopped You Regardless

"Coffee, or something stronger?" Mrs. Lily Gouch inquired of the official visitor who had been brought to her private living quarters in the brothel she ran with strict yet fair discipline and efficiency.

"You know you don't give no drinking liquor to an Injun," the deputy town marshal replied, his Texan's drawl having a pleasant tenor suggestive of a good singing voice and, despite the way in which the refusal was made, his manner was amiable. "But I wouldn't say no to a cup of your Arbuckles, please, ma'am."[1]

Lean and wiry, the Ysabel Kid was around six foot in height and gave the impression of possessing a whipcord strength which would not tire easily or quickly. Although some peace officers would not have considered such a courtesy necessary, he had removed his hat prior to entering and, so glossy it seemed almost blue in some lights, his hair was black as the wing of a Deep South crow. In his early twenties, but looking much younger—unless one noticed his curiously coloured red-hazel eyes, which gave a strong hint of a *vastly* different character—his Indian-dark features were handsome

[1]. Such was the availability of the brand of coffee known as "Arbuckle's," the majority of cowhands grew up without knowing there was any other kind. Therefore, they tended to call that beverage, "Arbuckle's" regardless of whatever Company's name might be on the label of the container in which it was purchased.
[1a]. An inexperienced and less than competent green hand on a ranch was sometimes referred to derisively by the cowhands as being an "Arbuckle;" on the principle that the boss must have sent off the Company's premium stamps to pay for his "extraordinary" services.

and seemed almost babyishly innocent. Even in repose, however, they offered a correct suggestion that he was of mixed bloodlines.[2] Every item of it being black—except for his sharp toed boots having low heels more suitable for walking than riding—including the headgear, his garb was of the style practically *de rigueur* for a cowhand from the Lone Star State. At the right side of his gunbelt, a Colt Dragoon Model of 1848 revolver hung with its plain walnut butt pointing forward in a low cavalry-twist draw holster. On the left was sheathed a massive ivory hilted James Black bowie knife. As if considering these somewhat archaic weapons might prove insufficient for his needs, he had a Winchester Model of 1866 rifle carried at the point of balance on its wooden foregrip by his left hand.

Matching the black clad Texan in height and far more bulky, there was nothing about Mrs. Gouch's outside appearance to indicate how she earned her living. Having dark brown hair tinged with grey and a good looking face, she was dressed in sober black and had none of the amounts of ostentatious jewellery sported by many of her contemporaries. All in all, she had the appearance one would expect from a middle-aged schoolteacher with a strong sense of discipline enabling her to control even the most rowdy of classes. While it was very much her nature when occasion demanded, she had acquired her demeanour of strictness when working as a prostitute and having elected to cater for those clients who enjoyed physical domination as part of her service.

In some of the other towns where she had operated similar premises as a madam, on receiving a visit from a member of the municipal or county law enforcement agencies, Mrs. Gouch would have wondered how much money it would cost her. However, she felt sure this was not the motive for the Kid coming to see her. Mulrooney was not that kind of community, nor were the members of the OD Connected ranch's floating outfit such self-seeking peace officers.

Based upon experiences elsewhere, Mrs. Gouch had hardly been able to believe what was said when greeted on her arrival by Freddie Woods and Captain Dustine Edward Marsden "Dusty" Fog in their respective official capacities. She was informed that, provided she kept a clean and honest establish-

2. The background and special qualifications of the Ysabel Kid are given in: APPENDIX THREE.

ment, she would not be subjected to any interference by the town marshal and his deputies. Since then, having lived up to the strictures—which had been termed as, "running an orderly disorderly house"—the promise had been kept. Until the brutal murder, she had contrived successfully to keep what few troubles had occurred confined to the premises and had never had a situation which required her seeking assistance from the peace officers.

"I wouldn't want you to think's I'm not *pleased* to see you, mind," the madam remarked, after having told the Negro maid who brought in the deputy to fetch coffee. She continued in a vein which she would never have been so ill-advised as to employ with some peace officers and the Earp brothers in particular. "But are you just hiding so's Cap'n. Fog won't find you some work for all that hard earned money's us good tax paying citizens hand over so's you can spend it in sloth and idleness?"

"You're starting to sound like Freddie Woods and Betty Hardin, which I don't know who-all's the worst 'tween 'em and I wouldn't want to wish such on *nobody*," the Kid replied in the manner of giving a warning he considered should be heeded and a change for the better made. He went on in a similarly light-hearted tone, "But my dropping by to say, 'Howdy, you-all' is some of that too."

"Too?" Mrs. Gouch queried, knowing a desire to avoid performing his duties was not what had brought her visitor to the brothel.

"Being a well-raised and taught proper lil ole Texas boy, I'm natural' against not earning my pay," the Kid claimed, with mock unctuous pride. Although there was little change on the surface, his voice took on a harder timbre as he got down to business. "You mind that son-of-a-bitch we're holding to the jailhouse?"

"The one who butchered poor lil Winnie?" Mrs. Gouch asked, her voice and manner showing a mixture of genuine remorse over the death of the girl and anger at the perpetrator. "I was inclined to go along with those folk's said we should come down there, hauled him out and stretched his neck on the nearest tree."

"Had you even *tried*," the black clad Texan said quietly. "We'd have *stopped* you regardless of how we'd reckon he deserved it, good tax paying citizens or not."

"That's *one* reason why I talked 'em out of it," the madam replied and, tough as she was, she felt a cold shiver run down her spine at the underlying menace with which the warning had been given. "Anyways, what about him?"

"Dusty allow's how he'll stretch hemp legal, comes his trial," the Kid obliged, his tone indicating he believed the source of the supposition made it undeniably correct. "Even though he's took on that snake-bellied law wrangler's was acting for the big *Metis,* 'til he got made wolf bait in the jail by his *amigos,* we've got enough evidence on him to make sure of that."

"Lena-Mae walked in on him and Winnie just as he was ripping at her with his knife," Mrs. Gouch said grimly. "Which she's ready and willing to swear to on oath any time she's asked."

"That's the main things we're counting on," the Kid admitted, then he apparently went off at a tangent. "By the way, ma'am. I hope you don't mind, but I've left my ole Nigger hoss in the trees out back."

"Isn't the livery stable good enough any more?" the madam inquired.

"He was real comfy there and that's a fact," the Texan replied. "But you couldn't expect me to *walk* all the way out here, now do you?"

"I'm surprised when I even see a cowhand *walking* to the backhouse and you're *worse* than most," Mrs. Gouch asserted, with a smile which still contrived to leave her face in its usual grimly determined lines. "Fact being, where *you* are concerned, I've always expected you to ride right on in."

"I *tried* one time, but there wasn't room for us both."

"Do you have a *special* reason for bringing that overgrown white goat out here?"

"You've heard that *hombre's* been allowing he's got kin's'll come get him loose afore we can haul him in front of the judge?"

"I've *heard.*"

"Well, 'less we've been told *wrong,* they could be in town."

"So you've come to warn me to have a watch kept on Lena-Mae?" Mrs. Gouch stated rather than asked. "Or does Cap'n. Fog figure on having her hid out some place where she'll be safe?"

"Well now, ma'am," the Kid replied and, suddenly, he no longer looked either young or innocent. "We don't have *neither* in mind."

"Hey, *old* man!" Kenneth Little called, having had his self assurance return—after it having been badly shaken by his capture—since finding he was not physically abused despite the obvious revulsion which all his captors felt towards him. It was augmented by something which had happened a short while before while he was left unobserved. "Do you and the tinhorn reckon it's *safe* for just the two of you to be here with me?"

"Well, now," drawled the man to whom the derisive comment was directed, looking from where he and the deputy town marshal to whom the prisoner was referring were seated at a small table playing cribbage. They were positioned so they had an uninterrupted view through the connecting door —which was propped fully open for just such a purpose—of the entrance from the street to the office at the front of the building. "When he was 'tending to that bad arm of your'n, which I'd've left to rot off, the doc did say's how you was close to being a 'hydrophoby' skunk's he'd *ever* come across, but we wasn't to worry 'cause what *you've* got ain't *catching*."

"You'll not be so smart-assed when Brother Sam 'n' Brother Saul 'n' the rest of our kin get here," Little warned, restraining himself from acting upon an inclination induced by anger over the response to what he had considered to be crushing sarcasm. He had just sufficient sense to know that to yield to his emotions would make his situation worse instead of better and was certain to jeopardize plans already made to secure his release. "'Cause I don't aim on leaving *none* of you alive when I get the hell out of here!"

"I wouldn't count any on getting out of here walking all spry and healthy, nor even just plain walking out," Deputy Sheriff Frank 'Derry' Derringer advised, almost mildly. "'Cause I'd be willing to lay good odds that there's a better than fair chance of *you* getting shot afore your kin can reach you."

"*Better 'n' fair*, you say, Derry?" the elderly man cackled and slapped his most prominent weapon. "Me 'n' lil ole Lulu-Belle here can practical' *guarantee* he'll get made wolf bait afore they come in."

Tall, lean, with what hair remained having been bleached white by years of exposure to the elements, Albert "Pickles" Barrel was leathery of visage and moved with a sprightliness of one much less than his undetermined age. As was his usual habit, although he had no intention of leaving that night, he had a battered and decrepit looking black Burnside campaign hat—decorated by an obviously ancient eagle feather tucked into a gaudy yet faded band of Indian manufacture around its crown—tilted back on his head. Despite having taken the post of jailer, he still retained it and the smoke-darkened buckskin shirt and trousers, which were tucked into Comanche-style leggings, and moccasins from the days when he rode scout for the Army.[3] Carried upon what had once been a military carbine sling, suspended from his left shoulder to the right hip, was the kind of sawed-off twin barrelled ten gauge shotgun known as "whipit gun."[4] To supplement this most efficacious close quarters' weapon, he had a well worn Colt 1860 Army Model revolver butt forward in the holster at the left side of his gunbelt.

About six foot in height, with a reasonable build suggestive of a hard physical condition rather than the effects of dissipation, Frank "Derry" Derringer had dark hair and a neatly trimmed moustache. Although he had never qualified for the derogatory designation, "tinhorn," with its implications of indulging in dishonest methods, he was undoubtedly a successful professional gambler. Because of the manner in which he normally earned his living, his pleasant face—schooled to show only such emotions as he considered warranted by any given situation—lacked the tan of the elderly jailer.[5] Bare

3. Due to an error in the material from which we first wrote about Albert "Pickles" Barrel, we inadvertently referred to him as "Pickle-Barrel" and implied he had been working as a swamper at the Fair Lady Saloon prior to being hired as jailer. In actual fact, he was already employed in the latter capacity by Freddie Woods before the members of the OD Connected ranch and Frank "Derry" Derringer became members of the town marshal's office.

3a. How the leggings and moccasins of a Comanche differed from those of other Indians is explained in: IS-A-MAN.

4. A detailed description of the modifications required to make a double barrelled shotgun qualify for the designation, "whipit gun," is given in CUT ONE, THEY ALL BLEED.

5. Deputy Town Marshal Frank "Derry" Derringer makes "guest" ap-

headed, as he had left his white "planter's" hat hanging on the rack by the front entrance to the office, he was wearing an open black "cutaway" tail coat, a white silk shirt, with a black string bow-tie, an unfastened vest which was multi-hued at the front and had a glossy dark green back, slim legged grey trousers having a black stripe down the seams of the legs and black Hersome gaiter boots. Designed for a fast withdrawal of the ivory handled Colt 1860 Army Model revolver in the holster tied to his right thigh, his gunbelt was black and well cared for. There was an elegant yet sturdy twenty-seven inch long black walking cane with a silver "claw and ball" handle leaning against the right side of his seat.

Being some ten years younger, because of some hereditary genetic trait, Kenneth Little did not resemble his brothers. Where the twins were not much over medium height, thickset and dark in complexion, he was tall, slender, blond and had a lighter skin pigmentation. Neither of his siblings could be called even moderately good looking, having surly and less than prepossessing countenances, whereas he was handsome; albeit with a suggestion of his true nature behind his ingenuous seeming features. If he felt any remorse for the heinous crime which had brought him to the cell, or concern for his future welfare, it did not show. Rather he was cocky and truculent. Bare headed, he had on a collarless and grubby white shirt from which the left sleeve had been removed to make way for the bandages swathing the arm reposing in a sling. He had neither galluses[6] nor belt to support the trousers of his three piece brown suit and, although he was wearing thick grey woolen socks through which his big toes whitely poked, his shoes too had been removed when he was incarcerated. His high crowned, somewhat dented, brown Derby hat, jacket and vest, hung on the end of the single bunk.

Being keen students of human nature, Derringer and Barrel had noticed the change which had come over the only remaining prisoner in the cell block at the rear of the building hous-

---

pearances in: QUIET TOWN, THE MAKING OF A LAWMAN, THE TROUBLE BUSTERS and THE GENTLE GIANT.

5a.   Frank Derringer "stars" in his own right in COLD DECK, HOT LEAD.

6.   "Galluses," also known as "suspenders;" the American term for what in the United Kingdom are known as "braces."

ing the town marshal's office.[7] Concluding he was far from being intelligent, they had put it down to his having been given to believe by Counsellor James S. Pitt—a notoriously unscrupulous attorney who had arrived claiming to have been instructed, by a source undisclosed to the peace officers on the grounds of legal secrecy, to act in his defense—that he had nothing to fear from the forthcoming trial. Or it was possible his improved spirits might have come because he too had heard rumours that members of his family were reported to have arrived in the vicinity with the intention of setting him free.

While correct in the latter assumption, the deputy and jailer were only partly so with regards to the other!

Being granted a private interview with the attorney, who had claimed when sure they would not be overheard to have been sent by his Brother Saul, Little had not received the slightest comfort from the assessment of his chances should he come up for trial. Instead, Counsellor Pitt—whose high prices resulted from supplying services which extended far beyond attending to the legal defense in court—had stated only a miracle could save him from the gallows. Having rendered the decision, the attorney had given *sotto voce* instructions for a contingency plan which had been made to save him from his well deserved fate.

Excellently though the building had been designed and constructed, it had a serious failing in the cells provided for holding prisoners awaiting trial or to be disposed of in other ways. The outside walls were very thick and sturdy, with a window for each cell to supply ventilation positioned too high for anybody to be able to look in without climbing in a conspicuous fashion. However, while supplied with thick bars too narrow to allow the passage of even the most slender human body, they did not have glass panes or anything else to prevent smaller objects being slipped through.

Having studied the situation when taking office, Dusty Fog had pointed out the serious discrepancy. Unfortunately, asserting that the jailhouse had already cost the town a considerably higher sum of money than was originally envisaged, Bruce

7. A detailed description of the building housing the office of the town marshal of Mulrooney and its specialized equipment is given in: THE TROUBLE BUSTERS.

Millan and his small coterie of adherents had said such an
addition was an unnecessary luxury when only miscreants
would be housed inside. The objections of the small Texan
had been to some extent justified by the murder of the *Metis*
prisoner being held and who was shot from the roof of an
adjacent building. In fact, as Millan was no longer in
Mulrooney, Freddie Woods had had no objections when ordering the modifications suggested by Dusty to be carried out.

Fortunately as far as Little was concerned, the protective
measures had not yet been taken!

Carrying out the instructions received from Pitt, the young
Bald-Knobber had responded to the call of a mocking bird
which came from outside the rear of the building by starting to
sing the song he was told to use. This had indicated he was
alone in the cell block and was acted upon with alacrity. A
heavy metal nut had been tossed through the window. Drawing in the string to which it was attached had brought in a
small rawhide bag containing the firearm he had been promised. It was a Colt Model of 1871 "Cloverleaf Cylinder"
House Pistol, a .41 Short calibre revolver in spite of its name.
While it was not as concealable as a twin barrelled Remington
Double Derringer would have been, it was less bulky than any
contemporary handgun of the same calibre and had the further
advantage of a four-shot capacity.

Giving the double tug on the string required by his instructions after removing the gun, Little had watched it and the
now empty bag whisked away in the direction from which it
had come. The absence of any commotion outside had indicated that whoever had presented him with the weapon had
done so and departed without being seen. Realizing he must
retain the element of surprise he had been granted, he decided
against keeping the Colt in the right side pocket of his trousers
and knew he was unable to tuck it into the back of the waistband because of having been deprived of the garment's support. He had been equally disinclined to try hiding it inside the
sling on his left arm. Instead, he had placed it beneath the
pillow on the bunk.

Armed and ready, the young Bald-Knobber was awaiting
the moment of liberation which he had been assured would
come that night!

Being the kind of person he was, Little had been unable to
keep his perked up feelings from being noticeable!

What was more, although he had come off worse in the exchange, the Bald-Knobber had yielded to the temptation to mock his captors!

Before Little could try to think up some suitably cutting witty response to the comments made by Derringer and Barrel, there was an interruption!

Although the front door was closed, the upper half of the window on either side of it was open sufficiently to allow the voice of the town marshal to be heard calling from the street!

"It's Dusty," Derringer announced unnecessarily.

"You'd best go see what he wants," Barrel suggested.

"I reckon I had at that," the gambler conceded and, picking up his walking cane, walked into the front office.

Guessing from what had been said that his promised liberation was about to take place, the young Bald-Knobber turned towards the bunk!

Promising himself the satisfaction of killing the elderly jailer, even if he should be prevented from according the gambler a similar fate, Little crossed to the bunk from where he had been standing at the barred door of the cell and, reaching beneath the pillow with his right hand, grasped the "bird's head" butt of the four-shot Colt!

CHAPTER TWELVE

You'll Get Your Brother Killed!

"Good evening, gentlemen," Mrs. Lily Gouch greeted, looking over the three men who had just entered the reception hall of her brothel. Their attire suggested the shortest was from a more affluent stratum of society than the others. Deciding the latter looked to be hired hands from a hill country district of Missouri, although the former could have been a prosperous owner of some kind of agricultural property from anywhere west of the Mississippi River, she went on in her usual manner without needing to think of what she was saying, "And in what way may my young ladies and I be of assistance to you?"

"We're wanting to have us a little party," Saul Little replied. "Us and a girl apiece."

"That seems a *reasonable* arrangement," the madam asserted, again giving a stock response. "May I have your names so I can present you to the ladies of your selection?"

"I'm Laurence Spigel, from Rockport in Atchison County, which's right up north in Missouri," the Bald-Knobber co-leader lied and, indicating his companions, continued, "These're my hired men, Jimmy Knapp and Tom Dalyell."

Knowing his accent would betray his place of origin, Little had not attempted to suggest he came from somewhere other than Missouri. However, he had selected a town far removed from the Mutton Hollow area in which he and his brothers had their home. Far from being his "hired men," the pair with him were distant cousins whose allegiance to family ties made them willing supporters in the efforts to save his younger brother from what would almost certainly be the gallows in the event of a trial. However, in their case, he did not offer an alias. Their qualities were loyalty and a lack of scruples rather than intelligence and he did not wish to take the chance of either inadvertently arousing suspicions by failing to respond when addressed by a summer name he had concocted.

"And what is the reason for your party, sir?" Mrs. Gouch asked. "A birthday, perhaps?"

"Be you allus this nosey?" asked the gangling red head who had been presented as Jimmy Knapp, his tone redolent of suspicion, moving his right hand until it was close to the walnut handle of a Colt 1860 Army Model revolver pointing forward in the low cavalry twist holster tied to the right leg of his faded Levi's pants.

"I'm *never* nosey, as *you* put it, *sir!*" the madam answered, her manner taking on the coldly authoritative demeanour which was second nature to her after being employed for so many years. "I merely wanted to know whether we could produce something *special,* such as a birthday cake."

"You'll have to forgive Jimmy, ma'am," Little requested, darting a prohibitive scowl at the red head. "It's the first time he's ever been anywhere this *fancy* and he doesn't know what to expect. But he's a good man and loyal as they come, as those blasted Bald-Knobbers found out when they tried to give me fuss back to home."

"Bald-Knobbers?" Mrs. Gouch queried, as if the name meant nothing to her. "And what might *they* be?"

"A bunch of thieving villains the like of which I hope you never come across, ma'am," Little explained, hoping his kinsmen would refrain from displaying any sign that they did not care for the description. He was better educated than anybody else in their band, even his one hour older twin, having been sent to live with relatives in Saint Louis where he had attended schools offering a more comprehensive curriculum than was available in their home town. Therefore, he was doing everything he could to prevent it occurring to the woman he was addressing that there was any possibility of him being connected with his younger sibling. "Jimmy downed two of them, neat's taking the head off a turkey gobbler called up for it, when they come 'round my place."

"Is *that* what you're celebrating?" Mrs. Gouch inquired, although feeling sure the answer would not be in the affirmative.

"No, ma'am," the stocky Bald-Knobber denied. Glancing into the parlour where several attractive and shapely girls in varying types of dishabille were lounging around, he noticed with satisfaction that the one he had arrived in search of was amongst them. "I've come to buy some of those longhorn cattle the Texans bring here and've made a choicely good deal. So I figured, them having helped me stand off those thieving Bald-Knobbers and all, I'd show them a good time."

"And you've come to the right place for that," the madam declared, again as she would to any visitor with such an avowed intention.

"I hear tell's how you've got a suite upstairs," the Bald-Knobber remarked in a casual fashion. "One room for sitting and socializing and two for having your pleasure."

"The Trail Boss Suite," Mrs. Gouch confirmed, being particularly proud of the special facilities she offered in the form described by the stocky visitor. "It's available. Now, have you any preference for your *company?*"

"I'll have that tall red haired girl in the blue robe," Little stated, pointing into the parlour.

"Lena-Mae Hoskins?" the madam asked, having noticed how quickly the selection was made and watching for any suggestion that the name meant something to the men.

"I don't care what she's called," the Bald-Knobber declared, trying to sound as if interested only in the pleasures which might lie ahead. "I've always been taken with tall red headed girls and she looks just the kind I'm smitten with."

"Well, she's——!" Mrs. Gouch began.

"I'm always willing to pay *high* for what takes my fancy," Little claimed, deciding the seeming reluctance was intended to get more money from him as a result of a natural misconception about the interest he had shown in the only eye-witness against his younger brother. "So name your price, or we'll go some other place to see happen they'll be more ready to oblige."

"It's fifty dollars for Lena-Mae," the madam obliged, although this was a far higher sum than she had ever suggested. "And, of course, there are the other two girls and the charge I'm afraid I have to ask for the use of the suite."

"You've got a deal," the Bald-Knobber assented, after having been quoted another sum in excess of the usual fee. Taking a thick wallet from the inside right pocket of his jacket, he counted out the required amount and, handing it over, went on, "Isn't *nobody* can say's how Laurence Spigel's a *piker* when it comes to having his wantings. Pick out the girls who take your fancy, Jimmy, Tom, and we'll go have us a *time*."

Accepting the money, Mrs. Gouch was prey to serious misgivings!

Having worked for a few years in Saint Louis, the madam was able to recognize a Missouri accent. She would have known "Spigel" and Knapp came from the so-called "Show Me" State even without having been informed of that fact.[1] On introducing himself and his companions, the stocky man had claimed they lived in Atchison County which was in the north of Missouri, and Kenneth Little hailed from Taney County situated at the extreme south. He had also professed a hatred for the Bald-Knobbers' bands, to one of which the murderer of Winnie had claimed membership.

Furthermore, as additional evidence that the trio could be what outer appearances suggested, the explanation for their presence in Mulrooney had a ring of validity about it. Missourians with sufficient land to make the proposition worthwhile, such as "Spigel" appeared to be, occasionally purchased longhorn cattle brought to Kansas to infuse new blood to their stock. Some of them were generous with their hired help and he might genuinely be meaning to repay the taller pair for having helped him fight off marauding attackers of the kind he mentioned. They looked capable of doing it, being typical of the poor and uneducated, yet hard bitten, fighting men, which the Ozarks' "hill country" spawned in great numbers.

While each of the taller men had an Army Colt in a tied down holster on the right and a J. Russell & Co. "Green River" hunting knife sheathed at the left of his gunbelt, "Spigel" did not have weapons of any kind displayed openly. In spite of this, having noticed from which pocket "Spigel" took his wallet—although he showed no signs of being left handed —Mrs. Gouch's keen and experienced gaze had detected a bulge under the left side of his jacket. It suggested he had a revolver of some kind in a shoulder rig. Of course, there was nothing unusual about the carrying of a weapon in concealment. Many completely honest and law-abiding businessmen went armed in such a fashion.

---

1. According to tradition, people from the State of Missouri would never accept anything at face value and had to be "shown."

Nevertheless, despite the evidence to support the possibility of the trio being what they claimed, Mrs. Gouch was equally aware of suggestions to the contrary!

The reference to coming from Atchison County and the apparent antipathy towards the Bald-Knobbers could have been intended to remove all suspicion of the trio being connected with the young man in the jailhouse. Being shorter, thickset and dark in complexion, "Spigel" looked nothing like Little. Nor, despite being tall and lean, did either Knapp or Dalyell. What was more, being a keen judge of character—especially where sizing up a potential customer was concerned—the madam had assessed "Spigel" as being shrewd and far from openhanded with his generosity. Yet he had accepted without comment, much less argument, the considerably higher than usual price she quoted for the services of Lena-Mae Hoskins and the suite he requested. As Mrs. Gouch knew all too well, most men had a particular type of woman to whom they were partial, but he did not strike her as being the kind who would pay out a considerable sum to gratify such a whim.

All of which left the madam with a problem of great importance!

Were the trio genuinely seeking an evening's pleasure?

Or had the visit a more sinister motive?

Having accepted that the information given to her by the Ysabel Kid must be acted upon, even if it should prove false, Mrs. Gouch had agreed precautions must be taken. She had been less enamoured of the suggestions he had made for observing those precautions. However, on hearing them, Lena-Mae had stated a willingness to play her part regardless of it entailing considerable risk.

The problem was, the request for the suite of rooms prevented the precautions from being put into effect!

To have refused the suggestion of such accommodation would have struck most people as being the obvious solution!

Unfortunately, the situation was more complex than that!

Should the offer be genuine, a considerable loss of revenue would be entailed, although, to give Mrs. Gouch credit, this was not a consideration she was taking into account!

On the other hand, if the trio had arrived on behalf of Kenneth Little, the refusal would be certain to arouse suspicion and might lead to an attempt to achieve their purpose by force, in a manner which would put the lives of everybody in the building at risk!

Thinking fast, the madam reached her decision!

"Well, that's all settled," Mrs. Gouch declared, hoping she sounded more cheerful than she was feeling. "I'll send upstairs to make sure the suite is ready, then I'll fetch out the ladies you've selected to meet you."

For a few seconds after regaining consciousness, Captain Dustine Edward Marsden "Dusty" Fog was unable to think of anything other than the pain which throbbed through his head. Then a remembrance of what had happened forced its way through his painful condition. Raising himself as quickly as he could manage into a kneeling position, he sent his right hand across towards the butts of the left side Colt 1860 Army Model revolver. His instincts warned that he was moving with less than the maximum speed he could attain when in full possession of his faculties. Before he could even reach the bone handle, his shoulder was seized in a powerful grip which prevented him, in his weakened condition, from being able to complete his draw.

"It won't do you no good at all!" Sam Little warned, retaining his hold until the small Texan's hand left the revolver. "We've emptied 'em *both!*"

Efficiently though Dusty could protect himself without the need to rely upon his Colts, he was too wise to attempt to do so in the present circumstances. Not only was he able to understand what was being said to him, but he could draw accurate conclusions with regards to his inability to react with requisite rapidity at the moment. He was still suffering sufficiently from the effects of being struck on the head, reduced as they had been by the hat lying near by, to be unable to move with the speed necessary to achieve anything other than further blows likely to render him unconscious again.

"Happen you fellers're figuring on rolling me for my trail herding pay——!" the small Texan began, putting a quavering tone into his voice and hoping to lead his assailants to assume he was the innocuous and easy-to-handle victim which the misleading appearance he presented often caused for the uninitiated.

"Don't hand us that bull-shit!" Little warned. "We know *who* you are!"

"Then you'll likely know you're breaking the law to hell and gone by whomping me over the head?" Dusty suggested. "Or didn't you-all find out who I am until after you'd started to roll me for my poke?"

"Like I said," the older of the Bald-Knobber co-leader twins replied. "We *knew* who you were when we did it."

"Then you must have a pretty good reason for doing it," Dusty assessed, noticing the trio were keeping just too far away for him to hope to take any effective offensive action against them. Realizing he could do nothing from his kneeling position, he went on, "Can I get up?"

"Feel free," Little assented and gestured with the Remington New Army Model revolver he had drawn. "Only don't figure on us being stupid chaw-bacon hill-billies's can be taken in easy. One wrong move and you'll be dead."

"I'll mind it," the small Texan promised, rising. Reaching with his right hand and starting to brush at the seat of his Levi's, his intention was not to remove dirt. However, although he satisfied himself that the *bois d'arc* stick was still in his back pocket, he made no attempt to take it out. Instead, he remarked, "I reckon's how you've got *something* in mind for what you're doing?"

"You can bet your god-damned life we have," Amos McDonnell confirmed, wondering how such a small and insignificant person could have attained the close to legendary reputation ascribed to Dusty Fog. "We're going to get Cousin Kenneth out of the pokey."

"Cousin Kenneth?" the small Texan said, in a tone of query.

"You *know* who he means," Little asserted, glancing to where John McDonnell was returning from around the corner where he had retrieved the twin barrelled shotguns the brothers had left there. "Start walking."

"Where to?" Dusty asked.

"The jailhouse," the stocky Bald-Knobber directed, returning the Remington to its holster. "Or do you reckon we figure you've had Brother Kenneth taken 'round to that fancy whore house for his pleasure?"

"So you reckon you can get him out of the jail, huh?" the small Texan inquired, doing as he was instructed.

"You'd best *hope* we can," Little warned, keeping to Dusty's left side, " 'Cause we'd soonest get him out peaceable and quiet. But, should that not work out, we're going to have him set free with as many dead 'n's as it takes. He's not being hauled in front of no judge in this stinking town and then hung after the kind of trial he'll get here. He'll be found guilty and laid up ready for a hang-rope afore he sets foot in the courthouse."

"It'll be a *fair* trial," the small Texan claimed dryly. "You can count on *that*."

"Us Littles don't count on *nothing* 'cepting ourselves and our kin," the stocky Bald-Knobber declared. "Now looky here, Fog, we'd sooner get Brother Kenneth from the jail without no killing, like I said. But, should that not come off, we'll shoot whoever and's many's it takes to do it."

"I'll mind it," Dusty promised, noticing the taller men were walking just too far to his rear and were separated from each other by enough distance to render any attempt against them doomed to failure.

"Then mind something else," Little ordered, nodding to the more populous portion of town they were approaching. "Anybody we come across'd best think we're all *real* friendly and sociable. 'Cause, happen you give them any notion of what's doing—or should they get to thinking along similar lines without your help—you 'n' them'll all get killed."

Having no doubt the threat would be carried out, Dusty did not reply. Instead, he and the men continued to walk through the business section which fringed the shipping pens. At that hour, there were few people about and none near enough to pay any attention to them. This state of affairs, which the small Texan considered more of a blessing than a disappointment, continued until they were approaching the jailhouse. However, although a man came from an alley before they arrived, his captors showed no concern. Nor, seeing how he was dressed, did Dusty believe he would be of any assistance or in danger of being shot for interfering.

"Got the gun to Cousin Kenneth, Cousin Sam," the newcomer reported, his Missouri accent confirming the supposition formed by the small Texan. "There's only two of 'em inside, what I can make out."

"That's to our favour," Little declared. "I don't want no killing, less'n we're give' cause for it and the more of 'em's there's on hand, the better the chance of getting it. Turn down the alley, Fog."

"Why?" Dusty inquired.

"You don't reckon we're going to walk up to the front door, like we was coming to ask your deputies to join us in a drink," the stocky Bald-Knobber said in a mocking tone. "Now do you?"

"I hadn't given it much thought one way or the other," Dusty lied. "So what *are* you figuring on doing?"

"Going in the back way when they open up for you," Little replied, but sounded less than sure of himself.

"You try *that*," the small Texan drawled. "And you'll get your brother *killed!*'

"How come?"John McDonnell asked, before his leader could pose the same question.

"The back door's locked and bolted at sundown *every* night," Dusty explained. "And my *orders* are, no matter who comes and for why—even if it should be *me*—that's the way it stops."

"They'll open up when we tell 'em what'll happen to you if they don't," Amos McDonnell claimed, with the air of one playing a trump card.

"Likely," the small Texan conceded. "Only before it's done, the jailer'll have that sawed-down whipit gun of his lined with a right true bead on *Brother Kenneth's* head and, at best, you'll have yourselves a greaser stand-off which'll take some breaking."

"He's *bluffing*, Cousin Sam!" the younger of the brothers assessed.

"You'd best *not* try to call it," Dusty warned."'Cause I'm telling you the truth. I don't 'specially want to get made wolf bait if there's another way—And there is, provided you go in the front door. That way, my deputies won't know anything's wrong and your brother won't be covered."

"We'll go in at the front!" Little decided, the words having been directed at him. "You've been keeping watch, Cousin Ezra. What do they do when they come up?"

"Huh?" the lookout grunted, looking puzzled.

"Do they just walk on in?" Little explained irascibly. "Or do they let who-all's inside know they're coming?"

"They allus shout out who it be," the lookout replied.

"Then that's what you're going to do, Fog!" the stocky Bald-Knobber ordered.

"Whatever you say," Dusty answered, his demeanour suggesting he knew he was beaten and was yielding to the inevitable, in the hope that he could get through the affair without sustaining an injury or being killed. "Was I you, though, I'd leave those scatter-guns outside. Should my deputies see them, they'll know for *sure* something's wrong."

"Do it!" Little ordered the pair who had helped him make the capture.

"Inside there, *Waco!*" the small Texan called, coming to a halt outside the door of the town marshal's office. "It's me, Dusty. Come and let me and these *four gents* who're with me in."

"Come ahead, *amigo!*" called a voice from inside the building, after a few seconds.

"Stop out here and cover us, Cousin Ezra," Little ordered, as the McDonnell brothers leaned their shotguns against the hitching rail. "Go on in, Fog. We'll be right behind you."

CHAPTER THIRTEEN

You Know Why I'm Here!

"Come on in, Mr. *Spigel*," Lena-Mae Hoskins requested, as she opened the door of the right side bedroom of the suite. Her accent was Southern and, although she came from a lower stratum of society below the Mason-Dixon line, suggestive of 'high-toned' origins. When Mrs. Gouch had made the introductions downstairs, Lena-Mae had felt more than usually suspicious of their names. Her voice held the suggestion that she knew she had received an alias.[1] "I trust you and I will have a most enjoyable *chat*. Please feel free to make yourself to home with my friends, you *two other* gentlemen."

Despite having volunteered to serve as a decoy and being told of the revised measures being taken to ensure her safety if the trio harboured evil intentions against her, the red haired prostitute was assailed by a sense of alarm as she started to guide the stocky man in accordance with her instructions. The room they were entering was furnished only by a comfortable bed and a small dressing-table with a chair in front of it. Although she had been assured protection would be available, she could see no sign of it. Nor did there seem to be anywhere her guardian could be hiding. In the sitting-room there was a set of French windows giving access to a small verandah upon which the occupants could step for a breath of fresh air, but this was a facility not offered where she was now. Even if the ordinary kind of window was not closed and bolted on the

1. Waldo "Waxahachie"Smith frequently commented upon the fact that he was almost invariably subjected to similar disbelief, even though it was not always expressed openly, when giving his surname: see: NO FINGER ON THE TRIGGER and other volumes of the *Waxahachie Smith* series.

inside, there was nothing beyond it upon which the Ysabel Kid could be waiting in concealment.

"Shall we go and have a couple of drinks *first?*" Lena-Mae suggested, halting instead of walking on.

Believing something must have gone amiss with the arrangements and sensing she was in the presence of a man about whom she had been warned, the red head wanted to remain in view of the other two girls until she could find a way of notifying Mrs. Lily Gouch of the situation and it could be rectified.

The desire failed to materialize!

"We'll do what I've come here for *first!*" Saul Little declared, giving the girl a push which sent her forward a few steps and kicking the door closed.

"W—What're you *thinking* of, sir?" Lena-Mae forced herself to demand, despite the alarm which was now assailing her. "I'll thank you not to be so *rough* with m——!"

"You *know* why I'm here!" the stocky Bald-Knobber snarled. "And, by God, I'm going to make sure you don't give no lying evidence against my Brother Kenneth!"

Having had his suspicions aroused both by the emphasis with which the girl had mentioned his "summer name" and her referring to, "you *two other* gentlemen," Little had realized her attempt to sound merely annoyed by his action was far from convincing and the words were provoked by a genuine fear which he felt sure could only mean she knew who he was. Startled by the possibility, instead of wondering how his purpose could have been suspected, he started to send his right hand under the left flap of his jacket.

"Y—You're going to *kill* me!" Lena-Mae gasped, preparing to throw herself at 'Spigel' in a desperate bid for salvation which she did not believe had a hope of succeeding.

The red head knew, as had been the case when her friend was being brutally murdered, that the walls were so effectively sound-proofed that her screams would not be heard in the second floor passage, downstairs, or anywhere else except the sitting-room from which she had come. Only having been unaware that Winnie had a client had caused her to walk in on the grisly scene and raise the alarm. She was sickeningly aware that no such circumstance would save her. What was more, even though the girls next door were sure to have their attention attracted by screams or a shot, the two lanky men would prevent them from either coming to try to help her, or going to summon more qualified assistance.

"Only happen you make fuss," Little replied, holding the three inch barrelled Colt Model of 1849 Pocket Pistol revolver he had drawn from its spring retention shoulder holster so its muzzle pointed towards the ground. "Keep quiet and all I'll do is give you a beating where the marks won't show, so's you'll know better'n tell *lies* about Brother Kenneth in the court-hou——!"

The words came to an end as the stocky Bald-Knobber received an indication that he and the red head might not have the room to themselves!

There was a scuffling originating from beneath the bed and the hanging covers on the side closest to Little were agitated by something coming through!

Snarling a profanity, the Bald-Knobber thumb-cocked and started to swing his Colt in that direction!

To point at a fancily decorated chamber-pot which slid into view!

"The hell you *will!*" stated a savage masculine voice, from a different direction.

Swinging his gaze towards the sound and starting to change the alignment of his revolver, Little saw a sight which chilled him to the marrow!

Accepting there was no other concealment available, the Ysabel Kid had hidden beneath the bed. He had been apprised that Mrs. Gouch had no proof the three Missourians who would be coming to the suite were other than what they pretended. Therefore, he had remained where he was until being given the requisite confirmation of their hostile intentions. Considering the threat being uttered was all he required, he was already holding the means to cope with the situation ready for use. Aware that he was in a position from which he would be unlikely to emerge without making sufficient disturbance to be detected, he had sought to create a diversion by using his right foot to thrust out the chamber-pot.

Then, going in the opposite direction, the Kid had rolled clear of his hiding place!

Having done so, the black clad Texan sat up and, without waiting to go any further, swung his big old Colt Dragoon Model of 1848 revolver held at arms' length with both hands across the bed!

Staring at the cause of the unexpected intrusion, Little saw nothing suggestive of babyish innocence about the Indian dark visage behind the massive old weapon!

Rather it was the face of a Comanche warrior preparing to make war!

That was the last impression of the stocky Bald-Knobber's violent and vicious life!

Already cocked, the big Dragoon boomed before its much smaller fellow product from "Colonel Sam's" Hartford factory could be turned upon its owner. Flying as was intended, the round soft lead .44 calibre ball—vastly more potent than any "shaped" bullet—was powered by forty grains of prime du Pont black powder, which was twelve *more* than was all considered safe to be used in the cartridges for the Winchester Model of 1866 *rifle*. Although low in velocity, it struck with a force which would rarely be improved upon until the arrival of "magnum" calibre handguns firing the more powerful "smokeless" powder of a later generation.

Taken in the left breast, losing his hold on the Pocket Pistol before it could be turned upon the intruder, much less aimed and fired, Little was pitched bodily against the door through which he had entered. Rebounding from it, under the impulsion of the bullet which tore his heart into fragments and killed him instantly, he sprawled face down and lifeless on the floor.

Masculine bellows and feminine shrieks of alarm arose from the sitting-room!

For once moving faster than his companion, who he told to "keep them god-damned gals quiet!", Tom Dalyell hurried to investigate. Although he drew his Army Colt, it was purely an instinctive reflex action. Being less than quick witted, he had not realized the sound of the shot from the bedroom was far too deep to have been made by the weapon with which he knew his cousin-cum-leader was armed. Throwing open the door and starting to lunge through, he discovered the error he had made in no uncertain fashion.

It was a lesson from which the red haired Bald-Knobber would not benefit!

Drawing back the hammer with both thumbs, the Kid changed the point of aim of his Dragoon. Although he would never have claimed to possess the skill with a handgun his *buenos amigos,* Dusty Fog, Mark Counter and Waco, could attain, he had no cause to be disappointed with the latest re-

sults. Sent through the somewhat worn rifling grooves of the
old revolver's seven and a half inch long barrel, the discharged ball took Dalyell between the eyes. Having sent it off,
controlling the far from gentle recoil and once more cocking
the single action mechanism, he thrust himself erect. With no
more than a cursory glance at Lena-Mae, having reverted in
the stress of the situation to the *Pehnane* Comanche upbringing of his childhood—when he had been taught a woman was
somewhat higher in the warrior's scale of values than a food
dog and a pack mule, but *far* below a good horse or a repeating rifle—he bounded across the bed and towards the still
open door through which his second victim had already returned.

Swiftly though the Kid moved, sounds coming from the
sitting-room suggested he would not be fast enough to deal
with the third of the party, which the comment made by Lena-
Mae as she had stepped into the bedroom had warned him was
there!

Being somewhat quicker witted than his red haired kinsman, although he was obeying the instructions he had received
instead of having been first to set off for the source of the
disturbance, the third member of the trio realized things were
going badly wrong!

Having his attention drawn from the two girls he was
watching by the second crash from the old Dragoon revolver,
Jimmy Knapp was startled and alarmed by what he saw when
he swung his gaze in that direction. Although they had grown
up together, he could hardly recognize the figure emerging
hurriedly backwards out of the doorway through which Dalyell had gone a moment earlier. The clothing was familiar, as
was the lanky figure. However, where the red hair covering
the top of the head had been was now a frightening mass of
blood and greyish brain tissue oozing from the shattered open
skull, torn flesh, splintered bone and raggedly dangling gory
scalp.

Letting out a strangled and nauseated croak, the surviving
Bald-Knobber's only thought was to avoid suffering from a
similar fate. Without waiting to ascertain what had happened
to Little, having drawn an accurate conclusion from there
having been no lighter sound to suggest the Pocket pistol was
being used in retaliation, he was sufficiently intelligent to realize that attempting to leave the brothel by the way in which he

had entered might now be inadvisable. With the disturbance having been heard, or so he assumed would prove the case, the way was certain to be blocked by enemies who would require him to fight his way through. With that in mind, knowing nothing of the effective sound-proofing which was preventing what was happening being heard beyond the walls of the suite, he raced in another direction.

Twisting his right shoulder around as he was approaching, paying no attention to the screams provoked from the girls by the hideous sight of his cousin's body crashing to the floor, Knapp charged at and rammed his way through the French windows. Vaulting over the verandah rail, he landed in a forward roll as he had learned when climbing rocky cliffs in the Ozark Mountains. Coming to his feet in a continuation of the move, he had no intention of trying to fight against whoever had killed his two kinsmen. Therefore, returning the Army Colt to its holster, he set off at a run towards the clump of trees he had noticed while approaching the brothel. He now considered they would offer much needed shelter.

There was no time for the Kid to do anything to aid Lena-Mae, who had fainted on seeing the ruination wrought to Dalyell's skull by his bullet. Nor, on entering the sitting-room just too late to prevent the third Bald-Knobber's departure, did he pause to offer any sympathy to the two close to hysterical prostitutes. Instead, he ran through the windows and on to the balcony. Looking over, he realized that the fleeing man must be prevented from joining any more of the Bald-Knobbers who were in the vicinity. If that happened, they would learn the attempt to deal with Lena-Mae Hoskins had been a failure and seek other means to prevent her giving testimony.

However, the black clad young Texan was equally aware of the difficulties involved in preventing this from happening. Already the man was beyond a distance at which he could expect to make a hit with his old Dragoon, except by more luck than he felt the situation should rely upon. Nor did leaping down and taking up the chase strike him as offering a much better solution. By the time he landed, the Bald-Knobber would have reached the trees and be hidden from view, then could make off in any direction.

However, even while reaching his conclusions, the Kid had already solved his dilemma!

A piercing whistle left the black clad young Texan!

Having been left untied and with its reins looped over the low horn of the double girthed Texas range saddle, instead of dangling free to form a "ground hitch"—having no need to be subjected to such means, or to be tied to something, to prevent it straying—the Kid's white stallion responded to the signal. A full seventeen hands at the withers, it possessed magnificent conformation. Seen in daylight, it looked as wild as any *manadero* leading a herd of wild mares, instead of being a domesticated and very well trained animal. However, in the stress of the moment, Knapp failed to notice the latter aspect. To him, the sight of the horse seemed like the answer to a prayer. It would, he believed, offer him the means of making good his escape. With that in mind, he hurried towards it.

"Nigger!" the Kid bellowed, placing his left hand on the balcony rail. As he jumped over, the next word was emitted in Comanche and the savage grunt of a *Pehnane* dog soldier; into which lodge of exceptionally competent warriors he had been initiated as a child. *"Attack!"*

Hearing the command, never taking kindly to strangers approaching it in such an over-familiar and incautious fashion, the stallion changed the lope at which it was obeying the summons given by the whistle into a determined charge. Although Knapp did not know what the second word he had heard might mean, he became aware of the change which had come over the animal. Letting out a startled profanity, he halted and his right hand twisted palm out to close about the butt of the Colt he had so imprudently returned to its holster. Before the weapon could be brought clear, the white stallion reached him.

Acting like the *manadero* it so resembled even when behaving peacefully, the big horse thrust out its neck. Its jaws closed about the man's wrist before he could bring his weapon from leather. A numbing sensation, caused by the teeth sinking through the sleeve of his threadbare jacket and cheap shirt into the flesh below, assailed him. Before he could get his mind to function again, he received a jerk which threw him in a staggering plunge to the ground. A moment later, giving him no chance to resist, four steel shod hooves were smashing down upon him. A couple of screams left his lips as bones were splintered by the stamping kicks. Such was the fury and efficiency of the attack, he had become silent and unmoving, apart from the jerks of his mangled body as the attack continued, by the time the Kid arrived to calm down the stallion.

"Back off, Nigger-hoss!" the Kid commanded. "Leave it, you blasted white goat and back away!"

While speaking, doing what would have been exceptionally dangerous for any other person under the prevailing conditions—even his three *amigos,* who could handle it with reasonable impunity at most other times—the Indian-dark young Texan went up to the horse. Grabbing the reins where they joined the *bosal* of rawhide just above its mouth, where the hackamore was employed to serve the same purpose as a bit on a conventional bridle, he drew down the head and exerted a pushing pressure. It said much for the control he was able to exert upon his powerful and fight-wild mount that he achieved his purpose without suffering injury in the attempt.

After the order was obeyed, paying no attention to the people who had heard the commotion—the downstairs' windows having had their upper sashes lowered as an aid to ventilation—and were emerging from the brothel to investigate, the Kid studied the gory remains with the dispassionate gaze of the *Pehnane* dog soldier warrior he tended to revert to by thought and deed in times of conflict. He needed only one glance to know that—like the pair in the suite—the third of the Bald-Knobbers now was past all thoughts of trying to dissuade Lena-Mae Hoskins against giving evidence at the trial of his kinsman held at the jailhouse.

"You know something, Con?" the Kid said to the burly headed bouncer who was the first of the crowd to arrive, needing time to allow the instincts which had guided his actions so effectively to die away. "I've *allus* wanted to hide under the bed in a gal's "buddy-wah" and tonight I got my wantings."

"I hope you didn't kick the chamber-pot over, 'case it was still full," the man replied, then became serious. "Are the gals all right upstairs, Kid?"

"Lena-Mae swooned off and the other two are having what I've been told's called the 'vapours' loud and copious," the black clad Texan answered, once more resuming the somewhat less dangerous character of the white man which changed conditions had led him to become. "But wasn't *none* of them so much as nicked nor bruised."

"Sounds like there's trouble in town!" the bouncer commented, as what he recognized as the clanging of the bells on fire engines rose above the excited comments of the people who had followed him.

"Sound like," the Kid admitted. "But I'll leave the other boys to 'tend to it and stay on here a while longer, just in case."

There was, the Indian-dark Texan realized, a possibility that he had not ended the attempt by Kenneth Little's kin to pervert the course of justice. Whatever the reason for the Mulrooney Fire Brigade being called out might be, it could have the ulterior motive of providing some other means of saving him from his well deserved fate.

Nevertheless, the Kid considered he would be better employed in continuing to guard the one witness who could put the murderous young Bald-Knobber's neck in a noose!

CHAPTER FOURTEEN

It's a Trick!

Alert for any suggestion of something happening to spoil his plan, which gave the impression of progressing in a most satisfactory fashion, Sam Little followed Captain Dustine Edward Marsden "Dusty" Fog into the town marshal's office!

Crossing the threshold, the stocky Bald-Knobber leader ran his gaze over the one deputy who was present and who, from his appearance did not expect any trouble. The peace officer was seated with both feet on the top of the large desk in the centre of the room, using a piece of cloth to polish a sturdy black walking cane. Nor did he stop this task and offer to get up as he looked, apparently without any particular curiosity, at the newcomers. The disinterest implied that he was drawing no conclusions from the way that, coming in behind Little and his captive—"Cousin Ezra" having remained outside as instructed—John and Amos McDonnell were positioned so each would have an unrestricted line of fire when the time for action arrived.

"Howdy, *Waco*," the small Texan greeted, showing no surprise over the way in which his subordinate was behaving. "These gents have come to see what kind of skunk that goddamned hill-billy shit-kicker from the son-of-a-bitching '*Who-Can't-No-How-Be-Shown*' State" we've got in the cells looks like and I see nothing *wrong* with them doing it."

"Nor me either, 'cepting he's no sight for honest and decent men, 'cepting to turn their stomachs, like all that scum's sneak out of Missouri," the deputy replied. Swinging his legs from the top of the desk and gesturing, with the cane he continued to hold in both hands, towards the big safe at the left side of the room, his accent was not that of a Texan as he went on, "But you'll have to fetch the keys to the cells. I can't open the box to get them."

Judging from his behaviour, the peace officer on duty was annoyed at having been compelled to give up the task of cleaning the cane. Despite returning his feet to the floor, he did not rise. Nor did he give any sign of noticing the trio behind Dusty were far from enamoured by the way in which Kenneth Little and Missouri had been described by his superior. What was more, he seemed equally oblivious that his own less than flattering comments did not appear to be changing their sentiments for the better.

"You can't at that," Dusty declared. As he started to walk in the appropriate direction without so much as glancing to his rear, or at the man who was to be seen through the open front door standing on the sidewalk, his right hand passed around his back. "It'll only take me a moment to get them, gents."

Considering everything was going along exactly as he wanted it, Little raised no objection to the small Texan moving from in front of him.

Then, suddenly and alarmingly, the stocky Bald-Knobber leader realized that things might not be going as smoothly as he had believed was the case!

More perceptive than either of the McDonnell brothers, particularly the younger, Little had been disturbed by the way in which their captive had behaved. He was aware that a man did not acquire the kind of reputation Dusty Fog had attained unless he was capable of at least a fair proportion of the qualities for which credit was given. Therefore, he had been surprised by the seemingly mild acceptance of a situation which he knew should have provoked him into some effort to change. Apart from the other successful law enforcement activities he had conducted since taking office, the small Texan had not too long ago rescued the beautiful Englishwoman who was the mayor of Mulrooney from three would-be kidnappers, and led a very successful posse against a bunch of *Metis* marauders threatening the peace of the town. Yet, having been captured by the Bald-Knobbers, he had made no attempt to turn the tables upon them.

In fact, the opposite had been the case!

Instead of trying to escape, or in some other way resist what he was told to do, the hitherto *very* competent marshal of Mulrooney had allowed himself to be marched through the town to the jailhouse. On approaching their destination, apparently afraid of the consequences he would suffer if anything went wrong, he had warned of the dangers inherent in trying to gain admittance by the rear entrance. If that was not enough to arouse suspicion, he had also pointed out how the brothers carrying their shotguns into the town marshal's office would produce a similar undesirable effect which had resulted in them being left behind.

None of which, now the co-leader of the Bald-Knobbers had taken the time to think, seemed to be in character with what he had heard about Captain Dusty Fog!

Having started such a disturbing train of thought, Little found something else which did not fit the facts as he knew them!

The appreciation struck home like the touch of an ice cold hand!

Realizing he needed to plan everything in advance with regard to his plans to save his younger sibling from the gallows, the stocky Bald-Knobber had made sure he could recognize every member of the town marshal's office on sight. Having gained admittance to the building where his brother was being held, he had noticed something which struck him as being strange about the appearance of the deputy sitting at the desk.

When announcing their arrival, the small Texan had put considerable emphasis when saying, *"Waco"*. Little had thought nothing of it at the time, as he knew there was a deputy with that name. While he was the youngest of them, yet by all accounts far from being ineffective on account of his youth, he was a Texan and a member of what, without understanding the term, the stocky Bald-Knobber had heard referred to as "Ole Devil Hardin's floating outfit". However, now that he had a feeling something amiss was going on, there were all too obvious indications that an incorrect identification might have been made.

The man seated at the desk did not have a Texan's accent and he was a few years *older* than Dusty Fog!

What was more, far from wearing the attire which municipal peace officers who were cowhands from Texas had always worn when Little had seen them around town, his clothes were that of a successful professional gambler!

However, the Bald-Knobber knew there was a fifth deputy who followed such a profession!

Therefore, the type of clothing suggested to Little that the man at the desk was Frank "Derry" Derringer and not the youngster who was supposed to be on duty!

The Bald-Knobber knew that peace officers sometimes changed duties and not always with the knowledge, or approval, of their superior. The name called by the small Texan on arrival outside suggested he was unaware of such a swop having taken place. However, on entering and discovering which of his subordinates was present, he had again given emphasis when repeating the incorrect identification.

All of which suggested the true facts had been known and the intention of the small Texan had been to alert whoever was inside the building that something was badly amiss!

Having arrived at that point in his reasoning, the stocky Bald-Knobber concluded the mistake had been deliberate and he had been led into what was almost certainly meant to be a trap!

However, Little decided the situation was far from desperate!

Despite having received an indication from Dusty Fog that things were not as innocuous as the reason given for the visit implied, it appeared the gambler-cum-deputy had not recognized it as a warning. He was still seated on the swivel chair at the desk, with the sturdy black cane—which the Bald-Knobber had seen him carrying when walking around the town— held in both hands. Unlike many of his kind, who selected ways of carrying a gun which enabled it to be used with ease while seated, he had always worn an ivory handled Colt 1860 Army Model revolver in his gunbelt's low hanging holster secured to his right thigh. It was not a position from which he could respond quickly to a hostile action. Nor, having had the percussion caps removed from the cylinders' nipples in his holsters and having no other weapons upon his person—as Amos McDonnell's search had established—was the small Texan any better placed to take action.

There was, Little concluded, only one thing to do under the circumstances!

"It's a *trick!*" the stocky Bald-Knobber bellowed, dipping his right hand towards the butt of the Remington New Model Army revolver. *"Get the bastards!"*

Although the connecting door with the office had been drawn almost closed when Frank Derringer went out, there was still sufficient of a gap for what was being said to be heard by the occupants of the cell block as Derringer had fully intended!

Having followed the conversation and drawn accurate conclusions from it, on hearing the words shouted by Sam Little, Albert "Pickles" Barrel started to move forward with his right hand closing around the butt of the whipit gun hanging on the carbine sling around his shoulders!

Doing so caused the elderly jailer to turn his back upon the young man in the cell!

Watching and waiting for just such an opportunity, Kenneth Little was only too willing and eager to exploit it!

Experiencing a sense of satisfaction as he grasped the "bird's head" handle of the Colt Model of 1871 "Cloverleaf Cylinder" House Pistol revolver concealed beneath the pillow on the bunk in his cell, although indifferent to the way in which his home State was mentioned, the young murderer was as annoyed by the derogatory references to himself as were his kinsmen still unseen in the office. On the point of yelling out a furious protest and demanding that something be done about the insult, he had just sufficient intelligence to realize that it would be inadvisable, and he had refrained. He did not, on the other hand, attach any significance whatsoever to the fact that the deputy in the front room was not being called by the right name. Instead, showing unusual self control for him, he waited until hearing the order given by his oldest sibling before bringing the weapon into view.

The warning of there being a trap laid and the demand to do something about it was followed almost immediately by the crash of a shot!

Having been informed of the intentions of the rescue party by "Cousin Ezra," while the revolver was being delivered through the window of the cell, Kenneth Little had no doubt these had been achieved. Satisfied he could do so with impunity, he set about extracting the revenge he had promised himself against the elderly jailer who—while never having abused him physically, such a thing being strictly prohibited by Dusty Fog he had discovered—had treated him with contempt and loathing from the moment of his arrival.

"Here's for *you*, you old son-of-a-bitch."

While snarling the words, snatching the Colt from its place of concealment and drawing back its hammer with his thumb, the youngest of the Little brothers lunged with it towards the barred door of the cell!

Even as Sam Little was reaching his conclusions, and was on the point of ordering the attack, Frank Derringer guessed what was coming! His usual way of earning a living had taught him to be very competent at reading expressions even when other people weren't aware they were showing their thoughts on their faces.

Realizing Dusty Fog must have a very good reason for calling out the name of a deputy he knew was engaged elsewhere that evening, the gambler had decided to take precautions to meet whatever turn of events was responsible for the error. The warning that four men were accompanying the small Texan had given him a clue of what was happening. Having delayed replying until seated at the desk in the way he had been discovered, he had succeeded in presenting an appearance of a lack of awareness which was far from the case.

Nor had Derringer felt he was behaving incorrectly when he saw Dusty still had the bone handled Army Colts in the holsters of the Joe Gaylin gunbelt. He had decided that, if his supposition was correct, they had been unloaded and left there to prevent arousing the suspicion which would have been incurred if they had been missing. As further confirmation to his suspicions, there had been the unwitting response which had followed the small Texan's untypical comments about the prisoner and Missouri. His own efforts along the same line had been greeted by a similar reaction. However, as the obvious animosity had not been given expression, he had concluded he was correct in his deductions.

Concluding there was no longer any point in retaining the pose suggesting a lack of awareness, Derringer did not even wait until starting to rise before taking action!

Instead, the gambler swung around the sturdy black walking cane he was holding!

To two of the Bald-Knobbers, the action did not appear to pose any danger!

Although Sam Little was better informed than his less worldly cousins and had thoughts along the correct lines, he too saw no reason to be concerned. The metal ferrule was being directed in his direction, but its end appeared solid instead of having the aperture which would have been visible if—as he had wondered, momentarily and with a sense of alarm, might be the case—it was a disguised firearm.

The few cane guns Little had seen had possessed one fault

which limited their use as a weapon of surprise. To prevent
dirt entering and clogging the barrel when being used for the
primary purpose as an aid to walking, they were equipped
with a wooden tampion to serve as a ferrule and plug the
muzzle. Such a device had two distinct different, yet connected, disadvantages. Fitted tightly, the plug would almost
certainly cause the barrel to burst if accidentally left in when
the weapon was discharged. On the other hand, if loose
enough to be shaken away easily in an emergency, it was
equally certain to fall out of its own accord and be lost.

Aware of these salient details, the stocky Bald-Knobber
considered he was in no danger. Either the gambler was turning the cane to throw at him, or—if it was a disguised firearm—due to the urgency of the moment, he had forgotten
the plug was still in position. No matter which, unless the
explosion of the barrel removed the need, he was convinced
he could complete his draw and cut the gambler-cum-deputy
down. What was more, while he was doing so, his cousins
could deal with Dusty Fog and the jailer, unless his youngest
brother saved them the trouble with the latter.

In accordance with an old adage, a little knowledge—no
pun intended—proved a dangerous thing!

Aiming the cane by instinctive alignment, it being the disguised weapon Little envisaged, Derringer pressed the small
button which served as a trigger!

Released by the action, the long striker flashed forward to
where a No.2, .32-100 calibre, cartridge was waiting in the
breach and caused the powder charge to detonate!

At which point, the error in the Bald-Knobber's summa-
tions became all too apparent to him!

Although other devices of the kind had the disadvantages
remembered by Little, Derringer was holding a Remington
Rifle Cane. Produced in accordance with a design patented on
February the 9th, 1858, by J.F. Thomas of Ilon, New York,
this offered a vast improvement over its predecessors and
competitors in the field. While it had a protective plug for the
barrel, this was a small piece of cork held by friction only.
Pushed out by the bullet propelled with the gasses created
when the powder was ignited, it proved no impediment to the
explosion inside the barrel.

Caught in the side by the flying lead, Little was hurt and
the completion of his draw was delayed!

However, the Bald-Knobber knew the weapon which inflicted the wound carried only a single bullet!

Aware that the man left outside would be coming to join them, probably bringing one of the shotguns they had left against the hitching rail, Little felt sure the McDonnell brothers could deal with the gambler!

Yelling his intention was only one of the mistakes made by Kenneth Little!

Although having acquired reasonable skill at using a revolver, the murderer was accustomed to the eight inch barrelled Army Colt. Intended for easy concealment rather than rugged stopping power, the weapon he was holding was much smaller and lighter than its better known fellow product. What was more, in addition to its compact shape, its bird's head grip was a very different proposition for holding than the hand filling butt of the Model of 1860. Therefore, its handling qualities were not the same. He discovered to his alarm that his instinctive movements, which would have turned the revolvers of his past experience to point where he wanted, were causing the one in his right hand to swing much further than he required.

There was something far more serious for Little to contend with!

For all his advanced years, Pickles Barrel had lost little of the faculties which had served to keep him alive when he had been riding scout for the United States' Cavalry in various Indian campaigns. Furthermore, he could still move with commendable speed when an occasion demanded. Although he had not suspected the prisoner had obtained a weapon, being aware such things happened even in the best regulated of jails, he concluded this was the case when he heard the clicking of the Colt's hammer being drawn until fully cocked. Therefore, without needing to turn and look, or wait to be shot at, he was already alert to the possibility of danger when Little supplied all the other confirmation he required.

Swivelling around fast, already grasping the wrist of the reduced butt and having his right thumb coiled around the twin hammers, the jailer liberated the stud on the frame of the whipit gun from the slot in a metal plate with which he had replaced the more usual hook on a carbine sling. As he was hauling them back to the firing position, his right hand's first and second fingers entered the guard so each was resting upon a trigger. Bringing the weapon upwards, his left hand crossed to take hold of the wooden foregrip and help support its not inconsiderable weight.

However, swiftly though Barrel moved, only Little's unfamiliarity with the House Pistol saved him from being shot!

Correcting the tendency to swing more than he required, the murderer turned back the small revolver. Thrusting it through the bars, he fired. The bullet missed, but not by many inches. Realizing this had happened, by the lack of response from his intended victim, he snarled a profanity and started to recock the action to try again.

"Let it drop!" Barrel barked, aligning the whipit gun at waist level.

"I'll kill you, you bastard!" was the reply.

Even though his incarceration had kept him sober, being imbued by the kind of rage which—having been drunk at the time—had caused him to brutally murder the girl at Mrs. Lily Gouch's brothel, the young man was oblivious to the danger posed by the weapon pointing his way. While making the declaration, having performed an adjustment to the way he was pointing the Colt, he fired again.

When the second bullet went past even closer than the first, which had only failed to make contact by a very narrow margin, the jailer decided he had taken all the chances he considered were justifiable. He had given the option to surrender and had it refused. Clearly the young man was too filled by rage to respond to verbal reasoning, so there was only one alternative if he was to be prevented from attempting to do as he had declared was his purpose.

One of the modifications for the weapon with which Barrel was going to defend himself had been the removal of the butt behind the curved "wrist". Therefore, it could not be fired from the shoulder like a conventional shotgun. Nor, under the prevailing conditions, would he have had time to do so. Instead, holding it in front of his midsection and well clear of his body, he pointed it towards the door of the cell.

On the second finger of the jailer's right hand depressing the rear trigger and allowing its drawn back hammer to snap down, flame and smoke gushed from the near side muzzle. The recoil would have been bad enough if the original three foot long ten gauge barrels had not been reduced. With only nine and a half inches remaining, it was far worse. The

weapon jerked upwards violently and there was nothing he
could do to prevent it happening. However, he had nothing to
fear from what might otherwise have proved a serious defect
to the efficiency of the whipit gun's performance in combat.

Because of the reduction to the length of the barrels, which
had turned a shotgun intended mainly for the sport of duck
hunting "on the pass"—at considerable distances—into a
most efficacious short range *weapon*, they no longer had the
"choke" narrowing the tubes slightly at the muzzle to reduce
the spread of the shot and increase the hitting power with
which its numerous components arrived. Nevertheless, being
at such close quarters, the nine .32 calibre buckshot balls had
not separated to any great extent when they reached their intended destination.

Having adjusted his aim, by raising the Colt to shoulder
height and looking along the barrel, Little was certain he
would not miss a third time!

However, even as the murderer's right forefinger began to
tighten, he was engulfed in the lethal spray of lead which was
erupted his way. Sending the revolver flying unfired from his
grasp, the impact literally lifted and threw him backwards
across the cell. He smashed into the wall below the window
through which the weapon was delivered, rebounded until
striking the barred door and spun off to sprawl lifeless on the
bunk.

"That's saved Mulrooney the cost of a trial and done the
good folks out'n seeing a hanging," Barrel commented dryly,
studying the effects of his shot as he brought the whipit gun
back into alignment. Concluding it would not be needed in
that direction, he continued, "But we'll for sure as shitting
have to get the bedding washed afore we can use it again!"

Even as the jailer was reaching the last conclusion, the
commotion from the office informed him things were still far
from being under control in there!

CHAPTER FIFTEEN

It Ain't Fair!

Being aware of the Remington Cane Rifle's potential, Captain Dustine Edward Marsden "Dusty" Fog had also realized what was expected of him when told the keys to the cell were in the safe!

Allowed to walk unchallenged from in front of his captors, the small Texan was alert and ready to take action when he estimated the time had come for it!

On hearing evidence which led him to consider the moment had come for the apparently passive behaviour to be brought to an end, Dusty showed how he had acquired his reputation for quick thought and even faster action!

Twisting around, the small Texan saw Sam Little struck by the bullet Frank "Derry" Derringer had dispatched. Although sure the wound would not prove immediately incapacitating, being inflicted by a conical piece of lead smaller and possessed of less "knock down" power than even one of "Navy" calibre—which he considered too light for serious combat work—he gave no further attention to the stocky leader of the Bald-Knobbers. Instead, glancing out of the open front door in passing and seeing something he had anticipated, he flung himself at the nearer of the two men who had followed them into the town marshal's office!

Hearing the shouted command, "Cousin Ezra" had concluded his intervention might be required. Forgetting his orders to remain outside and keep watch, he was about to dash in when he remembered the two shotguns left leaning against the hitching rail by the McDonnell brothers. Being far from a good shot with a revolver, he decided they offered a better choice of armament if his assistance should be needed to quell the resistance of the peace officers in the building. Therefore,

137

restraining his impatience, he turned to snatch up the one placed there by his Cousin John.

Behind the desk, aware he would not be granted sufficient time to reload, Derringer dropped the Remington Cane Rifle on to the desk. Even as it was leaving his grasp, he realized he had not dealt the man at whom he shot a mortal injury. Giving a thrust of his thighs, as he commenced to rise, he sent the swivel chair upon which he had remained seated sliding away from behind him. Coming to his feet, his right hand started dipping towards the ivory handled Army Colt in its low tied holster on his off side thigh. However, while doing so, he doubted whether he would be able to cope unaided when in contention against four assailants; especially as the one outside was picking up a shotgun on the sidewalk. However, even though the commotion in the cell block suggested Arnold "Pickles" Barrel was fully occupied and unable to render immediate assistance, he did not for a moment believe he would be left to attempt to face the quartet without receiving support.

The confidence of the gambler was not misplaced!

Rammed by a shoulder under the impulsion of a firmly fleshed body, which was possessed of solid muscles giving a power far in excess of what was suggested by the small size of his assailant, John McDonnell was knocked sideways to the right with his Colt 1860 Army Model revolver still not clear of its holster. Such was the force of the attack, he crashed against his younger brother. The collision did more than just prevent Amos from completing the drawing of a similar weapon. Spluttering out profanities, which were partially drowned by the sound of gun fire from the cell block at the rear of the building, the pair of them went reeling towards the right side wall.

Armed in a fashion he considered ideally suited for his needs, Cousin Ezra was diverted before he could go into the building. Suddenly excited shouts rang out from not too far away. They were mingled with the clamour of ringing bells and the drumming of several sets of hooves which put him in mind of a couple of occasions he had seen horse-drawn fire engines going into action elsewhere. Despite the urgency of the situation, he could not resist the temptation to try and find out whether his assumption of the cause was correct. However, the noises went away instead of approaching and he could see no red glow to suggest where they were heading. Hearing the profane exclamations of the McDonnell brothers returned his attention to the work in hand. Hauling back the hammers of the shotgun, he made for the open door. As he was crossing the threshold, he decided the deputy in the attire of a professional gambler behind the desk must receive the charge of at least the first barrel.

Digging the high heel of his forward boot against the floor, although meeting a surface as unyielding as the hard-baked ground upon which it was occasionally brought into contact when he was working on foot with cattle or horses, Dusty found it served one of the purposes for which it was supplied. Coming to a halt, while the two men he had charged were still reeling away, he spun around. Although as yet he could not see the man left outside, remembering what he had noticed in passing, he felt sure this desirable state of affairs was unlikely to continue for much longer.

Under the pretense of having reached for the key to the safe he was supposed to be going to open, the small Texan had slipped the six inch long piece of *bois d'arc* wood—which his captors, like others in the past, had dismissed as an unimportant, harmless toy of some kind—from the right back pocket of his Levi's pants. However, he did not put it to the use for which it was carried. Instead, reversing his direction, he sprang into the air. Rotating his body until it was close to parallel to the floor, he flexed and thrust out both legs vigorously. Struck by his feet, with all the power his physique of a Hercules in miniature could muster, the wide open door was slammed closed.

However, the leaping kick produced a very useful benefit beyond the original intention!

While the kick was delivered to prevent the man on the sidewalk from being able to open fire at Derringer, the solidly constructed door slammed into him as he was entering. Carrying the weapon he had picked up held at something close to what soldiers engaged in bayonet fighting practice refer to as the "high port" position, it and his knuckles received the full force of the impact. Letting out a pain-filled bellow, which merged with a double boom as the first and second fingers of his right hand inadvertently tightened upon the triggers, he was thrown backwards by the combination of the collision and the less than gentle recoil. Before he could regain control of his movements, he was precipitated backwards from the sideway. Crashing supine on to the hard-packed and wheel-rutted surface of the street, all the breath was driven from his body and, having the back of his head strike the unyielding surface, he was rendered unconscious.

Bringing out his Colt, Derringer guessed what course the events in the cell block were taking by listening to the guns which continued to be used there. Deriving satisfaction from his conclusions in that direction, he was just as relieved to see the man with the shotgun being refused admittance in such a fashion. What was more, past experience helped him to ascertain who was likely to be the next recipient of Dusty's attention. The removal of those two threats allowed him to give his full attention to the other participants in the conflict.

The McDonnell brothers had been taken unawares by both their captive's change from being passively obliging to most effectively hostile and the force his small body was capable of producing. Nevertheless, they managed to halt the stagger towards the right side wall, caused by the shove they had received, without losing their balance and falling. Regaining control of his equilibrium slightly faster than his young sibling, John showed more regard for self-preservation than family ties. The close proximity at which they were moving was restricting the freedom he required for his right hand to complete the interrupted draw.

Therefore, giving no thought to the adverse effect he might be creating, John gave his brother a shove which separated them. However, while it allowed the elder McDonnell to resume hostilities, the younger was driven even further onwards without being able to do the same. On the other hand, it also produced a reaction for which Amos might have counted himself grateful. Selecting the one he considered as now being the more dangerous of them, the gambler-cum-deputy threw a shot which found its mark in John's left shoulder. However, although he reeled under the impact, he neither fell nor dropped the Colt which had just cleared leather.

Dusty was not especially surprised to discover he was confronted by a serious and immediate threat to his well being!

In spite of having been wounded and sent staggering towards the wall on the left side of the door, Little swung his gaze around as it was closed with such violence. Even without needing the evidence of the double detonation followed by the heavy thud of his ejected kinsman landing on the street, he was still sufficiently in control of his faculties to see how badly the situation was going. What was more, he decided

there was a closer and potentially greater menace than the
deputy rising from behind the desk. Even though he knew the
bone handled Army Colts in the small Texan's holsters were
inoperative, due to having had the percussion caps removed
from the nipples of the cylinders, the discovery gave him
something of a shock.

Suddenly, the marshal of Mulrooney gave the impression
of no longer being small!

Instead, even though he was adopting a slightly crouching
posture, Dusty Fog appeared to have taken on a size and bulk
which caused him to appear to be the largest man present.
Although Little was sufficiently intelligent to realize the effect
was only produced by the sheer strength of the small Texan's
personality, even though he could not have expressed the sentiment in those exact words, he was unable to avoid being
affected by it. Therefore, the draw he had recommenced was
once more delayed.

Not by much, but more than sufficient to give an opportunity to a man with the small Texan's lightning fast reflexes and
knowledge of fighting techniques other than those involving
revolvers!

Because of the law enforcement duties which Dusty had to
perform where one section of the town's transient population
was concerned, he had the means upon his person to imple-
ment the scheme he formulated. As was the case with the
cowhands delivering trail herds to the shipping pens, the construction workers on the railroad frequently visited Mulrooney
to spend their hard-earned pay in celebrations which mostly
entailed excessive drinking. However, unlike the Texans, they
tended to rely upon bare hands and steel toed boots to settle
disagreements or resist arrest for legal infractions. Declining
to use the methods of such peace officers as the Earp brothers,
who never hesitated before using firearms even against unarmed men, he sought to quell such aggression without employing guns.

To this end, the small Texan had taken to carrying a most
effective—yet seemingly innocuous—albeit primitive,
weapon in his right hip pocket. The people who had designed
and perfected its technique, on the island of Okinawa, called it
a *"yawara* stick." Although he had never been there, he was
taught how to use it by a man who had. He had also learned
from Tommy Okasi, a Japanese *samurai* who acted as valet to

his uncle, General Jackson Baines "Olè Devil" Hardin,[1] certain other unarmed fighting techniques, including the leaping kick with which he had so effectively closed the front door, little known outside the country of their origin.

Thrusting himself forward and up like a sprinter leaving the starting block at the commencement of a race, Dusty launched himself towards the stocky Bald-Knobber. As he did so, he was aware that there was a serious problem to be solved. Unlike when he had been stunned by John McDonnell, he could not aim the blow he intended to deliver at the top of the head. While the curled brim was much smaller, the tall crown of the Derby hat with a Petersham band around it offered even more protection against an attack directed at that otherwise vulnerable area. Accepting this would place unacceptable limitations upon his intention of rendering Little *hors de combat*, he knew he must select another location for his attack. What was more, it must be one which would achieve the same purpose if he hoped to avoid being shot by his intended victim.

Responding as a trained peace officer invariably would under such circumstances, Derringer cocked his weapon and fired again. While his second bullet produced the required effect, hitting the older brother in the centre of the forehead, the time needed to aim and dispatch it had granted the younger an opportunity to halt and resume the fray. What was more, proving even faster and more competent than his now dead sibling, he seemed likely to be able to make the most of his chance as he brought up the Army Colt he had drawn and aligned it at the gambler.

Drawing his right arm until it was bent in front of his chest, Dusty whipped it outwards and around in an almost horizontal arc. Clasped in his clenched fingers and thumb, the rounded ends of the *bois d'arc yawara* stick emerged at either side. Driven in a backhand blow, the grooves around the centre rendering the grip upon it so secure it might have formed a

1. Some information about the careers of General Jackson Baines "Ole Devil" Hardin and his Japanese companion, samurai Tommy Okasi, can be found in the Ole Devil Hardin and Civil War series.

la. The eldest grandson of Captain Dustine Edward Marsden "Dusty" Fog, Alvin Dustine "Cap," received a similar education in the Japanese martial arts from Danny, a nephew of Tommy Okasi and also a samurai.
lb. Two occasions when Alvin Dustine "Cap" Fog put to use his skill with the yawara stick are recorded in: RAPIDO CLINT and THE RETURN OF RAPIDO CLINT AND MR. J.G. REEDER.

component of the hand, the part protruding from below the heel of his fist smashed against the side of Little's jaw. Breaking bone snapped audibly and the stocky Bald-Knobber's head was jerked violently to one side. Although his revolver was coming into alignment on his assailant, the force of the blow caused it to be deflected just enough. It roared and the muzzle blast singed the side of the small Texan's shirt. However, the bullet missed and buried itself harmlessly into the wall. Driven against the door, Little spun away from it and measured his length unconscious on the floor.

Even more than at any other moment in the affair, Derringer was in deadly peril!

Fortunately for the gambler, salvation was at hand!

Having dealt with Kenneth Little's attempt to kill him, Barrel had come into the office to render whatever assistance might be required. Taking in everything that was happening with a swift glance, he decided where his efforts would be most profitably directed. Accepting the danger of the powerful recoil sending the truncated butt crashing against his face, he raised the whipit gun rather higher than when he had dealt with the murderer as the distance was further. Looking along the shortened twin tubes to make certain of their alignment, he let out a yell.

On the point of firing at Derringer, Amos McDonnell looked around. Recognizing the danger posed by the elderly jailer, he wavered in his decision as to whether to carry out his original intention or to deal with the newer and, he realized, even more dangerous menace. A vacillation of that kind was fatal when opposed to two such competent fighting men. The whipit gun roared loud in the confines of the office, almost drowning the bark of the Colt which the gambler had swung around in order to deal with the threat he had known the last of the Bald-Knobbers was posing to his well being. Engulfed rather than merely being struck by a .44 bullet and six of the nine buckshot balls—each as large in calibre as the Remington Rifle Cane's charge—most of which would have inflicted a fatal wound, Amos was hurtled backwards. He was dead before his body struck the wall and ricochetted on to the floor.

"I'll 'tend to the jasper outside!" the gambler promised, thumb cocking his Colt after having added to the holocaust which ended the life of the younger McDonnell. Darting to the front door and throwing it open, he went through ready to deal with whatever eventuality he encountered. Studying the recumbent and unmoving body of Cousin Ezra, he concluded there was nothing to fear from that direction. Looking over his shoulder, he reported, "He's down and looks to be out cold, *Mark!*"

"Bueno, Cabrito," Dusty replied, smiling as he noticed the deliberate error in the name given by the gambler and employing in return the sobriquet employed by Hispanics on both sides of the Rio Grande to the Ysabel Kid. Glancing to his rear, he continued, "How's about that *hombre* you pair were *supposed* to be guarding, Pickles?"

"He's still back there, but he won't be standing no trial," Barrel replied, having contrived to thrust the whipit gun onwards when it recoiled thus causing the butt to strike the crown of his hat instead of his face. Then, retrieving and replacing his dislodged headdress, he continued in a mock irascible fashion, "It ain't *fair!*"

"What isn't?" the small Texan queried, putting away the *yawara* stick.

"While we was risking life and limb to uphold the law," the elderly jailer replied, returning the whipit gun to the slot on his carbine sling. "Mark 'n' Waco's off lolly-gagging in some danged saloon and the Kid's down to Mrs. Gouch's fancy house. How come *they* get all the *easy* chores like that?"

CHAPTER SIXTEEN

We've Been Looking For You!

Entering the bar-room of Honesty John's Tavern at eight o'clock on the evening of the day following her epic fight with Irene Beauville, as she had expected would be the case after the way she had put in her previous and more dramatic appearance, the beautiful young woman who called herself, "Miss Olga Chernyshevsky" was the subject for everybody's attention. Knowing she would receive such a scrutiny, being far from embarrassed or self-conscious over the incident, she had taken care to look her best. Before leaving her quarters in the hotel side of the establishment, she had dressed in a way she felt befitted the situation she anticipated.

To produce the desired effect, "Miss Chernyshevsky" had donned a light blue masculine shirt much more decorous than the blouse which had helped provoke the conflict—but which still proved she was physically well endowed, as was intended even when worn as part of her "prim and proper" pose while in disguise for business purposes—and a dark grey skirt. With the blonde wig having been tidied up and replaced, apart from limping slightly and displaying signs of being stiff, she was exhibiting no traces of her strenuous activities while in contention against the *Metis* girl. Carefully applied make-up concealed her blackened left eye, which was one less than she had inflicted upon her opponent. Her top lip was swollen, but not split as the yellowish-blonde's had been. However, this injury was not too noticeable.

At the conclusion of their fight the previous evening, the naked brunette and her totally unclad beaten opponent had been carried away from their sludgy final area of conflict by the saloon-girls. Then the owner of the establishment had had

145

a most lucrative evening. As he had anticipated, the spectators of as good a female fight as any of them had ever witnessed had become generous while discussing it at length. With the exception of the loser and, possibly the winner, both of whom had had the mud washed from them in a storeroom and received such medical attention as was needed, the only person to appear at all regretful over what had happened had been Arnaud *le Loup Garou* Chavallier.

That morning, the *Metis* had requested an interview with the globular man. Asking for credit, on account of having incurred considerable losses at the poker game and betting on the outcome of the fight, Chavallier had been far from pleased when reminded of the house rule, "In the Good Lord I trust, but mortals pay cash" and being refused. Hinting of possible reprisals, he had left with the still obviously suffering Irene. Although not unduly worried by the threat, but being cautious by nature, Turtle had sent a couple of his most trusted men who had kept an eye on the pair until they took a west-bound train in the afternoon. Except for making arrangements to find out should they return, or send others to take revenge, he had put the matter from his mind.

Studying the "blonde" like everybody else, Jonathan Ambrose Turtle was willing to concede she looked most attractive!

In fact, the globular man concluded he would not be wrong if he went further and assessed that she was the best looking and most shapely woman in the room!

Having reached this conclusion and found many eyes were turning his way, Turtle knew what was expected of him in his capacity of owner of Honesty John's Tavern. Ever willing to pander to public sentiment, so long as it was in concurrence with his own—which was the case on this occasion—he rose and left his comfortable armchair to greet "Miss Chernyshevsky" with, it was noticed and commented upon by those who had been present when she had put in her first appearance the night before, one more step than had been taken on her arrival. Having bestowed what everybody present knew was the seal of his approval upon her activities of the previous evening, politely declining an offer to join her for a meal on the grounds that he had already eaten and was trying to hold his not inconsiderable weight in "reasonable" bounds, he re-

turned to his point of vantage and resumed his surreptitious—
yet thorough—study of everything else taking place around
him. Selecting a seat at an otherwise unoccupied table near the
connecting door with the hotel side of the premises, "Miss
Chernyshevsky" had laid her bulky black reticule on it and,
signalling for a waiter, ordered a meal.

Having attended to the proprieties where "Miss Chernyshevsky" was concerned, Turtle found nothing else in the bar-
room worthy of more than passing interest. Therefore, despite
being alert to all that was going on, his thoughts went to the
fight between the two well matched physically and equally
beautiful and shapely young women. Not only had it been
quite a sight as they made their dramatic entrance to the bar-
room from the second floor, but its already erotic aspects had
been greatly enhanced by their conflict in the mud.

Wondering whether similar events would be worth putting
on, using his own saloon-girls, Turtle was jolted from his
pleasurable reverie by noticing something which was taking
place not too far away!

From what the globular man overheard, he was not alone
in his assessment of "Miss Chernyshevsky's" charms!

"Hey, there, feller," a newly arrived customer was saying,
in the accent of one raised in the State of Illinois, to the waiter
who had attended to the "blonde" on her arrival and again
when she took the table by the door. Having only arrived in
Brownton earlier that evening, he knew nothing of the fight
and considered her as no more than being the most attractive
and best endowed member of her sex in the bar-room. "You
tell that white haired gal with the big apples over there's
Rocky Todd, which same's *me*, Bad Bill Hamilton and Mean
Mick Meach wants for her to come on over 'n' take liquor
with us."

"That we do," supported the second of the trio seated at the
table, with just the trace of a Scottish burr in his voice. "Make
sure she know's how *I'm* Bad Bill Hamilton."

"And I'm *Mean* Mick Meach," introduced the third, in just
as loud a voice which made it obvious he too came from the
so-called 'Prairie State.' "So you just hop on over there and
get her."

There was more than a similiarity in the accents of the
speakers. All were tallish, well built without being exceptional and had fairly good looking faces which nevertheless

had lines suggestive of vicious natures. A few years earlier,
men such as them had formed the nucleus of the gangs of
Northern guerillas led by the likes of James "Redleg" Lane
and who were just as brutally unscrupulous as their counter-
parts riding with William Clarke Quantrell in an equally spurious pretence of serving the South. Deprived of this means of
acquiring money without the need to raise sweat doing honest
work, they had drifted to the West and, as such an occupation
was no longer lucrative in their home State, sought to earn a
living by hiring out their guns.

Of the three, Todd presented what some people might have
considered the most striking appearance. Having a slight advantage in height over his companions, he had clearly based
his appearance upon that of a man from Illinois who had acquired quite an impressive name throughout the West. Not
only had he allowed his mousey brown hair to grow shoulder
long, but he wore a flat topped and wide brimmed grey hat
with a shining leather band decorated by what looked to be
silver coins around its crown, a black cutaway coat, frilly
bosomed white shirt with a string bow tie, grey trousers and
black boots more suitable for walking than riding. The resemblance to James Butler "Wild Bill" Hickok was taken even
further. Two Colt Model of 1851 Navy Belt Pistol revolvers
were tucked through the scarlet cloth sash about his waist,
their walnut handles turned butt forward in the manner preferred by the famous gun fighter.[1]

Compared with their leader, although neither would have
been willing to confer such an exalted status on him despite
knowing he was a blood relation of a prominent outlaw, the
other two were far less flamboyant. Their round topped and
wide brimmed hats would never have been taken for the style
adopted by Texans, nor would they have wished this to be the
case being stout "Yankees" at heart, but their clothing was
much the same as worn by the cowhands who arrived at the
railroad towns in Kansas delivering herds of half wild longhorn cattle to the shipping pens. The gunbelt each wore was of

1. James Butler "Wild Bill" Hickok makes "guest" appearances in: Part
One, "The Scout," UNDER THE STARS AND BARS and Part Six,
"Eggars' Try," THE TOWN TAMERS.

1a. The circumstances of Wild Bill Hickok's death are recorded in: *Part
Seven, "Deadwood, August the 2nd, 1976"* J.T.'s HUNDREDTH.

a kind intended to permit the fast withdrawal of the Colt 1860 Army Model revolvers in the twin holsters.

"You mean you want for me to go over and ask *her* to come sit with you?" the waiter asked incredulously, looking to where the beautiful and *very* shapely "blonde" was still sitting alone—clad in a more decorous fashion than the female employees, yet which still emphasized she was most well-endowed—after having just finished her meal.

"The hell we do!" corrected Ronald Todd, who preferred to be known by what he assumed to be the tougher sobriquet, 'Rocky' instead of his given name. "You *tell* her to haul her ass over here."

"Do you know who she *is?*" the waiter queried and his manner was filled with thinly veiled disdain.

"We don't know, nor *care,*" asserted Michael Meacher, his preference for a more impressive sounding title having led him to adopt, 'Mean Mick' and abbreviate his surname. Wishing he could apply the question in the same context to himself, he continued, "Do *you* know who Rocky is?"

"Wild Bill Hickok, maybe?" the waiter suggested, in such a way that he might have been making a genuine error.

"Naw!" Meacher denied, trying and failing to decide whether he was being joshed. Still regretting being unable to claim a similar relationship to somebody of equal, or—more ideally—higher, prominence, he went on, "He's kin to *Dave Short,* is who."

"And if *that* don't fetch her running," supported William Dougal Hamilton, another who sought a nickname with a bolder sound. "I'll go over and *fetch* her here myself. Which she won't *like* one lil mite."

"I just *bet* she won't," the waiter said dryly. Although he was aware that David Short had acquired a better than fair reputation as a professional gunslinger, he had met so many with equal status that he was not unduly impressed by learning of the long haired youngster's relationship. Looking at the "blonde" again, he continued, "No, I reckon you can count on *that!"*

Before any more could be said, two men came through the batwing doors. Wearing Eastern style suits and hats, one was big and thickset, the other about the same height and lean, with a dour face. Halting once they had crossed the threshold, they subjected the bar-room to a sweeping gaze which, in each case, came to rest upon the "blonde."

On seeing the arrival of the newcomers and the commencement of the scrutiny, "Miss Chernyshevsky" looked away.

Not quickly enough, it soon became apparent!

Having left their equipment in the care of Arnold Godwin, "Professor" Oswald Cadwallicker and "Doctor" Angus Donald McTavish had made their way to Dodge City on foot. Night had fallen by the time they arrived and, as they had anticipated, an enquiry at the Prudential Hotel confirmed that the beautiful young woman who had called herself "Miss Olga Chernyshevsky" had been called away "unexpectedly." The only consolation they had been able to draw was that she had not taken the buckboard and, unless the clerk was misinformed, had boarded a west-bound train. Although there was one earlier that day, they had been delayed by the need to go and arrange a rendezvous where their assistant would meet them with the bulky tools of their trade.

Reaching Honesty John's Tavern, the pair's purpose was to try and discover the identity of the young woman who had so neatly tricked them. However, as they not infrequently made adjustments to their appearances, so that recognition and positive identification was rendered more difficult, they generally could recognize it in others. That they had failed to do so with 'Miss Chernyshevsky' was a tribute to the skill with which the wig she had worn was manufactured and her own not inconsiderable histrionic ability. She had played her part with a competence which completely took them in, experienced though they were.

However, such a state of affairs could only happen once!

Rankled by the thought of the loss they had suffered at the young woman's hands, which was made even worse by appreciating how she had taken them in, the two confidence tricksters had done more than just commit to memory the way she had looked during their meeting. Alerted to the truth by the dislodging of her hat and wig as she was dashing away, each had formed an image of what she might look like in real life. What was more, so successfully had they thought out the possibilities, it took more than what was obviously a blonde wig to hide her from them. This was especially true when, apart from the horn-rimmed spectacles having been discarded and the make-up employed to give her smooth skin an olive tint over its golden tan, she was dressed in much the same fashion as she had been in Dodge City.

"Come on!" Cadwallicker growled.

"Aye!" McTavish answered.

Exchanging the brief comments, the pair started to walk forward!

Having kept the newcomers surreptitiously under observation, her position at the table allowing observation of the door and the rest of the bar-room, the young woman swiftly dropped her still bulky reticule from the table into her lap and slipped her right hand inside. Then, giving no visible indication of having realized she was the subject of their attention, she remained seated and fingered the top of the empty coffee cup with her left.

If "Miss Chernyshevsky" showed no sign of knowing Cadwallicker and McTavish were approaching, the same did not apply to the three young men who had been so interested in obtaining her company.

"Just take a look at those two old bastards's just come in!" 'Rocky' Todd growled. "They're after *my* woman."

"Yeah!" 'Bad Bill' Hamilton agreed, although he intended to dispute the ownership of the 'blonde' once her acquaintance was made.

"We ain't going to let 'em get away with it, are we?" 'Mean Mick Meach' Meacher demanded, always one of the led rather than a leader.

"The hell we are," Todd declared and picked up the glass which he had just filled with whiskey in his left hand. "Come on and I'll show you one I learned from Uncle Dave."

"We've been looking for *you!*" Cadwallicker announced, coming to a halt so the table was between himself and the 'blonde.'

"I thought you might be," replied the young woman who, when she was not travelling under an alias, answered to the name of Belle Starr. She rested her thumb on the hammer of the specially adapted Manhattan Navy revolver in the reticule without drawing it to full cock.[2]

2. Resembling the Colt Navy Model of 1851, apart from having a spring plate interposed between the caps and the hammer, as produced by the manufacturers—who had gone out of business by the time of this narrative—the Manhattan Navy Model revolver had a barrel six and a half

Waiting in Dodge City for the associates she would need for a confidence trick of her own,[3] the lady outlaw had not been enamoured of the prospect of another team—especially one she deduced was freshly arrived from the East—working in the same area. If they began to fleece "marks" before she could locate a suitable victim, they would almost certainly cause an outcry which would cause the kind of men she was seeking to become excessively wary where anything to do with jewellery of any kind was concerned. Therefore, having the emeralds she would need in her room, she had decided to teach them a lesson.

Realizing her victims were likely to seek revenge, although quite able to take care of herself with firearms or—as she had proved against, amongst others, Irene Beauville—bare hands,[4] Belle had decided to avoid a confrontation with them while they were still in the heat of temper caused by discovering it was they and not she who had been fleeced. Leaving a message with a trusted colleague to inform her associates where to meet her, she had travelled to Brownton to await their arrival. What she had not anticipated was that, despite being only recently arrived from the East unless she missed her guess, Cadwallicker and McTavish had heard of Honesty John's Tavern.

Seeing the two confidence tricksters enter, the lady outlaw had hoped they would fail to recognize her as a result of the change of wigs and absence of make-up and spectacles!

Clearly this had not happened!

However, despite having taken the precaution of putting her revolver into a position of instant readiness, Belle had no

---

inches in length. The one carried by Belle Starr, when concealment was necessary, had had four and a half inches removed and the loading lever shortened accordingly. Should circumstances permit the wearing of a gun-belt and holster, she carried another which had not been modified.

3. What the confidence trick was to be is described, when performed successfully later, in CALAMITY, MARK AND BELLE.

4. Occasions when Belle Starr was compelled to defend herself in bare handed combat against other women are recorded in: *Part One, "The Bounty On Belle Starr's Scalp,"* TROUBLED RANGE; Its "expansion," CALAMITY, MARK AND BELLE; HELL IN THE PALO DURO; *Part Two, "We Hang Horse Thieves High,"* J.T.'S HUNDREDTH.; *Part Four, "Another Kind Of Badger Game,"* MARK COUNTER'S KIN and THE QUEST FOR BOWIE'S BLADE.

wish to use it!

Instead, the lady outlaw would have preferred to settle the affair amicably by returning an acceptable proportion of her loot and arranging with the pair to select itineraries which would avoid a clash of interests!

Laudable though the intention was, Belle was not permitted to bring it to fulfilment!

Just as she was on the point of commencing a placatory speech, the lady outlaw saw the three young men coming from their table. She had already noticed the attention they were paying to her and, in fact, guessed something of what had been said. However, she had not expected them to take such an active interest in her affairs. Nor, observing how they were advancing by a route which would bring them to the table behind the confidence tricksters, did she want them to do so.

"Hey, you pair!" Todd barked, coming to a stop with his companions on either side of him and a short distance from the men he was addressing. "That's *my* woman you're messing with!"

Starting to turn, Cadwallicker and McTavish moved their hands towards their concealed Remington Double Derringers. They were aware that people in their field rarely worked alone. What was more, the fact that she had inserted the advertisement in the local newspaper purporting to be a jeweller and had had the emeralds so readily available had suggested the confidence trick she was employing required assistants. Therefore, they assumed one was speaking and preparing an excuse for using a gun to protect her.

Inadvertently, the pair were playing into Todd's hands!

"Don't pull that gun!" the long haired young man bellowed, before he could see this was being attempted.

While the words were leaving Todd's lips, he flung the contents of the glass into Cadwallicker's face. Blinded by the fiery liquid splashing into his eyes, the bulky man staggered back and his hand left the Remington's butt. He was not granted an opportunity to recover. Twisting the off side Colt from the cloth sash at a reasonable speed with his right hand, dropping the empty glass while doing so, the long haired youngster sent a .36 calibre soft round lead ball into the centre of his victim's chest. Inflicting a mortal wound, it spun the recipient sideways and to the floor.

Surprised by the unexpected response, McTavish still managed to extract his Double Derringer. However, with it out, he faced the problem of who to use it against first. Having expected their companion to start hostilities immediately they were close enough, Hamilton and Meacher had their hands on the butts of their revolvers before they stopped. On the heels of the shot fired by Todd, they jerked out the weapons. Seeing this, the Scottish confidence trickster was unable to decide which of the three posed the greater danger. Nor was he allowed to reach a conclusion. The outside youngsters of the trio fired at him almost simultaneously and, thumb cocking the smoking Colt, their companion followed suit an instant later.

Thrust backwards by the triple impacts, any one of which would have created a fatal wound, McTavish was flung to sprawl across the table. Seeing him coming, Belle thrust back her chair and dived sideways from it. Alighting on the floor, despite the pain caused by her, of necessity, hurried movements (pain caused more from alighting without being able to employ the skill which had reduced the impact of falls during the earlier stages of her fight) she threw the reticule away and brought the Manhattan into view.

"Take it easy there!" Todd growled, as several members of Turtle's staff brought out guns to cover him and his companions. Replacing the Colt in his sash as an indication of his pacific intentions, while the other two holstered their revolvers, he continued, "We are only helping the gal there."

"Did you *need* their help, Belle?" the owner of the Tavern asked, nursing a sawed-off shotgun which he had produced from its readily accessible hiding place on the side of the armchair and, for once, foregoing his rule of anonymity unless permission for a correct identification had been granted.

"Not *that* quick," the lady outlaw replied, giving no suggestion of gratitude. Coming to her feet, she retrieved the reticule in a way which showed she was suffering as a result of her evasive tactics. Replacing the Manhattan, she went on just as coldly, "If at all."

"*Belle!*" Todd ejaculated, staring at the young woman with eyes which came close to bulging as realization struck home and he understood what the waiter had meant by the sardonic statement about how the 'blonde' would not like being ordered to join himself and his companions. "A—Are you *Belle Starr?*"

"I am," the lady outlaw confirmed, her tone less than amiable. "And I'll take it you acted as you thought *best*, so I'll thank you for doing it."

"Maybe you could use m—*us* in your gang?" Hamilton hinted, showing just as much surprise and fascination.

"I've got all the help I *need*," Belle stated definitely, then swung her gaze to Turtle. "I'm going back to my room, Jonathan. If any of the boys get in, please have somebody come up and let me know."

"Certainly," the enormous man assented pleasantly, as he always did when addressing somebody he considered important. The gaze he directed at the three young men was less amiable and his voice became cold as he went on, "I don't take kind to having customers shot up *before* they can spend money here. So I reckon you'd best take your trade someplace else."

"I'm Dave Short's nephew—!" Todd began.

"Say hello to him from *me* the next time you meet," Turtle replied, making it obvious he was completely unimpressed by the information. "And the sooner you start to look for him to do it, the better I'll be pleased."

Scowling at the dismissal, but realizing the futility of attempting to ignore it, the three young men slouched towards the exit from the bar-room!

Watching the trio go, Belle noticed an apparently long haired and bearded man wearing range clothing of the Texans' style rise and follow as they went by his table. Seeing that every item of his attire appeared to be brand new, she gave him a closer scrutiny. Wondering why he should be wearing false whiskers and a wig, she decided to see whether Turtle could satisfy her curiosity. However, before she could do so, she was diverted by the arrival of three men who had been participants in the poker game the previous evening. Feeling it incumbent upon herself to apologize for being in part responsible for it being broken up—although she felt sure they would have no objection under the circumstances—and ensuring her winnings were returned safely, she changed her immediate plans and put the matter from her mind.

The lady outlaw was to remember the incident in the not too distant future![5]

5. Why Belle Starr remembered the incident is recorded in: THE CODE OF DUSTY FOG.

CHAPTER SEVENTEEN

I Want To Hire You to Kill a Man

"That lard-gutted son-of-a-bitch beefhead has his nerve telling us to leave the way he did!" Ronald 'Rocky' Todd protested furiously, as he and his companions walked through the moonlight away from Honesty John's Tavern.

"We *should* go back and teach him respect for his *betters!*" William Dougal 'Bad Bill' Hamilton suggested, but his voice lacked conviction.

"Why don't we?" Michael 'Mean Mick Meach' Meacher inquired, although his tone implied he was really hoping to be given a reason to refrain.

"Naw!" Todd declined, also having no desire to accept what all three of them realized would be the considerable risks entailed by such a course. "He's *nothing* by his-self, but he's got all them hired guns on hand to guard him."

Having been supplied with what they regarded as a satisfactory reason for allowing their dismissal by Jonathan Ambrose Turtle to go unpunished, the three young men continued with their search for somewhere which would offer greater hospitality!

Hearing footsteps hurrying after them, the trio turned with hands moving towards the butts of their guns!

"Excuse me, gentlemen!" a harsh and close to croaking masculine voice called. Suggesting no hostile action was intended, it continued, "I have something I'd like to say to you!"

Starting to turn, all three hoped that either Turtle had seen the error of his ways and sent an invitation for them to return, or Belle Starr had reconsidered her refusal and was going to ask them to go into partnership with her!

Neither contingency materialized!

Clad after the fashion of a cowhand from Texas, the man who was approaching was about average height and build, with what appeared to be longish hair straggling from beneath his hat and a bushy beard which concealed much of his features. However, being less perceptive and seeing him in lighting conditions not so suitable for drawing deductions as had been the case in the bar-room, they failed to reach the conclusions which Belle "Miss Olga Chernyshevsky" Starr had arrived at. Instead, they were all wondering what a man they assumed to be from the Lone Star State might want with them.

"What'd it be?" Todd demanded truculently.

"I saw what you-all did back to the saloon there," the 'bearded' man replied and, if his audience had been as worldly as they pretended to be, they would have noticed his accent was less than authentic. However, his next words prevented them from even considering such a point. "It was's good a piece of work as I've *ever* seen. You took those two *hombres* like Grant took Richmond."

"It warn't *nothing* special," Todd asserted, with blatant false modesty, but failing to see anything unusual about a person who sounded something like a Texan adopting such a Northern simile. "We've took down better men than either of 'em."

"Plenty of times," Hamilton claimed, giving support to the lie.

"Anybody could see *that*," the disguised man declared, with what the trio considered to be genuine respect and admiration. "Fact being, as soon as I saw them going down, I said to myself, '*Will Little*,' I said, 'Those gents are the *men* for you.'"

"In what way, *Mr. Will Little?*" Todd inquired, glaring at his companions. Then he realized belatedly that the man he was addressing did not sound like any of the few Texans he had met. "You got something wrong with your voice?"

"I've just been down with the grippe," the 'bearded' man replied. "But you asked why I thought you're the men for me."

"Why do you?" Meacher put in, not wishing his long haired companion to appear to be the leader of their small group.

"I want to hire you to kill a man for me," the disguised man replied.

"Who'd it be, Mr. Little?" Meacher asked, deciding the

potential employer for the first paid killing in which he was to be engaged deserved politeness.

"First things first!" Hamilton interrupted, before the question could be answered. Wanting to appear more nonchalant and practical than the previous speaker, he went on, "How *much* are you going to *pay?*"

"The price'll be *high,*" the 'bearded' man affirmed. "And, when you hear who I want killing, you'll see why it *must* be."

"Who is it?" Todd asked, speaking quickly to beat his companions seeking the information.

"Dusty Fog!" answered the disguised man who had said his name was "Will Little."

Appendix One

Following his enrolment in the Army of the Confederate States,[1] by the time he reached the age of seventeen, Dustine Edward Marsden "Dusty" Fog had won promotion in the field to the rank of captain and was put in command of Company "C," Texas Light Cavalry.[2] At the head of them throughout the campaign in Arkansas, he had earned the reputation for being an exceptional military raider and worthy contemporary of Turner Ashby and John Singleton "the Grey Ghost" Mosby, the South's other leading exponents of what would later become known as "commando" raids.[3] In addition to averting a scheme by a Union general to employ a virulent version of what was to be given the name, "mustard gas" following its use by Germans in World War 1[4] and preventing a pair of pro-Northern fanatics from starting an Indian up-rising which would have decimated much of Texas,[5] he had supported Belle "the Rebel Spy" Boyd on two of her most dangerous assignments.[6]

---

1. Details of some of Dustine Edward Marsden "Dusty" Fog's activities prior to his enrolment are given in: *Part Five, "A Time For Improvisation, Mr. Blaze,"* J.T.'S HUNDREDTH.

2. Told in: YOU'RE IN COMMAND NOW, MR. FOG.

3. Told in: THE BIG GUN, UNDER THE STARS AND BARS, *Part One, "The Futility of War,"* THE FASTEST GUN IN TEXAS and KILL DUSTY FOG!

4. Told in: A MATTER OF HONOUR.

5. Told in: THE DEVIL GUN.

6. Told in: THE COLT AND THE SABRE and THE REBEL SPY.

6a. More details of the career of Belle "the Rebel Spy" Boyd can be found in: THE BLOODY BORDER: BACK TO THE BLOODY

At the conclusion of the War Between The States, Dusty became the *segundo* of the great OD Connected ranch—its brand being a letter O to which was attached a D, OD—in Rio Hondo County, Texas. Its owner and his maternal uncle, General Jackson Baines "Ole Devil" Hardin, C.S.A., had been crippled in a riding accident and was confined to a wheelchair.[7] This placed much responsibility, including the need to handle an important mission—with the future relationship between the United States and Mexico at stake—upon his young shoulders.[8] While carrying out the assignment, he met Mark Counter and the Ysabel Kid. Not only did they do much to bring it to a successful conclusion, they became his closest friends and leading lights of the ranch's floating outfit.[9] After helping to gather horses to replenish the ranch's depleted remuda,[10] he was sent to assist Colonel Charles Goodnight[11] on

---

BORDER—Berkley Books, New York, August, 1978 edition re-titled, RENEGADE—THE HOODED RIDERS; THE BAD BUNCH; SET A-FOOT; TO ARMS! TO ARMS! IN DIXIE!; THE SOUTH WILL RISE AGAIN; THE QUEST FOR BOWIE'S BLADE; Part Eight, "Affair Of Honour," J.T.'S HUNDREDTH and Part Five, "The Butcher's Fiery End," J.T.'S LADIES.

7. Told in, *Part Three, "The Paint,"* THE FASTEST GUN IN TEXAS.

7a. Further information about the General's earlier career is given in the *Ole Devil Hardin* and *Civil War series*. His death is recorded in, DOC LEROY, M.D.

8. Told in: THE YSABEL KID.

9. "Floating Outfit": a group of four to six cowhands employed by a large ranch to work the more distant sections of the property. Taking food in a chuck wagon, or "greasy sack" on the back of a mule, they would be away from the ranch house for long periods and so were selected for their honesty, loyalty, reliability and capability in all aspects of their work. Because of General Hardin's prominence in the affairs of Texas, the OD Connected's floating outfit were frequently sent to assist such of his friends who found themselves in difficulties or endangered.

10. Told in: .44 CALIBRE MAN and A HORSE CALLED MOGOL-LON.

11. Rancher and master cattleman Charles Goodnight never served in the Army. The rank was honorary and granted by his fellow Texans in respect for his abilities as a fighting man and leader.

11a. In addition to playing an active part in the events recorded in the books referred to in *Footnotes 13* and *14*, Colonel Goodnight makes "guest" appearances in: Part One, "The Half Breed," THE HALF BREED; its "expansion," WHITE INDIANS and S-A-MAN.

the trail drive to Fort Sumner, New Mexico, which did much
to help Texas recover from the impoverished conditions left by
the War.[12] With that achieved, he had been equally successful
in helping Goodnight convince other ranchers it would be possible to drive large herds of longhorn cattle to the railroad in
Kansas.[13]

Having proven himself to be a first class cowhand, Dusty
went on to become acknowledged as a very competent trail
boss,[14] roundup captain,[15] and town taming lawman.[16] Com-
peting in the first Cochise County Fair in Arizona, against a
number of well known exponents of very rapid drawing and
accurate shooting with revolvers, he won the title, "The Fastest Gun In The West."[17] In later years, following his marriage
to Lady Winifred Amelia "Freddie Woods" Besgrove-Woodstole,[18] he became a noted diplomat.

Dusty never found his lack of stature an impediment to his
achievements. In fact, he occasionally found it helped him to
achieve a purpose.[19] To supplement his natural strength,[20] also

11b. Although Dusty Fog never received higher official rank than Captain, in the later years of his life, he too was given the honorific, "Colonel" for possessing the same qualities.
12. Told in: GOODNIGHT'S DREAM—Bantam Books, U.S.A. July
1974 edition re-titled, THE FLOATING OUTFIT, despite our already
having had a volume of that name published by Corgi Books, U.K., see
Footnote 19—and FROM HIDE AND HORN.
13. Told in: SET TEXAS BACK ON HER FEET—although Berkley
Books, New York re-titled their October, 1978 edition VIRIDIAN'S
TRAIL, they reverted to the original title when re-issuing the book in
July, 1980—and THE HIDE AND TALLOW MEN.
14. Told in: TRAIL BOSS.
15. Told in: THE MAN FROM TEXAS.
16. Told in: QUIET TOWN, THE MAKING OF A LAWMAN, THE
TROUBLE BUSTERS, THE GENTLE GIANT, THE SMALL TEXAN
and THE TOWN TAMERS.
17. Told in: GUN WIZARD.
18. Lady Winifred Amelia Besgrove-Woodstole appears as "Freddie
Woods" in: THE TROUBLE BUSTERS; THE MAKING OF A LAW-
MAN; THE GENTLE GIANT; BUFFALO ARE COMING; THE FOR-
TUNE HUNTERS; WHITE STALLION, RED MARE; THE WHIP AND
THE WAR LANCE and Part Five, "The Butcher's Fiery End," J.T.'S
LADIES. She also "guest" stars under her married name, Mrs. Freddie
Fog, in: NO FINGER ON THE TRIGGER.
19. Three occasions when Dusty Fog utilized his small size to his advan-
tage are described in: KILL DUSTY FOG!; Part One, "Dusty Fog And

perhaps with a desire to distract attention from his small size, he had taught himself to be completely ambidextrous.[21] Possessing perfectly attuned reflexes, he could draw either, or both, his Colts—whether the 1860 Army Model,[22] or their improved "descendant," the fabled 1873 Model "Peacemaker"[23]—with lightning speed and shoot most accurately. Furthermore, Ole Devil Hardin's "valet," Tommy Okasi, was Japanese and a trained *samurai* warrior.[24] From him, as was the case with the General's "granddaughter," Elizabeth "Betty" Hardin,[25] Dusty learned ju-jitsu and karate. Neither

---

The Schoolteacher," THE HARD RIDERS; its "expansion", MASTER OF TRIGGERNOMETRY and Part One, "The Phantom of Gallup Creek," THE FLOATING OUTFIT.

20. Two examples of how Dusty Fog exploited his exceptional physical strength are given in: MASTER OF TRIGGERNOMETRY and THE PEACEMAKERS.

21. The ambidextrous prowess was in part hereditary. It was possessed and exploited with equal success by Freddie and Dusty's grandson, Alvin Dustine "Cap" Fog who also inherited his grandfather's physique of a Hercules in miniature. Alvin utilized these traits to help him be acknowledged as one of the finest combat pistol shots in the United States during the Prohibition era and to earn his nickname by becoming the youngest man ever to hold rank of Captain in the Texas Rangers. See the Alvin Dustine "Cap" Fog series for further details of his career.

22. Although the military sometimes claimed derisively it was easier to kill a sailor than a soldier, the weight factor of the respective weapons had caused the United States' Navy to adopt a revolver of .36 calibre while the Army employed the larger .44. The reason was that the weapon would be carried on a seaman's belt and not—handguns having been originally and primarily developed for use by cavalry—on the person or saddle of a man who would be doing most of his travelling and fighting from the back of a horse. Therefore, .44 became known as the "Army" calibre and .36, the "Navy."

23. Details about the Colt Model P of 1873, more frequently known as "The Peacemaker" can be found in those volumes following THE PEACEMAKERS in our list of Floating Outfit series' titles in chronological sequence.

24. "Tommy Okasi" is an Americanised corruption of the name given by the man in question, who had left Japan for reasons which the Hardin, Fog and Blaze families refuse to divulge even at this late date, when he was rescued from a derelict vessel in the China Sea by a ship under the command of General Hardin's father.

25. The members of the Hardin, Fog and Blaze families cannot—or *will not* make any statement upon the exact relationship between Elizabeth "Betty" and her "grandfather," General Hardin.

form of unarmed combat had received the publicity they would be given in later years and were little known in the Western Hemisphere at that time. Therefore, Dusty found the knowledge useful when he had to fight with bare hands against larger, heavier and stronger men.

25a. Betty Hardin appears in: Part Five, "A Time For Improvisation, Mr. Blaze," J.T.'S HUNDREDTH; Part Four, "It's Our Turn To Improvise, Miss Blaze," J.T.'S LADIES; KILL DUSTY FOG!; THE BAD BUNCH; McGRAW'S INHERITANCE; Part Two, "The Quartet," THE HALF BREED; THE RIO HONDO WAR and GUNSMOKE THUNDER.

Appendix Two

With his exceptional good looks and magnificent physical development,[1] Mark Counter presented the kind of appearance many people expected of a man with the reputation gained by his *amigo*, Captain Dustine Edward Marsden "Dusty" Fog. It was a fact of which they took advantage when the need arose.[2] On one occasion, it was also the cause of the blond giant being subjected to a murder attempt although the Rio Hondo gun wizard was the intended victim.[3]

While serving as a lieutenant under the command of General Bushrod Sheldon in the War Between The States, Mark's merits as an efficient and courageous officer had been over-

1. Two of Mark Counter's grandsons, Andrew Mark "Big Andy" Counter and Ranse Smith inherited his good looks and exceptional physique as did two great-grandsons, Deputy Sheriff Bradford "Brad" Counter and James Allenvale "Bunduki" Gunn. Unfortunately, while willing to supply information about other members of his family, past and present, "Big Andy" has so far declined to allow publication of any of his own adventures.
1a. Some details of Ranse Smith's career as a peace officer during the Prohibition era are recorded in: THE JUSTICE OF COMPANY "Z" and THE RETURN OF RAPID CLINT AND MR. J.G. REEDER.
1b. Brad Counter's activities are described in: Part Eleven, "Preventive Law Enforcement," J.T.'S HUNDREDTH and The Rockabye County series, covering aspects of law enforcement in present day Texas.
1c. Some of James Gunn's life story is told in: Part Twelve, "The Mchawi's Powers," J.T.'S HUNDREDTH and the Bunduki series. His nickname arose from the Swahili word for a hand held firearm of any kind being, *"bunduki"* and gave rise to the horrible pun that when he was a child he was, *"Toto ya Bunduki,"* meaning, "Son of a Gun."
2. One occasion is recorded in: THE SOUTH WILL RISE AGAIN.
3. The incident is described in: BEGUINAGE.

164

shadowed by his unconventional taste in uniforms. Always something of a dandy, coming from a wealthy family had allowed him to indulge in his whims. Despite considerable opposition and disapproval from hide-bound senior officers, his adoption of a "skirtless" tunic in particular had come to be much copied by the rich young bloods of the Confederate States' Army.[4] Similarly in later years, having received an independent income through the will of a maiden aunt,[5] his taste in attire had dictated what the well dressed cowhand from Texas would wear to be in fashion.

When peace had come between the North and the South, Mark had accompanied Sheldon to fight for Emperor Maximilian in Mexico. There he had met Dusty Fog and the Ysabel Kid. On returning with them to Texas, he had received an offer to join the floating outfit of the OD Connected ranch. Knowing his two older brothers could help his father, Big Ranse, to run the family's R Over C ranch in the Big Bend country—and considering life would be more enjoyable and exciting in the company of his two *amigos*—he accepted.

An expert cowhand, Mark had become known as Dusty's right bower.[6] He had also gained acclaim by virtue of his enormous strength. Among other feats, it was told how he used a tree-trunk in the style of a Scottish caber to dislodge outlaws from a cabin in which they had forted up,[7] and broke the neck of a Texas longhorn steer with his bare hands.[8] He had acquired further fame for his ability at bare handed roughhouse brawling. However, due to spending so much time in the company of the Rio Hondo gun wizard, his full potential as a gun fighter received little attention. Nevertheless, men who were competent to judge such matters stated that he was second only to the small Texan when it came to drawing fast

4. The *Manual of Dress Regulations* for the Confederate States' Army stipulated that the tunic should have "a skirt extending half way between hip and knee."

5. The legacy also caused two attempts to be made upon Mark's life, see: CUT ONE, THEY ALL BLEED and Part Two, "We Hang Horse Thieves High," J.T.'S HUNDREDTH.

6. "Right bower;" second in command, derived from the name given to the second highest trump card in the game of euchre.

7. Told in: RANGELAND HERCULES.

8. Told in: THE MAN FROM TEXAS, this is a rather "pin the tail on the donkey" title used by our first publishers to replace our own, ROUNDUP CAPTAIN, which we considered far more apt.

and shooting accurately with a brace of long barrelled Colt revolvers.[9]

Many women found Mark irresistible, including Martha "Calamity Jane" Canary.[10] However, in his younger days, only one—the lady outlaw, Belle Starr—held his heart.[11] It was not until several years after her death that he courted and married Dawn Sutherland, who he had first met on the trail drive taken by Colonel Charles Goodnight to Fort Sumner, New

---

9. Evidence of Mark Counter's competence as a gun fighter and his standing compared to Dusty Fog is given in: GUN WIZARD.

10. Martha "Calamity Jane" Canary's meetings with Mark Counter are described in: Part One, "The Bounty On Belle Starr's Scalp," TROUBLED RANGE; its "expansion," CALAMITY, MARK AND BELLE; Part One, "Better Than Calamity," THE WILDCATS; its "expansion," CUT ONE, THEY ALL BLEED; THE BAD BUNCH; THE FORTUNE HUNTERS; THE BIG HUNT and GUNS IN THE NIGHT.

10a. Further details about the career of Martha Jane Canary are given in the Calamity Jane series, also; Part Seven, "Deadwood, August the 2nd, 1876," J.T.'S HUNDREDTH; Part Six, "Mrs. Wild Bill," J.T.'S LADIES' and she makes a "guest" appearance in, Part Two, "A Wife For Dusty Fog," THE SMALL TEXAN.

11. How Mark Counter's romance with Belle Starr commenced, progressed and ended is told in: Part One, "The Bounty On Belle Starr's Scalp," TROUBLED RANGE; its "expansion" CALAMITY, MARK AND BELLE; THE BAD BUNCH; RANGELAND HERCULES; Part Two, "We Hang Horse Thieves High," J.T.'S HUNDREDTH; THE GENTLE GIANTS; Part Four, "A Lady Known As Belle," THE HARD RIDERS and GUNS IN THE NIGHT.

11a. Belle Starr "stars"—no pun intended—in: WANTED! BELLE STARR. She also makes "guest" appearances in: THE QUEST FOR BOWIE'S BLADE; Part One, "The Set-Up," SAGEBRUSH SLEUTH; its "expansion," WACO'S BADGE and Part Six, "Mrs. Will Bill," J.T.'S LADIES.

11b. We are frequently asked why it is the "Belle Starr" we describe is so different from a photograph which appears in various books. The researches of the world's foremost fictionist geanologist, Philip Jose Farmer—author of, amongst numerous other works, TARZAN ALIVE, A definitive Biography of Lord Greystoke and DOC SAVAGE, His Apocalyptic Life—with whom we consulted have established the lady about whom we are writing is not the same person as another equally famous bearer of the name. However, the Counter family have asked Mr. Farmer and ourselves to keep her true identity a secret and this we intend to do.

Mexico.[12] The discovery of oil on their ranch brought an added wealth to them and his commodity now forms the major part of the present members of the family's income.[13]

Recent biographical details we have received from the current head of the family, Andrew Mark "Big Andy" Counter, establish that Mark was descended on his mother's side from Sir Reginald Front de Boeuf, notorious as lord of Torquilstone Castle in Medieval England[14] and who lived up to the family motto, *Cave Adsum*.[15] However, although a maternal aunt and her son, Jessica and Trudeau Front de Boeuf, behaved in a way which suggested they had done so,[16] the blond giant had not inherited the very unsavory character and behaviour of his ancestor.

12. Told in: GOODNIGHT'S DREAM and FROM HIDE AND HORN.
13. This is established by inference in: Case Three, "The Deadly Ghost," YOU'RE A TEXAS RANGER, ALVIN FOG.
14. See: IVANHOE, by Sir Walter Scott
15. "Cave Adsum;" roughly translated from Latin, "Beware, I Am Here."
16. Some information about Jessica and Trudeau Front de Boeuf can be found in: CUT ONE, THEY ALL BLEED and Part Three, "Responsibility to Kinfolks," OLE DEVIL'S HANDS AND FEET.

Appendix Three

Raven Head, only daughter of Chief Long Walker, war leader of the *Pehnane*—Wasp, Quick Stinger, Raider—Comanche's Dog Soldier lodge and his French Creole *pairaivo¹* married an Irish-Kentuckian adventurer, Big Sam Ysabel, but died giving birth to their first child.

Baptized "Loncey Dalton Ysabel," the boy was raised after the fashion of the *Nemenuh.²* With his father away from the camp for much of the time, engaged upon the family's combined businesses of mustanging—catching and breaking wild horses³—and smuggling, his education had largely been left in the hands of his maternal grandfather.⁴ From Long Walker, he learned all those things a Comanche warrior must know: how to ride the wildest freshly caught mustang, or make a trained animal subservient to his will while "raiding"—a polite name for the favourite pastime of the male *Nemenuh*, stealing horses—to follow the faintest tracks and just as effectively conceal signs of his own passing;⁵ to locate hidden enemies, or keep out of sight himself when the need arose; to

1. "Pairaivo:" first, or favourite wife. As is the case with the other Comanche terms, this is a phonetic spelling.
2. *"Nemenuh,"* "the People," the Comanches' name for themselves and their nation. Members of other tribes with whom they came into contact called them, frequently with good cause, the *"Tshaoh,"* the "Enemy People."
3. A description of the way in which mustangers operated is given in: .44 CALIBRE MAN and A HORSE CALLED MOGOLLON.
4. Told in: COMANCHE.
5. An example of how the Ysabel Kid could conceal his tracks is given in: Part One, "The Half Breed," THE HALF BREED.

move in silence on the darkest of nights, or through the thickest cover; to know the ways of wild creatures[6] and, in some cases, imitate their calls so well that others of their kind were fooled.[7]

The boy proved a most excellent pupil at all the subjects. Nor were practical means of protecting himself forgotten. Not only did he learn to use all the traditional weapons of the Comanche,[8] when he had come into the possession of firearms, he had inherited his father's Kentuckian skill at shooting with a rifle and, while not *real* fast on the draw—taking slightly over a second to bring his Colt Second Model of 1848 Dragoon revolver and fire, whereas a tophand could practically half that time—he could perform passably with it. Furthermore, he won his *Nemenuh* "man-name," *Cuchilo,* Spanish for "Knife," by his exceptional ability at wielding one. In fact, it was claimed by those best qualified to judge that he could equal the alleged designer in performing with the massive and special type of blade which bore the name of Colonel James Bowie.[9]

Joining his father in smuggling expeditions along the Rio

6. Two examples of how the Ysabel Kid's knowledge of wild animals were turned to good use are given in: OLD MOCCASINS ON THE TRAIL and BUFFALO ARE COMING!

7. An example of how well the Ysabel Kid could impersonate the call of a wild animal is recorded in: Part Three, "A Wolf's A Knowing Critter," J.T.'S HUNDREDTH.

8. One occasion when the Ysabel Kid employed his skill with traditional Comanche weapons is described in: RIO GUNS.

9. Some researchers claim that the actual designer of the knife which became permanently attached to Colonel James Bowie's name was his oldest brother, Rezin Pleasant. Although it is generally conceded the maker was James Black, a master cutler in Arkansas, some authorities state it was manufactured by Jesse Cliffe, a white blacksmith employed by the Bowie family on their plantation in Rapides Parish, Louisiana.

9a. What happened to James Bowie's knife after his death in the final assault of the siege of the Alamo Mission, San Antonio de Bexar, Texas, on March the 6th, 1836, is told in: GET URREA and THE QUEST FOR BOWIE'S BLADE.

9b. As all James Black's knives were custom made, there were variations in their dimensions. The specimen owned by the Ysabel Kid had a blade eleven and a half inches in length, two and a half inches wide and a quarter of an inch thick at the guard. According to William "Bo" Randall, of Randall-Made Knives, Orlando, Florida—a master cutler and authority upon the subject in his own right—James Bowie's knife weighed forty-

Grande, the boy became known to the Mexicans of the border country as *Cabrito*—the Spanish name for a young goat—a nickname which arose out of hearing white men refer to him as the "Ysabel Kid," but it was spoken *very* respectfully in that context. Smuggling was not an occupation to attract the meek and mild of manner, yet even the roughest and toughest of the bloody border's denizens came to acknowledge it did not pay to rile up Big Sam Ysabel's son. The education received by the Kid had not been calculated to develop any over-inflated belief in the sanctity of human life. When crossed, he dealt with the situation like a *Pehnane* Dog Soldier—to which war lodge of savage and *most* efficient warriors he had earned initiation—swiftly and in an effectively deadly manner.

During the War Between The States, the Kid and his father had commenced by riding as scouts for Colonel John Singleton "the Grey Ghost" Mosby. Soon, however, their specialized knowledge and talents were diverted to having them collect and deliver to the Confederate States' authorities in Texas supplies which had been purchased in Mexico, or run through the blockade by the United States' Navy into Matamoros. It was hard and dangerous work,[10] but never more so than the two occasions when they became engaged in assignments with Belle "the Rebel Spy" Boyd.[11]

Soon after the War ended, Sam Ysabel was murdered. While hunting down the killers, the Kid met Captain Dustine Edward Marsden "Dusty" Fog and Mark Counter. When the mission upon which they were engaged was brought to its

---

three ounces, having a blade eleven inches long, two and a quarter inches wide and three-eighths of an inch thick. His company's Model 12 "Smithsonian" bowie knife—one of which is owned by James Allenvale "Bunduki" Gunn, details of whose career can be found in the *Bunduki* series—is modelled on it.

9c. One thing all "bowie" knives have in common, regardless of dimensions, is a "clip" point. The otherwise unsharpened "back" of the blade joins and becomes an extension of the main cutting surface in a concave arc, whereas a "spear" point—which is less utilitarian—is formed by the two sides coming together in symmetrical curves.

10. An occasion when Big Sam Ysabel went on a mission without his son is recorded in: THE DEVIL GUN.

11. Told in: THE BLOODY BORDER and BACK TO THE BLOODY BORDER.

successful conclusion, learning the Kid no longer wished to go on either smuggling or mustanging, the small Texan offered him employment at the OD Connected ranch. It had been in the capacity as scout rather than ordinary cowhand that he was required and his talents in that field were frequently of the greatest use as a member of the floating outfit.

The acceptance of the job by the Kid was of the greatest benefit all around. Dusty acquired another loyal friend who was ready to stick to him through any kind of peril. The ranch obtained the services of an extremely capable and efficient fighting man. For his part, the Kid was turned from a life of petty crime—with the ever present danger of having his illicit activities develop into serious law breaking—and became a useful and law abiding member of society. Peace officers and honest citizens might have found cause to feel grateful for that. His *Nemenuh* upbringing would have made him a terrible and murderous outlaw if he had been driven into a life of violent crime.

Obtaining his first repeating rifle—a Winchester Model of 1866, although at first known as the "New Improved Henry," nicknamed the "Old Yellowboy" because of its brass frame— while in Mexico with Dusty and Mark, the Kid had soon become an expert in its use. At the First Cochise County Fair in Arizona, despite circumstances compelling him to use a weapon with which he was not familiar,[12] he won the first prize in the rifle shooting competition against stiff opposition. The prize was one of the legendary Winchester Model of 1873 rifles which qualified for the honoured designation, "One Of A Thousand."[13]

12. The circumstances are described in: GUN WIZARD.

13. When manufacturing the extremely popular Winchester Model of 1873 rifle—while they claimed to be the "Gun Which Won The West"— the makers selected all those barrels found to shoot with exceptional accuracy to be fitted with set triggers and given a special fine finish. Originally, these were inscribed, "1 of 1,000," but this was later changed to script, "One Of A Thousand." However, the title was a considerable understatement. Only one hundred and thirty-six out of a total production of 720,610 qualified for the distinction. Those of a grade lower were to be designated, "One Of A Hundred," but only seven were so named. The practice commenced in 1875 and was discontinued three years later because the management decided it was not good sales policy to suggest different grades of gun were being produced.

It was, in part, through the efforts of the Kid that the majority of the Comanche bands agreed to go on the reservation, following attempts to ruin the signing of the treaty.[14] It was to a large extent due to his efforts that the outlaw town of Hell was located and destroyed.[15] Aided by Annie "Is-A-Man" Singing Bear—a girl of mixed parentage who gained the distinction of becoming accepted as a *Nemenuh* warrior[16]—he played a major part in preventing the attempted theft of Morton Lewis' ranch provoking trouble with the *Kweharehnuh* Comanche.[17] To help a young man out of difficulties caused by a gang of card cheats, he teamed up with the lady outlaw, Belle Starr.[18] When he accompanied Martha "Calamity Jane" Canary to inspect a ranch she had inherited, they became involved in as dangerous a situation as either had ever faced.[19]

Remaining at the OD Connected ranch until he, Dusty and Mark met their deaths whilst on a hunting trip to Kenya shortly after the turn of the century, his descendants continued to be associated with the Hardin, Fog and Blaze clan and the Counter family.[20]

14. Told in: SIDEWINDER.
15. Told in: HELL IN THE PALO DURO and GO BACK TO HELL.
16. How Annie Singing Bear acquired the distinction of becoming a warrior and won her "man-name" is told in: IS-A-MAN.
17. Told in: WHITE INDIANS.
18. Told in: Part Two, "The Poison And The Cure," WANTED! BELLE STARR.
19. Told in: WHITE STALLION, RED MARE.
20. Mark Scrapton, a grandson of the Ysabel Kid, served as a member of Company "Z," Texas Rangers, with Alvin Dustine "Cap" Fog and Ranse Smith—respectively grandsons of Captain Dustine Edward Marsden "Dusty" Fog and Mark Counter—during the Prohibition era. Information about their specialized duties is given in the Alvin Dustine "Cap" Fog series.

Appendix Four

Left an orphan almost from birth by an Indian raid and acquiring the only name he knew from the tribe involved,[1] Waco was raised as one of a North Texas rancher's large family.[2] Guns were always part of his life and his sixteenth birthday saw him riding with the tough, "wild onion" crew of Clay Allison. Like their employer, the CA hands were notorious for their wild and occasionally dangerous behaviour. Living in the company of such men, all older than himself, the youngster had become quick to take offense and well able, eager even, to prove he could draw his revolvers with lightning speed and shoot very accurately. It had seemed only a matter of time before one shootout too many would see him branded as a killer and fleeing from the law with a price on his head.

Fortunately for Waco and—as was the case with the Ysabel Kid—law abiding citizens, that day did not come!

From the moment Dusty Fog saved the youngster's life during a cattle stampede, at some considerable risk to his own, a change for the better had commenced.[3] Leaving Allison, with the blessing of the "Washita curly wolf," Waco had become a member of the OD Connected ranch's floating outfit. The other members of that elite group treated him like a favourite younger brother and taught him many useful lessons. Instruction in bare handed combat was provided by Mark Counter. The Kid showed him how to read tracks and other secrets of the scout's trade. From a friend who was a profes-

1. Alvin Dustine "Cap" Fog informs us that at his marriage to Elizabeth "Beth" Morrow, Waco used the surname of his adoptive family, "Catlan."
2. How Waco repaid his obligation to the family which raised him is told in: WACO'S DEBT.
3. Told in: TRIGGER FAST.

sional gambler, Frank Derringer,[4] had come information about the ways of honest and dishonest followers of his chosen field of endeavour. However, it was from the Rio Hondo gun wizard that the most important advice had come. *When,* he already knew well enough *how,* to shoot. Dusty had also supplied training which, helped by an inborn flair for deductive reasoning, turned him into a peace officer of exceptional merit. After serving in other official capacities,[5] then with the Arizona Rangers[6]—in the company of Marvin Eldridge "Doc'" Leroy—and as sheriff of Two Forks County, Utah,[8] he was eventually appointed a United States' marshal.[9]

4. Frank Derringer appears in: QUIET TOWN, THE MAKING OF A LAWMAN, THE TROUBLE BUSTERS, THE GENTLE GIANT and COLD DECK. HOT LEAD.
5. Told in: THE MAKING OF A LAWMAN; THE TROUBLE BUSTERS; THE GENTLE GIANT; Part Five, "The Hired Butcher," THE HARD RIDERS; Part Four, "A Tolerable Straight Shooting Gun," THE FLOATING OUTFIT; Part Two, "The Invisible Winchester," OLE DEVIL'S HANDS AND FEET; THE SMALL TEXAN and THE TOWN TAMERS.
6. During the 1870's, the Governor of Arizona formed this particular law enforcement agency to cope with the threat of serious organized law breaking in his Territory. A similar decision was taken by a later Governor and the Arizona Rangers were brought back into being. Why it was considered necessary to appoint the first force, how it operated and was finally disbanded is recorded in the Waco series and Part Six, "Keep Good Temper Alive," J.T.'S HUNDREDTH.
7. At the period of this narrative, although having acquired a reputation for knowledge in medical matters, Marvin Eldridge "Doc" Leroy had not yet been able to attain his ambition of following his father's footsteps by becoming a qualified doctor. How he did so is recorded in: DOC LEROY, M.D.
8. Told in: THE DRIFTER, which also describes how Waco first met Elizabeth "Beth" Morrow.
9. Told in: HOUND DOG MAN.

Appendix Five

Throughout the years we have been writing, we have frequently received letters asking for various terms we employ to be explained in greater detail. While we do not have the slightest objection to such correspondence and always reply, we have found it saves much time consuming repetition to include those most frequently requested in each new title. We ask our "old hands," who have seen these items many times in the past, to remember there are always "new chums," coming along who have not and to bear with us. J.T.E.

1.   We strongly suspect the trend in movies and television series made since the mid-1950's, wherein all cowhands are portrayed as heavily bearded, long haired and filthy arose less from a desire on the part of the productions companies to create "realism" than because there were so few actors available—particularly to play "supporting" roles—who were short haired and clean shaven. Another factor was because the "liberal" elements who were starting to gain control over much of the media seem to obtain some form of "ego trip" from showing dirty conditions, filthy habits and unkempt appearances. In our extensive reference library, we cannot find even a dozen photographs of actual *cowhands*—as opposed to civilian scouts for the Army, old time mountain men, or gold prospectors—with long hair and bushy beards. In fact, our reading on the

subject and conversations with friends living in the Western States of America have led us to the conclusion that the term "long hair" was one of opprobrium in the Old West and Prohibition eras just as it still tends to be today in cattle raising country.

2. We consider at best specious—at worst, a snobbish attempt to "put down" the myth and legends of the Old West—the frequently repeated assertion that the gun fighters of that era could not "hit a barn door at twenty yards." While willing to concede that the average person then, as now, would not have much skill in using a handgun, knowing his life would depend upon it, the professional *pistolero* on either side of the law expended time, money and effort to acquire proficiency. Furthermore, such a man did not carry a revolver to indulge in shooting at *anything* except at close range. He employed it as a readily accessible *weapon* which would incapacitate an enemy, preferably with the first shot, at close quarters, hence the preference for a cartridge of heavy calibre.

2a. With the exception of .22 calibre handguns intended for casual pleasure shooting, those specially designed for Olympic style "pistol" matches, the Remington XP100—one of which makes an appearance in: Case Two, "A Voice From The Past," THE LAWMEN OF ROCKABYE COUNTY—designed for "varmint" hunting at long distances, or medium to heavy calibre automatic pistols "accurized" and in the hands of a proficient exponent of modern "combat" shooting, a handgun is a short range *defensive* and not an *offensive* weapon. Any Old West gun fighter, or peace officer in the Prohibition era and present times expecting to have to shoot at distances beyond about twenty *feet* would take the precaution of arming himself with a shotgun or a rifle.

3. "Make wolf bait," one term meaning to kill. Derived from the practice in the Old West, when a range was infested by stock killing predators—not necessarily just wolves, but coyotes, the occasional jaguar in southern regions, black and grizzly bears—of slaughtering an animal and, having poisoned the carcase, leaving it to be devoured by the carnivores.

4. "Up to the Green River": to kill, generally with a knife. First produced on the Green River, at Greenfield, Massachusetts, in 1834, a very popular type of general purpose knife had the inscription, *"J. Russell & Co./Green River Works"* on the blade just below the hilt. Therefore any edged weapon thrust into an enemy "up to the Green River" would prove fatal whether it bore the inscription or not.

5. "Light a shuck," a cowhand term for leaving hurriedly. Derived from the habit in night camps on "open range" roundups and trail drives of supplying "shucks"—dried corn cobs—to be lit and used for illumination by anybody who had to leave the campfire and walk about in the darkness. As the "shuck" burned away very quickly, a person needed to hurry if wanting to benefit from its illumination.

6. The sharp toes and high heels of boots worn by cowhands were functional rather than merely decorative. The former could find and enter, or be slipped free from, a stirrup iron very quickly in an emergency. Not only did the latter offer a firmer brace against the stirrups, they could be spiked into the ground to supply added holding power when roping on foot.

7. Americans in general used the word, "cinch," derived from the Spanish, *"cincha,"* to describe the short band made from coarsely woven horse hair, canvas, or cordage and terminated at each end with a metal ring which—together with the *latigo*—is used to fasten the saddle on the back of a horse. However, because of the word's connections with Mexico, Texans tended to employ the term, "girth," usually pronouncing it as "girt." As cowhands from the Lone Star State fastened the end of the lariat to the saddlehorn, even when roping half wild longhorn cattle or free-ranging mustangs, instead of relying upon a "dally" which could be slipped free almost instantaneously in an emergency, their rigs had double girths.

8. "Chaps": leather overalls worn by American cowhands as protection for the legs. The word, pronounced, "shaps," is an abbreviation of the Spanish, *"chaperejos,"* or "chaparreras," meaning "leather breeches." Contrary to what is frequently shown in

Western movies, no cowhand ever kept his chaps on when their protection was not required. Even if he should arrive in a town with them on, he would remove and either hang them over his saddle, or leave them behind the bar in his favourite saloon for safe keeping until his visit was over.

9. "Hackamore": an Americanised corruption of the Spanish word, *"jaquima,"* meaning "headstall." Very popular with Indians in particular, it was an ordinary halter, except for having reins instead of a leading rope. It had a headpiece something like a conventional bridle, a brow band about three inches wide which could be slid down the cheeks to cover the horse's eyes, but no throat latch. Instead of a bit, a *"bosal"* — a leather, rawhide, or metal ring around the head immediately above the mouth—was used as a means of control and guidance.

10. "Right as the Indian side of a horse"; absolutely correct. Derived from the habit of Indians mounting from the right, or "off" and not the left, or "near" side as was done by people of European descent and Mexicans.

11. "Mason-Dixon line," erroneously called the "Mason-Dixie line." The boundary between Pennsylvania and Maryland, as surveyed from 1763-67 by the Englishmen, Charles Mason and Jeremiah Dixon. It became considered as the dividing line separating the Southern "Slave" and Northern "Free" States.

12. "New England": the North East section of the United States—including Massachusetts, New Hampshire, Connecticut, Maine, Vermont and Rhode Island— which was first settled by people primarily from the British Isles.

13. "Gone to Texas": on the run from the law. During the white colonization period, which had commenced in the early 1820's, many fugitives from justice in America had fled to Texas and would continue to do so until annexation by the United States on February the 16th, 1846. Until the latter became a fact, they had known there was little danger of being arrested and extradited by the local authorities. In fact, like Kenya Colony from the 1920's to the outbreak of World War II—in

spite of the number of honest, hard working and law abiding settlers genuinely seeking to make a permanent home there—Texas had gained a reputation for being a "place in the sun for shady people."

14. "Summer name": an alias. In the Old West, the only acceptable way to express doubt about the identity which was supplied when being introduced to a stranger was to ask, "Is that your *summer* name?"

15. In the Old West, the jurisdictional powers of various types of law enforcement agencies were established as follows. A town marshal, sometimes called "constable" in smaller communities, and his deputies were confined to the town or city which hired them. A sheriff—who was generally elected into office for a set period of time—and his deputies were restricted to their own county. However, in less heavily populated areas, he might also serve as marshal of the county seat. Texas and Arizona Rangers could go anywhere within the boundaries of their respective States. But technically were required to await an invitation from the local peace officers before participating in an investigation. As we explain in our *Alvin Dustine "Cap" Fog* series, by a special dispensation of the Governor during the Prohibition era, Company "Z" of the Texas Rangers were allowed to initiate operations without requesting permission under certain circumstances. Although a United States Marshal and Deputy U.S. Marshal had jurisdiction everywhere throughout the country, their main function was the investigation of "Federal" crimes. Information about the organization and duties of a modern day Texas sheriff's office can be found in the *Rockabye County* series.

16. "Burro": in this context, a small wooden structure like the roof of a house upon which a saddle would be rested when not in use. Being so dependent upon his rig, a cowhand preferred to use a burro when one was available instead of laying it down or hanging it by a stirrup.

16a. Despite the misconception created by western movies —even the late and great John Wayne being an offender—a cowhand would *never* toss down his saddle on its skirts. If no burro was available, he would either lay it on its side, or stand it on its head, somewhere it would be safely clear of anybody inadvertently stepping upon it.

THE END